DEAD IN THE WATER

DEAD IN THE WATER

Glenda Carroll

Beachbreak Press
Marin County, California

Cover Design: Richard Burns

Beachbreak Press, Marin County, California

beachbreakpress@yahoo.com

DEDICATION

To Eddie and Ricky

ACKNOWLEGEMENTS

DEAD IN THE WATER began with a simple question, "what if?" It took me more than a year to answer that question and I didn't do it alone. No writer does.

Editorial analyst Martha Engber and proofreader Iwonka Kelly gave the manuscript a professional polish.

Many thanks to D.P. Lyle, MD, forensic specialist, and to Rebecca Salazar, MD, Tucson, AZ, for their medical expertise. Officer Wilson Ng, San Francisco Police Department; Doug Farley, firefighter, EMT, City of Fort Lauderdale, Florida, David Robinson, Aquatic Specialist, Sonoma County Parks, Sonoma, Ca and Frank Oliveto, hot rod aficionado, Mill Valley, Ca answered my many questions.

Kudos to Steve Munatones, international open water swimming guru, for sharing meaningful statistics and to Nancy Ridout for her thoughtful comments.

Authors and cousins, Charlee Ganny and Joan Ganny, need acknowledgement for their virtual handholding.

This mystery is about open water swimming. I want to thank Pacific Masters Swimming, the open water event hosts and the swimmers that I've met over the years. A special thanks to Tamalpais Aquatic Masters, head coach Marie McSweeney and my teammates, especially the women in the locker room who kept asking, 'when do I get to read your book?'

CONTENTS

DEAD IN THE WATER

1

I was sitting on the shore of Lake Joseph, a startling green lake in the California Sierra foothills, far enough in the shade to be protected from the bone-melting sun but still feel its warmth. The toasted scent of dry pine needles filtered through the air. On the radio was a San Francisco Giants game. They were winning. I was dozing. But, the shouts from a man across the beach kept drowning out the announcer's take on a lead-off double. Very annoying. I wished he'd shut up—the shouter—not the announcer.

I opened my eyes. Lake Joe, as it's called, was stretched out in front of me, bordered by tall pines working their way up neighboring small mountains. Spray, like glitter thrown into the air, bounced off the river of swimmers—maybe two hundred in all—making a beeline toward the beach. My thirty-eight year-old sister, Lena, was out there somewhere. This was her fourth open water swim of the season.

I sat up a little straighter and leaned forward. One swimmer near the front of the pack had turned left while the others kept moving straight toward the finish line. He was swimming the wrong way. He paused for a minute, treading water. Then he swam calmly, stroke after stroke, toward a nearby dock anchored on the edge of the course.

When he was within five feet of the wooden dock, he turned over on his back and floated. His body slowly began to rotate until he was face down in the water, arms and legs spread out. He never moved again.

Standing in the hot sun at the side of the course closest to the floating swimmer, was the shouter. He waved his hands wildly. His voice cracked as he yelled.

"Here...help. He needs help. Get a lifeguard. Now. Quick! Damn it, hurry!"

Jumping up and down, he pointed at the face down figure in the water. He continued loudly, frantically. "Hey, over here... hurry...hurry."

My corner of the beach erupted. Sunbathers ran down to the water's edge. Sand was kicked everywhere. I ran with them, tripping over my own feet. Two lifeguards on stand-up paddleboards moved quickly through the water to the unconscious man. One guard jumped off his board, swam a few short strokes, tucked a thick red rescue tube under his arms to keep his head afloat. He pushed him onto the other board. Then, side-by-side, the paddlers stroked in unison, their long paddles flashing in the sun. Even three hundred yards away, I saw the determined look on their sunburned faces.

Moving into the shallows close to where the shouter stood, one guard jumped into knee-deep water. He pulled the body onto the beach.

Two women dashed past me, legs pumping, arms flying. They reached the limp swimmer at the same time he was pulled across the sand into the shade. They were a doctor and a nurse from the event's safety team. Still breathing hard from the sprint, they bent over the body.

The shouter, a tall man in a striped polo shirt, stood there, nervously running his hands through his cropped brown hair. His eyes were hidden behind reflective sunglasses. He took a step back when an ambulance pulled up and the paramedics brought out resuscitation equipment.

"There's Cody Stephenson," said a thirty-something swimmer standing next to me. He pointed at a man with a clipboard jogging toward the growing group of people surrounding the swimmer. "Bet that's the guy's coach."

Along the whole beach, voices grew louder. Then softer. Then louder again, like the ebb and flow of a wave. Some words were clipped, the edges hard; others reduced to whispers. The beachgoers stared at the downed swimmer.

Off to one side, I saw my sister run through the yellow finish arch, pull off her goggles and cap. Shading her eyes with her hands, she looked out to the lake at the rest of the pack heading toward the finish line. I walked over to her.

"What's going on?" she asked, nodding to the group at the side of the course.

"Not sure," I said. We walked back up the beach to where I had been sitting. "They just pulled that man out of the water. I think he's unconscious."

Lena grabbed a towel, drying her face and mop of short strawberry blond corkscrew curls. A stocky dark-haired man as solid as a side of a mountain and wearing dark blue jammers, (a knee length swim suit) walked up to Lena.

"Mario, you know who it is?" she asked.

"It's Dick Waddell. We're on the same team."

"The new guy, you know the one from Texas I told you about, burning up the course," Lena said to me. Her first words were muffled from beneath the towel. "Glad there's an ambulance here. Trish, this is Mario, a reformed body builder. Now an open water swimmer. Mario, this is my sister, Trisha, Trisha Carson. She's my swim chauffeur and current roommate."

We nodded, smiled briefly, and he continued walking to another picnic table nearby. Lena settled down on the splintery bench and began to peel off her suit under the towel.

"Think I'll walk around and see what's up," I said.

"Trish, stay out of it."

"I'm not going to bother anyone. I'm curious, that's all."

"That's what you always say. Then you do something stupid. Don't get involved."

I've heard that from my sister since we were kids—and there have been times I've overstepped some boundaries. But, she likes to pretend that life is all blue sky and sunshine. I see the storm clouds and grey sky, so I need to be prepared.

I tiptoed across the hot sand in my bare feet to the edge of the lake. Swimmers were still racing down the last leg of the course, then high-stepping through the shallows before they crossed the finish line.

When I reached the shade, it was 10° cooler. As I walked by the ambulance, I glanced inside. There, on the driver's seat, was a clipboard with some forms. I wondered if they had anything to do with the swimmer. A quick look, that's all I needed. I rested my palm near the door handle and pretended to crane my neck to see around the other looky-lous. I slipped my hand down to the handle, ready to open the driver side door.

"Excuse me, ma'am, I need to get something." said an EMT with short, trim black hair.

He pulled open the door, reached in for the clipboard and walked away. So much for more information. I joined a circle of onlookers a discreet distance away, but completely hypnotized by the scene. The yeller, the tall man in the polo shirt, was a few feet behind me.

"He'll be okay?" the man asked quietly. No one answered him. No one seemed to hear him but me. Everyone's focus was on the swimmer on the ground. I turned to reassure him, but he was walking quickly away through the pines toward the parking lot.

The man lying on his back was tall and muscular. But now his stomach was distended from the air pumped into him by the paramedics. He was pale and tinged with blue. He wore jammers, black with a green lightning bolt on the outside of each leg. One of the race directors who helped carry the man from the rescue surfboard to the shore was standing outside the circle of onlookers. He shook his head.

"This is terrible," he said to himself. He picked up a cell phone, punched in some numbers and started to talk quickly as he walked closer to the ambulance.

"Awful…not sure what happened. He's unconscious, but has a weak pulse. Great conditions here. Flat water, sunny, no wind. Water temp was about 68° at the start."

The EMTs were talking about a thready pulse and a drop in blood pressure. Maybe this wasn't as bad as it looked. One emergency worker tried reviving the swimmer by rubbing his knuckles on his sternum. It didn't work. Then another opened an ammonia inhalant packet, crushed the ampoule and held it under his nose. I'd seen these inhalants waved under the nose of semi-conscious athletes before. They always worked. But, now, nothing.

Quickly but carefully, the medics placed the swimmer on a backboard, and loaded him into the ambulance. I stood to the side and watched as they inserted an IV drip filled with a clear solution into his arm. An oxygen mask was placed over his mouth and nose. He was hooked up to a heart monitor. As they closed the back door to the ambulance, one EMT spoke in a flat steady voice to a doctor at the Lake Joseph Hospital, alerting him to the patient's condition and their arrival. Then they drove off the beach through the crowded parking lot, turning on the piercing siren when they reached the road out of the park.

Next to me, watching the ambulance disappear was a man I'd seen before. His name was Mike Menton and he was always picking up awards. He held his reflective silver goggles first in one hand, then the other; back and forth, back and forth, the goggles went. He was staring after the ambulance, when his teenage daughter approached. "What happened, Dad?" she asked.

"I don't know," Mike said. "Wad…"

"Who?"

"Uh, Dick was right behind me…I thought. I passed him and I could swear he was right behind me. I'm sure it was him hitting my feet with each stroke. It was going to be a close race, like always. I wanted to win, but not like this."

He shook his head and took the towel that his daughter held out. Then he moved slowly over to where the results of the swim would be posted. Swimmers walked by, patted him on the back and congratulated him on the win. He grimaced and shook his head again.

I watched his daughter, a skinny fifteen-year-old in a red and pink bikini, hop across the blistering pebbly sand until she came to her large striped towel. She sat down next to her boyfriend—some geeky kid, pale as can be. He doesn't get outside much, I thought. I could see them talking, heads close together. He reached over to pat her hand.

Just running out of the water was a tiny curvaceous woman in a wetsuit. She couldn't be more than five feet. Smiling, she glanced from side to side, scanning the crowd waiting at the finish line. Pulling off her cap, she tossed her thick black hair with one hand, waved to the crowd with the other. How she managed a fashion model jog across the timing mat, I don't know. But she did. As the volunteers bent over to take off her timing chip, two women approached. Talking to her quietly, they led her away from the finish arch. She abruptly stopped walking, tilted her head and stared at both of them. The smile evaporated. She covered her mouth with her hands and her knees began to buckle. The two women held her arms and eased her down to the sand. Not good. Must be a relative. Maybe his wife.

I watched as the women helped her back up and then they disappeared into the shade.

Still floating at the water's edge was a pair of green reflective goggles. The black straps had a lightning bolt on either side. They floated so easily on the water, the straps swaying with the movement of the tiniest of waves hitting the beach. I bent down to pick them up. Turning them over in my hands, I wondered if their owner would ever wear them again.

What happened to him? Was it a heart attack? Stroke? Ok, he was moving up the age ladder to be sure. I remember Lena telling me that he was in his early fifties. But...it didn't make sense. Had he been sick? Was it just his time? Was it something else?

I was standing in the middle of a group of people. A little overweight, my baggy black shorts and even baggier Giants tee shirt, were a perfect camouflage. I was invisible. Sunglasses and a base-ball cap completed the picture. I could move around, stop, look the opposite direction and tune in on conversations next to me. Not the most sought-after talent in the world, but I heard things people didn't know I was hearing. And I have a unique ability. I never forget a face...never...ever.

Out in the water, the last few swimmers were stroking toward the water's edge. Following them were two lifeguards aboard a small Zodiac. They had picked up the large orange and yellow course buoys and were dragging them to the shore where they would be deflated. I watched, but mostly I listened to the conversation behind me.

"He's still alive," a man said. "I know him. He swims with a good friend of mine. He is in great shape."

"Weekend warrior. Aging boomers, you know," said a female voice.

"No, not him."

"Right," she said. "I have a friend, a dispatcher for the Santa Miguel Sheriff's department. She was telling me that every week-end, there are at least three or four boomers—mostly men—falling off their bikes. Heart attacks. Dead on the spot. They still think they're twenty years old."

"No, Dick was known for taking care of himself. I thought he was a hypochondriac, always running to the doctor's with some kind of sport's ailment. I told him, he was looking for the silver bullet, the one that would keep him young, strong and faster than not just the swimmers in his age group, but a few age groups below him. He would laugh, but he never denied it. He knew all his num-bers—cholesterol, blood pressure, resting heart rate."

The conversation grew fainter as the couple walked away.

———

The athletes, hungry after the long swim, surrounded some tables heavy with food. They descended like diving seagulls on deep trays full of juicy watermelon slices, sweet strawberries and yellow bananas. Close by, were bagels, three different kinds of cream cheese and plates of chocolate chip cookies. There was even a booth offering samples of a new neon orange rehydration drink.

I squeezed in, and grabbed a handful of strawberries. Mario, the body-builder turned swimmer, reached a thick arm in front of me for a bunch of grapes.

"For a new guy, you must be pretty fast. You were out of the water before my sister," I said.

"There were two races today, a one mile and a two mile. I only did the first race, the one miler. I was on shore waiting for everyone to finish the longer swim. I saw the whole thing with Dick—the rescue, everything."

"Did Dick do both swims?"

"Yeah, he did. This is his ninth or tenth swim for the year. Two first place finishes would almost guarantee him an overall win this season."

"How many swims are there?"

"About twenty. The number of races changes every year."

I knew from attending swims with Lena that the open water season started in late spring and went to the end of September. During that time, more than 3,000 swimmers, ages 18 to 80-plus drive around Northern California, jump into cold water, tear through a course, then do the same thing again the next weekend, the weekend after that and the weekend after that.

"Maybe it was just too much for Dick's body."

"Not likely. He can do double this distance in his sleep."

Mario walked over to the results board a few yards away. It was surrounded by a crowd of people, trying to peer around the swimmers in front of them or standing on their toes to look over someone's head, so they could read the spreadsheet of names and find out where they placed.

Does it matter that much? I wondered as I watched the crowd. All that effort for a glass mug that says second place?

From across the beach, there was a loud whistle. It was my sister, Lena. She was waving that ratty towel of hers and pointing to the parking lot. She didn't care where she placed or if she picked up an award. She was ready to go home.

The long circular parking lot was full of cars since most swimmers were still pecking through the free food and drinks. Not one, but two, additional ambulances were stationed there. Paramedics, solid looking guys dressed in dark blue shirts and trousers, arms crossed, were standing outside, chatting with each other.

"Just another day at the beach?" said Lena to one as she walked by.

"You'd be surprised how often this occurs," said the paramedic. "The same thing happened to a guy less than a month ago, right here, at this lake."

I walked ahead to open up the car while Lena continued her conversation with the medics. I personally think she was more interested in them than in what they had to say.

The dark seats of Lena's '99 Camry were vibrating from the heat. I threw down a towel to cover the driver's seat and then another to cover the steering wheel. I slid in and within a few seconds, sweat began to drip down the back of my neck. Pulling my hat off and holding my hair away from my neck with one hand, I quickly turned the key, lowered the windows and switched on the air conditioner with the other. By the time Lena reached in to retrieve her old towel from the steering wheel and went around to sit in the passenger's seat, the car had cooled down enough to put the windows up. Still, my black tee shirt was plastered to my chest.

"So?"

"So, what?" Lena replied, her head back on the seat rest, her eyes beginning to close.

"This could be a new record. You might be asleep before we even get out of the parking lot," I said. "So...what did they say about the swimmer, the guy in the ambulance?"

"They took him to the Lake Joseph city hospital. But it doesn't look good. He never regained consciousness. You know, I can't remember there ever being a death at one of these swims. Odd though. I asked why they didn't use the defibrillator if it was a heart attack. They said it wasn't called for. Not much more to tell...just need to rest a bit.....good swims, tough swims...tired."

I pulled out of the parking place and drove down the narrow two-lane road out of the park. In my mind, I was back in the shade near the beach. All I saw was the swimmer on the ground—his pale stomach stretching like a balloon about to explode. I never noticed the three guys on mountain bikes directly in front of me. I stomped on the brake with both feet. The Camry violently jerked to a stop less than 10 feet from the cyclists.

Lena's eyes flew open. "What?"

One cyclist in a black and yellow jersey flipped me off. "Hey, watch it," he yelled. "You trying to kill us?" The other two swerved to the side and glared back at the Camry.

"Sorry...so sorry," I mumbled.

I pulled off the gravel road and stopped under the pines. My heart was pounding. I came that close to hitting three people. Why didn't I see them? They were right in front of me.

"The swimmer...I keep thinking about him. I hope he's going to be all right." I glanced over at Lena who was staring at me.

"Want me to drive?" she asked.

I didn't respond. Instead, I started up again, going slowly, hearing the crunch of the tires on the unpaved road and forcing myself to focus until I reached the park exit.

Okay, I thought. This should get easier.

The three-hour trip home would be a quiet one. I took a quick look over at my sister before I aimed the car toward Highway 80. Her eyes were shut. Back to normal. I switched on the Giants game. Bottom of the fourth. Giants had slipped one run behind.

"Do you have to listen to that?" said an irritated Lena, opening one eye and reaching for the radio. "It is so annoying."

I smacked her outreached hand. "Hey, leave it be. Who am I supposed to talk to? You?"

With closed eyes, she turned her hands into puppets having a conversation.

"Blah, blah, blah...strike zone. Blah, blah, blah...outfield. Blah, blah..."

"Go to sleep already," I said. In less than five minutes, she was out cold. Definitely back to normal.

The four-laned highway heading west was chiseled into the rolling hills. It wrapped around bare granite outcroppings and bordered a wide fast moving river. It was mid-afternoon and there were only a few other cars on the road. As the road straightened out, the mountains moved miles off to each side and straw-colored flat farmland took their place. The drive became long and monotonous.

For almost thirty years, I've been driving my sister to swimming events. She was a little girl then and just learning to put her face in the water. Lena is a natural athlete. Me, I'm a natural fan... of her...of baseball...of most sports. There's just the two of us left in our family; her boyfriend might increase it to three, but the jury's still out on that.

I've been away from the San Francisco Bay area for about ten years. I was married and had a pretty good job as an executive assistant in a healthcare firm. Brad, my husband, and I lived way outside of Denver, surrounded by mountains and pines. A good life, I thought. A few uneasy spots, but basically solid. Then, Brad disappeared. Just disappeared. One day, he never came home from work. He was a well respected consulting software engineer. No one ever figured out what happened. Not the police. None of his clients. Not even his brother on the East Coast. I haven't heard anything from him since.

"Just like dad," I said out loud to the radio sports announcers.

When Brad left, I couldn't make myself do anything. I didn't want to work any more. I'd wander through the house at night with the lights off and end up sitting in my kitchen, wearing the same clothes I had on two days before. I couldn't eat during the day, but at night, bags of Oreos were my best friends. Then Lena sent me a cryptic text that said, "I'm moving out of SF back to Marin. Bought a small house, cottage, really, two bedrooms. I only need one. Want the other one?"

That's all it took. In less than two months, I was back living in San Rafael off Wynnwood Drive, only a mile from where we grew up.

2

The baseball game was over when I turned onto our short street. In our driveway was Terrel Robinson and the love of his life, his mortician black '70 Dodge Charger. T. or Dr. T, as my sister called him, was Lena's boyfriend. The hood was up and Terrel was underneath, long legs sticking out. A post-game talk show was blaring out of a small radio somewhere in the garage.

I got out of the car, opened up the trunk and pulled out my red and white cooler. Lena, still half asleep, pushed her side door open with both feet.

"Take your swim bag," I called to her as she walked over to Terrel and lightly kicked his shoe.

"Hey, doc. Missed you today. When are you going to start coming to my swims?"

"Never. They're too white for me. Besides, I'm on call," mumbled the voice from under the car. He scooted out, stood up, stretched and wiped his hands on the rag sitting next to the five yellow quart bottles of engine oil. Then he wiped the oil smears off his black rimmed glasses on his tee shirt.

"You're such a phony," said Lena, easily falling into a long-running, but congenial argument. "Skin color has nothing to do with it. You can't swim. That's your problem."

Terrel glanced at her and then looked at me, cocked his head, held out his hand and smirked.

"Pay up. Your wonderful Giants lost…again. Those two World Series wins were a fluke."

"They just ran out of innings," I said, heading for the door.

"They choked. Pay up."

"Double or nothing the next game…"

"They got nothing. A bet's a bet," he said. "Pay up."

Terrel Edward Robinson, the product of a white mother and a black father, was an emergency room doctor in San Francisco. His road to and through medical school had not been easy. With his long lanky arms and legs, his aptitude for cars and 'don't mess with me' stare, he was often thought of as a pick-up basketball player, a potential mechanic or a probable thug. He could be all of those things, when needed. But it was his dogged determination and savage intelligence that got him that M.D. after his name.

"You should have been there today," Lena continued. "Someone nearly drowned or something. I'm really not sure. Maybe you could have helped."

The baseball bet was quickly forgotten.

"What happened?" he asked.

Lena began to explain what she knew as they walked toward the front door.

"Forgetting something? Your swim bag? I'm not your maid," I called out.

Lena glanced over her shoulder at me standing by the car, hands on hips, "Don't worry about dinner, Trish. I'm calling in for Chinese."

———

When the food was delivered, we placed the white cartons on the dining room table. Well, you couldn't really call it a dining room table in the formal sense. It looked more like a sturdy oak work table found in a country kitchen decades ago. Lena's chairs were mismatched, all with different color cushions she'd picked up at garage sales. That's the way the rest of her house looked. Colorful, comfortable, but at times a little odd.

On the walls were framed enlarged samples of typography; Helvetica E, Garamond I, Century Gothic G and Tahoma M. A mobile made up of tarnished silverware hung by the window and swayed and clinked in the afternoon breeze.

Lena was a graphic designer, sought after and well paid. She specialized in web sites. About 50% of her clients were related to the swimming world. She had a great eye for color and design and understood what made readers come back to a site time after time.

Terrel came out of the kitchen carrying forks, two sets of chopsticks, serving spoons and a six pack of Tsingtao beer. "Confucius say, 'Hot food, cold beer lead warrior over Great Wall to paradise. Kung Pao, Tsingtao.'"

"That is lame," said Lena, reaching out for a bottle of beer.

"I suppose you can do better," said Terrel.

"I'm sure I can."

"Go ahead. Now, do it. Now. Don't think about it. Just say it… go ahead."

"Well, ah…"

"Can't deliver…I knew it."

As they sparred across the table, I dug into a carton of food. Thanks to a suggestion from Lena who kept the website for the Northern California Swimming Association humming along, the organization hired me for some temporary work. It wasn't much of a job, but at least I had money coming in. Nor Cal Swimming was the group in charge of today's open water event.

"You know, I found the swimmer's goggles floating right at the water's edge. T, give me your best guess. What do you think happened?" I asked.

Terrel was eating the Kung Pao chicken and decided not to let medical questions come between him and his dinner. He didn't answer.

"Come on, T. Here's the situation. Older guy…," said Lena.

"I'd say he was more middle-aged."

Lena rolled her eyes.

"Okay, middle-aged guy in good shape, swims hard and then drowns, almost. He is pulled from the water, put in the ambulance; they hook him up to some machines and then run some tests. So what happened?"

T looked up at Lena, then down at his plate. He was about to take another bite.

"I'm eating here. Can't you see that?" Terrel said. "Look, he'll probably recover. Maybe he was just dehydrated."

"Dehydration can lead to unconsciousness?" I asked.

"It can," he said. "You've seen marathon runners who can't stand on their feet at the end of a race, right? Dehydration has a lot to do with that. Maybe his blood pressure dropped. Caused by…who knows what?"

"I heard the paramedic talking to the ER before they drove off to the hospital. They were talking about blood sugars."

"Okay," Terrel said, staring first at Lena, then at me. "Do you know if his blood sugar was too low? If so, he may be hypoglycemic. That could be the underlying reason he lost consciousness. It's very dangerous if not treated. Did he have any known medical conditions? Any heart abnormalities?"

"How would I know," Lena said. "I never met the guy, not really."

"What medications was he on? Was he taking them? Was he taking something else? Something he shouldn't have been taking. He's an athlete. Athletes are known to take drugs, performance enhancing drugs."

"You're talking steroids? In Masters swimming? Oh, please," I said.

But Terrel had started diagnosing and once he started, it was hard to stop him. I watched as he began to free associate, something he liked to do.

"Ok...then...maybe he had too much coffee. Coffee...caffeine...one of those high powered energy drinks...maybe there was some kind of interaction. Stimulants, good possibility, amphetamines, speed. Whatever he took might have stimulated his heart into an arrhythmia, an irregular heartbeat. Maybe he was juiced. It doesn't take more than 60 seconds to find performance enhancing drugs—PEDs—on line."

"T," I said "You keep coming back to these...PEDS...or whatever you called them. This is Masters swimming. They don't do drugs for that."

"Well," said Lena. "That's what I thought, until I went to Australia for the World Games a few years back. They had an open water swim as the last event. I was standing at the train station in Perth with some swimmers from Costa Rica trying to get to the venue.

"The woman pointed to a baldheaded man at the end of the platform. She said, 'I know him from home. He's on 'roids. Everyone knows it. He looks different and he acts crazy.' That was the first time I heard talk about performance enhancing drugs in Masters. I couldn't believe it then. Still can't."

"There are many reasons for a fit athlete to collapse, whether in the water or on a playing field," said Terrel. "Cardiac arrest is only one of them. Maybe the water was too hot, hyperthermia."

"Not here," said Lena.

"Okay…maybe it was too cold. Hypothermia. Blood clot. Cramps. Panic. You know, there's a new drug on the streets based on a synthetic testosterone derivative. It is supposed to help with muscle retention and growth, but it can make someone very sick if too much is absorbed into the body. It is primarily injected. Street junkies call it High Test. You use it to top off your tank."

"Back to steroids again," said Lena. "Testosterone, High Test, top off your tank. You're making this up, aren't you? You've been in the ER in downtown San Francisco too long. Not every death is caused by street drugs, guns or gangs," said Lena.

"What do you know? Ah, right, you're the Marin expert on downtown street life. If this man is as fit and as clean and upstanding as you think and he dies, and the family thinks something seems off, they may ask for an autopsy. Autopsies aren't done as a matter of course anymore. Otherwise, if he lives and doesn't want to talk about it, you'll never know."

I watched as they quibbled and snapped at each other. It was like this all the time. From a distance, it was disconcerting. But for them, this was foreplay. The fight would often finish in bed.

I picked up a bottle of beer and wandered off to my room. Bedrooms can be depressing places when you can't sleep and there is no one to talk to. Each night I tensed up when I headed in that direction. My bedroom held a tempting promise of rest and relaxation. That's what I wanted and desperately needed. But that's all it was...just a promise. Each night, I thought it would be different. But no matter how tired I was, I could sleep only an hour or two at a time, if that.

I heard Terrel call out 'later'. The front door shut. Next came the deep throaty rumble of the Charger's engine followed by the sound of its tires crunching over the small pebbles in the driveway. The noise soon faded, as he drove down the street.

I stretched out on my bed and picked up a book. After reading the same words over and over, I found myself gazing out the window to the gentle uneven peaks of Mt. Tamalpais. At 2,571 feet, it wasn't much more than a bunny slope, if you compared it to the Colorado Rockies. But Mt. Tam, with its sensual curves was soothing to look at. Tall Douglas fir and oak dotted the hills and there was a promise of the Pacific Ocean just on the other side.

My eyes closed. Hours passed as I dozed, woke up, dropped back into a light sleep, and then woke again. The house was dark. It was three in the morning and sleep seemed as elusive as the swirling grey fog that was sitting on top of Mt. Tam. I pulled on a sweatshirt and sweatpants, slipped on a pair of socks and started my nightly cruise through the house. First to the living room. I wandered from the front window to the bookcase and back to the window. Inside my head, a hamster was running an endless loop on his wheel.

How did I get back here, not more than one mile from where we lived as kids? No husband. An on-call temporary delivery job that paid next to nothing. No place of my own. An expanding waistline. And I'm living with my sister, my younger sister. This isn't how I pictured my life. I tried the positive thinking approach. 'It won't be this way forever. I can change it, I know I can.'

I moved into the kitchen. The tangy aroma of soy sauce still hung in the air from the empty food cartons. Opening up the refrigerator, I pulled out the last beer and headed back to my room.

Warm milk does nothing for me, but a beer could sometimes put me to sleep. I began to doze again. The open water swim drifted into my dream. I was waiting at the lake's edge; the warm sun on my face; the cool water swirling around my toes. Flecks of fool's gold glittered in the water and the tiniest of fish, no wider than a toothpick and half the length, swam around my ankles.

I was the only one on the beach. It was completely empty, just me standing there looking out at Lake Joseph. The wind was blowing. I could see it in the trees, but it remained deathly quiet, as if I were standing in a vacuum.

The swimmers were spread out across the lake, silently coming toward me. Then, they stopped and calmly, serenely began to disappear, one by one, sinking slowly below the surface. There was no panic, no screams, no thrashing of arms and legs. Only deep stillness. The ripples that spread out from their movements in the water began to subside until the water grew tranquil as if no one had ever been there. And I was frozen on the shore, not able to move, not able to help any of them.

3

Off in the distance, the phone was ringing. Lying there with eyes closed, the dream kept repeating itself. I was still on the sunny, hot, sandy beach; no noise except the deadly lull of the small waves whispering their way up the beach—and the ringing phone. Disgusting tasting stomach acid lurched into my mouth. I was queasy and dizzy. Normally, I don't answer phones, but I was eager to get away from the drowning swimmers' dream. Using every bit of energy I had, I sat on the side of the bed, head in hands, stood up and stumbled toward the phone.

Before I even had a chance to say hello, a harried voice on the other end asked for Lena.

"She's not home. She left about two hours ago for swim practice," I said, willing myself to listen.

"Trish, Bill, here. Bill Rutherford, Nor Cal Swimming. Lena promised to work on our website later today. I need her now. The whole system crashed. I had just uploaded the results from yesterday's open water swim and it froze. No one can get into our site. Swimmers are calling for results. This machine is a piece of shit. I've tried her cell phone, but she's not answering."

I smiled at that. Lena's not crazy about talking on phones either.
"Okay. Listen, I'll text her and tell her to call you."

"This is the wrong day, wrong day for this. My assistant, Chris, left me a message over the weekend, saying he had to go 'work on himself' for a while. So what does he do? He quits, says he is leaving for some beach on the Pacific Northwest. Who does things like that anymore? Look, I need you to pick up some swim caps, and medals for next weekend's swim. You up for that?"

"Of course," I said with a clarity and chipperness I didn't feel. "I've got some free time and gas in the car."

I hung up and the hamster sprinting around on his wheel in my head came to an abrupt stop. Then, he turned around and started galloping in the other direction. Got to shower, get directions online. I jogged back to the bedroom and pulled out a clean pair of cargo pants and a long sleeve yellow tee shirt. One set of racing thoughts smothered the other, as I forced myself to set up a plan for the morning.

With my baseball cap pulled down as far as it could go and dark sunglasses perched on the brim, I picked up my car keys from the kitchen counter. I should eat. But my stomach reeled at the thought of food. Maybe later. Instead, I grabbed a bottle of water and a handful of saltine crackers as I headed for the door.

The swim caps and medals were ready at the sports store. With a quick signature, I was back on the road. Wispy fog rolling down the hills above Sausalito was beginning to burn off. The sun was out and with the next curve of the road, I could see the houseboats in Richardson Bay off the Sausalito waterfront. The top of the two towers of the Golden Gate Bridge popped into view while I was still in the Waldo Tunnel.

On the Bridge, I slowed down to the obligatory 45 miles an hour. I glanced to my right at the Pacific Ocean, disappearing into a hazy horizon. There was a container ship moving toward the mouth of San Francisco Bay, propelled by the incoming waters.

To my left were the white crisp lines of the San Francisco skyline. Three piers and four concrete warehouses of Fort Mason jutted out into the Bay. Behind them were red-tiled roof buildings. One of those housed the office for the Nor Cal Swimming Association. That's where I was headed.

I pulled into Fort Mason's large outdoor parking lot, grabbed the box of caps, found the right building and climbed three flights of no-frills stairs to the swimming office. The hallway was sparse, the stairwell whitewashed.

Inside, director Bill Rutherford was on one phone, while two others were ringing. He glanced at me and the box of caps and motioned for me to come in. "Thank you," he mouthed. Bill was a compact muscular man about 5'8", in his forties, who vibrated with energy. His prematurely thinning grey hair combed straight back, rimless glasses, designer jeans, and crisp white dress shirt, sleeves rolled up to the elbows gave him more of a hip accountant look than that of a sports director.

He switched to his headset and continued talking, hands moving constantly. I looked around the one room office. Tall narrow uncluttered windows faced the Bay. Like the stairs, the office walls were whitewashed. Photos of swim meets, swimmers, and awards ceremonies hung on the concrete walls. I put the box of caps and medals on an empty chair near the door.

Finally, Bill stopped talking. Immediately, the phone rang again.

"It's been like this all morning. We had a problem yesterday at the open water swim. People are calling to find out what happened. The press is even calling."

"I know. I was there," I said. "How is the swimmer? Do you know what happened?"

Bill sat down on the edge of this desk. "He died this morning."

"That's terrible. A heart attack?" I asked.

"I can't really talk about it at this point," he said. "In thirty years, we've never had a death at an open water swim."

I was struck by the fickleness of life. What would Waddell's family do? How would their lives be different? During that first month after Brad walked out, I wondered how many pills it would take to put me asleep permanently. Watching this swimmer fade before my eyes yesterday, I realized what a terrible mistake I almost made. That could have been me. If that was the case, Lena would be alone. It would have destroyed her.

I started for the door.

"Would you like to expand the work you're doing for me... maybe help out in the office, until I can settle the 'Chris' question?" Bill asked. "You'd still have to run errands and deliver supplies, but the rest of the time, you'd be here answering the phones."

"Sure, I've worked in offices for years."

For the next three minutes, I became a talking resume, focusing not only on my office abilities from my last job, but the incredible way (or so I thought) I tiptoed between the sparring healthcare executives, union leaders and frontline workers.

"It probably won't be full time. But, it would be a big help. Tomorrow morning? Could you start then?"

I nodded.

"One more thing. I need another delivery done today. It's about an hour away."

Since there was nothing else on my very blank calendar, I agreed to make the run.

"Some swim items were left at the event yesterday. They need to get back to the family."

"Do you usually do a door-to-door delivery service for lost and found? I think it would be the swimmer's responsibility to watch over their own things."

"Normally, that's what happens. But the office needs to get them back to the Waddell family." He paused.

"The Waddell family, as in Dick Waddell, the swimmer who died?"

"Yes, that's the one."

4

The hour's drive out to Martinez, birthplace of joltin' Joe DeMaggio, the famous New York Yankee ballplayer, home of naturalist John Muir and of the recently departed swimmer Richard Waddell was surprisingly relaxing—radio on, weather warming up, a bottle of water and saltines within my reach. Waddell lived in a quiet suburb—small one-story homes with flat roofs and well kept front lawns. The neighborhood was sandwiched between two shopping centers with trees used as a vision and sound buffer. Nice, simple, not overly fancy or memorable. Since most people were at work, the neighborhood streets were empty.

As I parked, I wondered what I had gotten myself in for. What do I say to these people that just lost an important part of their family?

I had put Dick Waddell's swim bag in the car trunk, but it had fallen over and everything was scattered. What a mess. Half-used sample packets of sunscreen and shampoo had oozed out and were mixing together in the trunk. As I scraped up the sticky lotions, I noticed a small baggie with two white capsules in it and three gel packs. The gel packs I'd seen before. Lena used them all the time before a swim to keep her energy up. But never the capsules. I picked the baggie up and held it at eye level, rubbing the capsules between my thumb and forefinger through the light plastic bag.

Maybe this had something to do with Waddell's death.

I could help the family. I could give the baggie to Dr. T and ask him to test the capsules. It might answer some questions. Questions they haven't even asked yet. Maybe, it could even save other swimmers. I didn't want to see anyone else die.

I looked at the baggie again. I could hear Lena's voice echoing in my head, "Stay out of it." She was right. Dick Waddell, his death, these capsules had nothing to do with me. It was none of my business.

"I have to put you back," I said to the baggie as I stuffed it and the rest of the gear into the swim bag.

I followed the walkway that curved around to a front door located on the side of the house. I rang the bell and counted 'one Mississippi, two Mississippi'—if I got to 'three Mississippi,' I was going to leave the swim gear on the front step. But, no such luck. A man wearing khaki trousers with creases so sharp they'd cut paper, a snappy blue blazer and rich brown leather boat shoes, opened the door.

"Hi, I'm Trisha Carson…from the Nor Cal Swimming Association. These were left yesterday, at the open water swim. They belong to Richard Waddell."

I stood there awkwardly, not knowing what to do or what else to say.

"Come in," said the man. He introduced himself as Spencer Matthews, Waddell's brother-in-law. Deeply tanned with brown wavy hair, Spencer was surprisingly short, probably under 5'4". I was taller than he was.

"I'm sorry to hear about Mr. Waddell," I said.

Spencer led me into the living room. "Sit down, sit down," he said. "The family is still at the hospital. I just got back here myself. Terrible tragedy. Excuse me, but I'm on the phone with his employer."

I looked around the half-empty living room. There was a nondescript brown and blue couch, one straight back chair, a large HDTV on the wall and a small bookcase. Waddel was a minimalist or someone who didn't spend much time at home.

Spencer walked back into the room.

"Dick worked as a financial analyst. This came as a shock to his staff as well as his supervisor. Hard to believe he's gone. Dick was in the best of shape. Pamela, his sister, and I—of course—were so glad when he moved here. About a year ago, a Texas transplant. He used to crew for me. Sailboat races…not too comfortable on the foredeck but he was pretty decent in the cockpit."

Spencer stopped and looked at me.

"An all-around water person, it sounds like. I'm so sorry," I said again, not sure what else to say.

"Did you know him?" Spencer asked.

"No, no, I didn't. But I happened to be at the swim yesterday. I can tell you that the paramedics, the ambulance, were right there as soon he was brought to shore. You couldn't have asked for a quicker response."

I'm not sure Spencer was listening. He was pulling things out of Waddell's swimbag: an extra swimsuit, towel and the plastic baggie.

"What's this," he asked, pointing to the gel packet and capsules.

"Probably energy supplements. Swimmers, runners, lots of athletes use them all the time. It helps with endurance and performance, completely legal." I felt I needed to add that, remembering the conversation I just had with myself a few minutes ago.

Spencer smiled. "No doubt. Richard wouldn't think of doing anything out of the ordinary to stretch his performance. He was a by-the-book kind of guy...straight laced, very religious...spiritual mostly. Not quite my style."

Too much information. It was time to get out of there.

———

By 9:00 a.m. the next day, I was back at the swim office in Fort Mason. This morning, I was the one answering phones while Bill looked on. He gave me about fifteen minutes of orientation, mostly on how to work the phone headset. Then he left with an off-hand comment about never being in the office, that I'd be by myself most of the time and did I understand?

I opened my mouth to answer. He was gone. I could hear his footsteps hurrying down the three flights of stairs. I understood all too well. I was on my own.

"Nor Cal Swimming," I said over and over to each caller. More than one person asked about Dick Waddell. I tried to sound sympathetic without giving anything away. Not an easy thing to do. Even Mike Menton, the swimmer who placed first in Waddell's age group, left a message asking for an address so he could send flowers. It didn't sound like he knew that Waddell was dead.

About an hour later, the phones quieted down. This gave me a chance to really look around. The office was just one big room with two desks, mine at one end, Bill's at the other with bookcases in between.

I took the phone messages for Bill and put them on his cluttered desk. It was covered with papers, folders, crumbled up napkins and empty coffee cups.

A folder labeled Richard Waddell was off to the side on the one semi-clear spot. I picked it up and leafed through the papers. There was a preliminary report for Nor Cal's insurance company, a list of names and phone numbers, probably the event director and key swimmers who had been on the scene, the name of the ambulance company that took Waddell to the hospital and the name of a doctor, probably from Lake Joseph's emergency room. Interesting, but also sad. Someone's life came down to impersonal forms, lists, and in this case, lawyers—Dick Waddell's humanness had begun to fade away. I glanced back at the names and phone numbers. Was the Good Samaritan in the striped polo shirt on the list? He had been the first to notice the distressed swimmer and the first to disappear. A coincidence? Maybe. But maybe not.

The office extended to a small storage room across the hall with a huge copy machine, reams of different colored paper, boxes of old trophies, ribbons, and medals that had never been picked up. Floor to ceiling industrial styled bookcases were crammed full. There was even some extra equipment for pool meets and open water swims and a box full of tools—wrenches to tighten and loosen lane lines, buckets filled with dried cement that could be used as anchors for buoys, different lengths of synthetic rope, a series of red, yellow, green starting flags, a bullhorn and some large banners.

Before Bill left, he had handed me a swim magazine opened to a page that listed open water swimming statistics in a snappy graphic format under the heading, *Did You Know?*

According to an international open water expert, in 2011, approximately 60,000 people competed in open water swims in the United States and another 2.3 million people competed in triathlons, which have a swimming leg. There were more than 4,000 open water swims around the world, from Japan to Mexico, Australia to Hungary, and Cuba to Singapore.

Next to those numbers, Bill had scribbled, *"Northern California Masters offers more open water swims than any other area in the United States. People look to us for leadership on how to do things."*

I was impressed. At times, I thought the open water swimming consisted of only Lena and me spending weekends on the road. But I was wrong. This was a growing sport with international connections.

The computer on my desk was a relic, but I needed to check into the office's email. I couldn't answer much in the way of questions, but at least I could read them and get a sense of what went on.

The subject line of many said *Dick Waddell*. Most wanted to know what happened. One email was clearly different. I couldn't tell who it was from. The return address was "Do Not Reply" with a school system name in the Sacramento area. There was no message, just a subject line.

Subject: Waddell death. ??????

Did the sender know that Dick had died? Or was it a question wondering if he was dead. Maybe it was a query about how he died. If the office was getting these inquiries, certainly the Waddell family was. It must be painful for them to handle this right now. If I had gone through with my 'too many pills' scenario, Lena would have switched off her computer and phone immediately, headed for her bedroom and stayed there. I didn't want the Waddell family to struggle with requests for information, no matter how well-meaning. Forget Lena's warning to leave things alone, I felt compelled to help this family in any way I could.

I hit Reply and the Do Not Reply message came up. Then it reverted back to the Inbox. I clicked on the message again to open it. When I hit Reply, the same thing happened. On the third try, my computer restarted.

"Welcome to day one of the new job," I sighed.

Later, when Bill called into the office, I told him about the email. "Who knows? Maybe they hit the send button before they had time to write anything," he said "We get strange emails all the time."

"But nobody knows that Dick Waddell has died. What if his death isn't so cut and dried?"

"The family probably called his swim coach and a few of his close friends. Look, your job is to mind the office and answer the phones," said Bill. "Don't get involved with this. I know you mean well, but when there's a death, lawyers are often close behind."

"Well, now that you mention it, Waddell's coach, Cody Stephenson did call and so did an attorney for the Waddell family." I gave him her name and number. When I heard Bill muttering to himself, I quickly said goodbye and hung up.

Dick Waddell intrigued me. I looked up his information on our database. It didn't tell me more than the basics: date of birth, home address, phone number and how he placed in past swims.

Then I did a web search. Waddell was an accomplished swimmer and there were articles and records for him that dated back to his college days. He'd even gone to the Olympic trials, but missed making the team by a fraction of a second. An international swimming magazine did a profile of him a few years back when he was still in Texas. The photo showed a man doing a powerful butterfly stroke, biceps flexed as he moved through the water. Then there was a picture of him after an open water swim in Chicago. He was wearing a broad-brimmed cowboy hat, a pair of tight-fitting jeans that hung precariously low on his hips and cowboy boots. That was it. The word 'Lucky' was tattooed on his back.

The most recent piece about him mentioned that after a brief break from swimming, he had moved to Northern California to be closer to family. There was no mention of a wife or kids.

On the surface, this seemed plausible, but something was missing. Did he come to the Bay area to be close to his sister and the nattily-dressed brother-in-law? I guess, if there is no one else. Who could I talk to without bothering the Waddell family? I thought of the call from Mike Menton. They were competitors. From what I'd seen during my sister's swimming career, competitors were often good friends. I could give out the address he wanted and maybe, just maybe, have a little conversation.

Looking down at my notepad, I dialed his phone and waited.

"Hello," said a girl's high voice.

"Is Mike there?" I asked.

"No, this is his daughter, Daisy. Can I take a message?"

"Hi, Daisy. My name is Trisha Carson from the Nor Cal Swimming office. I think I saw you at the open water swim at Lake Joseph this past weekend."

There was a long pause.

"My dad's not here right now."

"He called for an address. Can I give it to you?"

For a minute, it sounded like she had put her hand over the phone and was speaking to someone nearby.

"I'll tell him you called," she said. Then the line went dead.

"What in the world?" I thought to myself. Most kids past the age of eight know how to take a message. I wondered if this was the teenager in the bikini with the nerdy boyfriend I had seen at the swim. Or maybe it was another daughter? Whoever it was needed some serious lessons in telephone etiquette.

I walked back over to Bill's desk, picked up the Waddell file and headed for the storage room. I copied the four sheets of paper with the names and phone numbers, then put it back on his desk. I placed my copies in a file folder and stuck it in my backpack.

5

My first week of work went by at a frantic pace. Bill was out of the office, more than he was in it. Phone calls about everything related to swimming, from pool meets, to upcoming swim clinics for officials and coaches, even questions about chlorine—were non-stop.

Although I didn't make a habit of talking about Dick Waddell, Bill did. I eavesdropped on phone calls between Bill and the insurance company, Bill and the Waddell's lawyer, Bill and the Waddell family and Bill and the event director.

Things weren't going smoothly.

The last thing Bill said to a caller about the Waddell death before he bolted out the door to yet another meeting was, "That's in the hands of the insurance company now. There is nothing I can do. If you think there is a question about the cause of death, maybe you should talk to the doctors again."

One afternoon, before heading for home, I left work early to pick up a few cartons of tee shirts for an upcoming pool meet. The summer sun was still high in the sky when I pulled into our driveway in

San Rafael. Lena was there, intently staring at a computer screen, her fingers flying over the keyboard, creating lines of code.

"You need a break."

She didn't look up.

"Take a drive with me. I have to return Dick Waddell's goggles."

"I've got a deadline for a project. I can't figure out how to make the interactive part of this website work the way I want. I've been trying different things all afternoon."

"Like I said, you need a break. We'll be gone for only an hour or two. Your mind will be fresh when we come back."

"Maybe you're right. Where are we going?"

———

As we drove out toward Martinez, I told Lena that I'd checked in with Pamela, Waddell's sister, to set up the meeting and that she had suggested her brother's house because she would be there, cleaning up. That was a partial truth. The location was my suggestion. I wanted to get back into Dick Waddell's house.

"So who is his sister? Does she swim, too?" asked Lena.

"I don't know about the swimming. But her name is Pamela Matthews. I met her husband when I dropped off Waddell's swim bag."

"Right," she said, already losing interest.

Early evening traffic made the drive almost twice as long. When we pulled up to the home in Martinez, Lena said, "The house looks closed up. Pamela knows we're coming, right?"

"She does."

We walked down the pathway around the house to the front door. I rang the bell and went through my 'one Mississippi, two Mississippi, three Mississippi' routine.

"Nobody's here. Did you get the time right? You said she would be here."

"I said 'will be.'"

"She's not supposed to be here yet?"

"She should show up in about forty-five minutes," I said, looking at my watch.

"I don't understand," said Lena.

"Let's walk around to the backdoor." I lifted the latch on the gate of the tall wooden fence and we walked into the empty sunless backyard.

"What are you doing?"

This backyard wouldn't be featured in any home improvement or gardening magazines. Rusted metal lawn chairs were piled one on top of the other. The grass hadn't been watered in a long time and it was dried and straggly. At one end of the yard were large dark green garbage bags used for yard clippings. Four of them were brimming over. There was no greenery anywhere, except for the garbage bags. Five cardboard boxes were piled by the back door.

"Not very inviting," Lena said. "It's creepy back here."

I walked up the three steps to the back door and knocked. It was eerily quiet.

"We know no one's home. Let's wait in the car."

"Give me a minute."

I tried to open the door. Locked. I walked back down the steps and moved over to the kitchen window around the corner from the back door. I couldn't quite see inside.

"Lena, get me one of those chairs."

"No."

"Lena, get me a chair. I need to see what it looks like inside."

"You do not and I will not." She sat down on the back steps and crossed her arms.

"I'm cold. There isn't a spot of sunshine anywhere in this yard. I want to get out of here."

"Lena."

"No. If you want a chair, get it yourself. Someone is going to see us. We—make that you—are going to end up in jail."

"It won't be the first time," I mumbled.

"What did you say?"

"Nothing...nothing important. This yard is a dump. Nobody is watching us. Look around. I can't see any windows from the houses on either side. So they can't see me or you."

Lena sat there staring at me. "You said something about jail."

"No, you did."

"Trisha?"

I walked over to one of the rusted metal chairs and dragged it back to the window. It almost toppled over on the uneven ground. Not the steadiest of platforms, but I could stand on it and look inside.

In stark contrast to the unkempt backyard, the kitchen was neat and clean. No dishes in the sink. No empty pizza boxes on the kitchen table. I did see two more dark green garbage bags full of trash. It looked like someone, probably sister Pamela, had been there and cleaned up.

Mail was piled on the counter by the sink. Three, maybe four envelopes. I could almost see the return addresses. I jiggled the screen until it pulled off. Then, I pushed against the sliding glass window. It didn't give. I pushed again harder. A small white plastic lock that held the window shut, popped off and landed in the sink.

"Hmmm."

"What did you do?"

"I broke the window lock. It was nothing but a cheap piece of plastic. How could that keep anyone out of here?"

"Get down. Let's go."

"Just one more minute," I said pulling the window open and peering inside. "Not a bad kitchen."

"Are you a decorator now? Let's go."

"I need to get in the house, alone, for a few minutes. I want to go through Waddell's swim bag. There were capsules in a baggie. I didn't have the nerve to stick them in my pocket when I brought the bag back. If I could find them, Terrel could test them."

I propped myself against the open window.

"There is some unopened mail right here on the counter. Maybe something from the hospital at Lake Joseph. Maybe an itemized bill. Maybe test results."

"That's why we're here now, isn't it? You didn't want her to be here, did you?"

"You're right, I didn't want her here. I'm sure there is something inside; something that, I don't know, that could explain his death."

The envelopes were just out of reach. I leaned in and stretched out my arm. Another inch of two, that's all I needed. My fingertips almost, almost touched the pile of mail. I was balancing now on the window ledge. My legs and feet were up in the air outside; the top of my body was completely inside.

Stretch. A bit more. Stretch. Got it. The fingers of my right hand touched the edge of one envelope. I inched in closer until I could get a better grip on it. With the letter in my hand, I slowly moved out of the window. Lena was still sitting on the steps with her arms crossed, staring at me.

"Trish, what do you care? Let's get out of here."

"It's become very important to me, very personal."

I held the envelope up like a trophy, then turned it over so I could see the return address. It was an advertisement from a local bank.

"Not what I wanted. Not what I wanted at all. I'm putting it back." The top half of me disappeared, once again, through the kitchen window.

Lena hopped off the steps and lunged at my legs.

"Get out. Now, get out. Trish, I can hear a car coming down the road. Maybe it's Dick's sister. Please get down."

I hated to admit it, but Lena was right. I could spend the rest of the evening trying to convince Pamela, or even worse, a police officer that I meant no harm. Still holding on to the envelope, I pulled myself out of the window, slid it shut, put the screen back in place and climbed off the chair.

A car stopped in front of the house.

Lena and I stared at each other. We looked through a slat in the fence and saw a solid, big-boned, short blond woman get out of a car, pop the trunk open and take out some cleaning supplies.

"Pamela?" Lena mouthed. She looked like she was going to faint.

"Probably, but I don't know. I never met her before," I whispered. "When she opens the front door and goes in, I'll flip up the latch and we will quietly walk toward the car."

We heard the front door open and shut. Her footsteps moved into the living room. She stopped. We waited. Then she started walking again. That was the cue. I lifted the latch. We crouched down low and snuck out, hiding between the greenery that divided the Waddell home from the next house. Instead of heading directly for the car, which was parked across the street, I grabbed my sister's arm and led her to the corner.

"Where are we going? Let's get back into the car."

"Just a minute."

We stood there for about thirty seconds. Then, I led the resistant Lena slowly back to the Waddell house, up the winding path to the front door at the side of the house and knocked.

———

Pamela Matthews opened the front door and stood there with a garbage bag in each hand.

"Two down and I don't know how many more to go," she said. "Come in. I was expecting you."

"Yes. We're here a little early," I said.

"You're the neighbors who called yesterday?"

"No, I'm from the swim office. I called this morning."

"My mistake. Neighbors have been stopping by to pay their respects. Let me go put these bags into the kitchen." She disappeared down the hall as we followed close behind. I spotted the pile of mail on the kitchen counter not far from the window.

"Must have been a beautiful yard once," I said, straining my neck to look out to the backyard. I blocked her view of the letters and dropped the bank advertisement on top of the pile. Then, I inched the mail toward the counter's edge.

"Maybe before my brother moved in. Dick was no gardener," Pamela said following my gaze to the back yard.

I pulled the envelopes closer. Lena stood behind me. I turned to her and mouthed, "pick them up."

She shook her head 'no.' She put her hand's up, traffic cop style, and gave me the smallest of shoves. That's all it took. The mail fell on the floor.

"Here, let me get that out of your way," said Pamela as she bent down and scooped up the envelopes, looked at them briefly, then stuck them in her pocket. As she stood up, she glanced into the sink.

"What is this?"

In the sink were two sponges and the small white plastic lock I had knocked off the window. She reached in to pick it up and turned it over in her fingers.

"I didn't really introduce myself properly," I said quickly. I held out my hand. "I'm Trisha Carson, from Nor Cal Swimming Association. There was something of Dick's that I wanted to return. It was left at the Lake Joseph swim. This is my sister, Lena."

Lena managed a weak smile and a nod.

Pamela led us back to the living room. "Sit down. Let me get you something to drink."

She placed the narrow piece of plastic on the table. We both just stared at it; then glanced at each other. Lena whispered "This is crazy. Give her the goggles and let's get out of here. Say you got a call and we have to leave, now."

Pamela walked back in carrying a tray with tall glasses of lemonade and some shortbread cookies.

"I've been existing off this for the last week. No real time or interest in food right now."

We nodded our heads in understanding.

"So what did you say you are returning?"

"Mr. Waddell's goggles."

I put them on the table. She picked them up and turned them over in her hands. A ghost of a smile moved across her face.

"You know when Dick was little, goggles weren't around yet. He used to come home from swim practice with red, burning eyes all the time. So hard to do his homework. But by the time he was about 17 or 18, right around the time of the 1976 Olympics, they became the thing to have, if you were a swimmer. They were worn at the Olympics in Montréal and records were shattered. The coaches loved them. That meant their swimmers could practice longer. Dick's goggles made all the difference. His speed increased dramatically."

Lena leaned forward to listen. The conversation was about something that interested her.

"I'm wondering," I said. "Did the hospital ever tell you what happened to Dick? Did he have a stroke or a heart attack?"

"Well, the official cause of death was drowning. They found fluid in his lungs. That doesn't satisfy me. I want to know what caused the drowning. Dick was an exceptionally good swimmer. I told the doctors he was a type A personality, driven to succeed. They suggested that he could have had a cardiac event that led to the drowning. But we—Spencer and I—don't think he went out there and had a heart attack."

"If it wasn't a heart attack, what do you think it could have been?" I asked.

Pamela paused and glanced around the room, then down at her brother's goggles still in her hand.

"Some of the test results I received from the medical examiner don't make sense to me. I asked for them to be redone and I've requested an autopsy. My brother was an incredible athlete. He liked winning. And if truth be told, he didn't mind telling you how good he was."

The conversation was cut short when the front door opened and in walked Spencer Matthews, the man I met when I returned the swim bag.

"Hey, girls. What's going on?" He looked at us curiously. Pam started to introduce us.

"We've met," he interrupted, staring at me, then shifting his eyes to Lena.

"My sister, Lena," I said. He nodded.

I think he was wearing the same clothes as before. Knife-edge khakis, blazer, boat shoes. Maybe that's all he owns. He certainly wasn't dressed to help his wife clean up the house.

Pamela walked over to a low cupboard and opened a drawer. It was crammed full of medals, ribbons, even some photos. She pulled out a photo of Dick's high school swim team.

"See, there he is," and she pointed to a tall skinny kid in the back row.

"Look at those big bushy sideburns," Lena said.

"I remember those things," Spencer said, looking over Pamela's shoulder at the picture.

"You knew Pam and Dick back then?" I asked.

"We all grew up together," he said.

"Bet his swim coach gave him grief for those," Lena said.

"There was a compromise. Remember the Olympic swimmer from around that time, Mark Spitz? He had a dark mustache. Dick's coach wouldn't let the boys on the team have long hair, but if Spitz had facial hair, then the guys could have sideburns," she chuckled.

"Who's the white guy with the Afro?" asked Lena.

"Justin Rosencastle. Not a very nice person, even to this day. Big competitor of Dick's, but always in his shadow. He thought he didn't get as much of the coach's attention as Dick did.

Spencer turned and walked out of the room. Pamela looked as if she had just swallowed sour apple juice.

I scanned the high school swim team photo. The swimmers were sitting on bleachers near a pool. At the bottom was a list of names. There was Richard Waddell, third from the left in the back. In front of him was Justin, the kid with the Afro.

"Do you know him?" Pamela asked. "He's still swimming and he is in this area."

Lena shook her head.

"Don't think so," I said. "We need to go. Do you mind if I use your bathroom? It's a long drive home."

Pamela pointed toward the hallway and I passed Spencer coming out of what looked like Waddell's bedroom. I closed the bathroom door and waited a few minutes. Then, I quickly pulled open the drawers on the pine vanity. Toothpaste, floss, super strength deodorant. A brush with strands of blond hair. Soft earplugs. A homeopathic salve for sore muscles. An electric razor. A few throw-away razors. In the bottom drawer were a variety of different colored condoms.

The large area under the sink held cleaning supplies, as well as shampoo, mouthwash and an extra large bottle of liquid soap. That was it. No medicine for cholesterol or blood pressure. No prescriptions at all. And nothing that looked the least bit illegal. I could hear the muffled voices of Spencer talking with Pamela and Lena in the dining room.

I opened the bathroom door and moved quietly down the hall to the room that Spencer had just left. I paused. The three of them were still talking.

I put my hand on the silver doorknob and slowly turned it. It gave a slight click. I pushed the door open, first an inch, then two inches, then wide enough to slip through.

The setting sun created long shadows in the big room. Wall-to-wall carpet swallowed up the sounds of my rapid breathing and shuffling feet. There was a California king sized bed covered with a navy blue bedspread near the window. Sitting directly in the middle of the bed was Waddell's red, white and blue swim bag.

A grey towel was resting on top. I pulled it out. Underneath were two caps, one yellow, one red. I put them on the bedspread. Stuffed into the corner of the bag I could see the edge of a plastic sandwich bag. I reached in and gave it a tug.

"What are you doing?"

Spencer walked into the room and stood near the doorway. He moved toward the window and turned to face me. His body blocked the sun and his face was hidden in black shadows.

"I…uh…The other day, Dick's swim bag fell over in the trunk of my car. I think when I was putting things back, I stuffed in one of my tee shirts by mistake. I wanted to find it."

I strained to see his face.

He walked over to the bed and picked up the bag. He looked down at the baggie I held between my thumb and forefinger.

"That doesn't belong to you," he said and held out his hand.

I dropped it into his open palm.

"I'll check on your shirt later. Now, your sister's waiting. She's outside. It's time for you to leave."

Spencer's eyes never left my face as he opened Waddell's closet and put the swim bag on the floor way in the back behind several pairs of cowboy boots, tasseled loafers, and running shoes.

Spencer followed me out into the living room. His phone rang and he walked into the kitchen to answer it.

I was alone with Waddell's sister.

"Pamela, I…uh…have to confess. I went into your brother's bedroom. I thought I had stuffed one of my old shirts into his swim bag by mistake before I dropped it off. I noticed a baggie with a few capsules in it. I don't want to insinuate that your brother did anything wrong, but maybe they were the cause of his death. A bad interaction with, maybe, other prescription drugs he was taking. It might be worth getting them tested. I'd be glad to…"

Spencer walked back into the room, glanced at me and then at Pamela.

"You'd be glad to—what? Trish…it is Trish, isn't it?"

I nodded.

"In the past and in my current business, I have had numerous dealings with lawyers. Some have been on my side; some not. Everything can be litigated. So it has become my policy…our policy…that neither Pamela nor I discuss anything unless a lawyer is present. Nothing against you. It's just better for everyone."

———

"What took you so long?" Lena asked.

We were flying down the freeway headed back to Marin. The visit was full of discrepancies. For starters, an outstanding swimmer with a squeaky clean reputation drowned, according to his doctors.

"What's with Spencer? He couldn't get us out of there fast enough."

"Seems that he doesn't talk to anyone unless there is a lawyer present. Understandable, I guess. I don't think they have any real answers yet on Dick's death. Oh, and he found me in Waddell's bedroom. I was looking for…"

"What? You were looking for what? A pill bottle with a skull and crossbones on it? No wonder they threw us out. I'd do the same thing."

"I saw the baggie. I had it in my hand. That's when Spencer walked in. I think those capsules have something to do with

Waddell's death. I told Pamela as much and asked her to have them tested."

"I can't believe you did that."

Checking the speedometer, I noticed that if I went any faster, we would soon be airborne. I backed off my 85 miles an hour pace and just hoped I hadn't passed a highway patrol hiding by the roadside.

"By the way, do you want to explain that comment you made about jail," said Lena.

"I don't want to talk about it."

I kept my eyes on the road and ignored my sister. There is no way she would understand what it was like after mom died and our dad left. I was old enough to take care of her, but we didn't have much money. Some of my friends—acquaintances, really—were burglarizing homes. They paid me to keep the things they stole until they could get rid of them. We needed the money, so I did it. Not the smartest of moves. Once I even went with them on a job. But I couldn't take anything. Not one thing. My life of crime ended that night. Well, not quite and jail did come later.

Lena didn't need to know any of this. I looked in my rear view mirror and kept driving.

6

Friday evening before the next open water swim, Lena, dressed in sweats and wrapped in a comforter, was stretched out on the couch. She had come down with a bad summer cold. Her nose was red and her voice had dropped three octaves. The closest she would come to water was drinking a cup of hot herbal tea. That meant I was going it alone.

I checked and rechecked everything I needed for the next day. I had the evaluation form, the name of the event director, a copy of the open water guidelines and directions to get to the swim. I was even bringing a digital camera in case I needed to visually document anything. I put everything on the kitchen table. Then I moved the lot to the table by the front door. When I shifted the papers and camera for a third time, Lena said, "What are you so nervous about? You're not even swimming? You are going as an evaluator. That's it."

"Well, I want to do it right. Everything perfect."

"This is no big deal. Most of these swims have been running for over ten years. The event directors are pros. Talk with them if you have a question. Just follow that check-list you showed me. Before you, they used to have volunteers do the evaluating. I've even done it once, a few years back. It's not that hard."

"But you're a swimmer. You know how things run. Who do I call if there is another accident?" I said, still walking around the living room with the folder in my hand.

"Not gonna happen," said Lena. "Last weekend was a once in a lifetime event. What is wrong? You can do anything. I've seen you."

"I didn't expect to go to this swim without you."

Lena laughed. "I'm your security blanket? I thought you were my security blanket. Okay, here's the down and dirty about the Cold Water Clash. It's a one mile swim around the Santa Cruz pier. It's in the Pacific Ocean. It's crowded and the water's cold, like the name indicates, about 60°. End of story."

With that, she struggled off the couch, a box of tissues under one arm and the comforter thrown over her shoulders.

"I'm going to sleep. That's what you should do. You need to be at the swim when they open registration and that's around 7:00 or 7:30 a.m., right?"

I nodded. She disappeared into her bedroom. The hamster sprinting around its wheel was back in my head.

———

I pulled out of our driveway at 5:00 a.m. I'd been pacing the floor since three o'clock in the morning. My head was throbbing but I managed to get dressed, grab the ever ready box of saltines, a bottle of water, and head for the door. Stress was doing nothing for my sleep patterns, but I was losing weight, whether I wanted to or not. Darkness enveloped our small neighborhood. The sliver of moon was hazy with an uneven circle of mist surrounding it. Mt. Tam was still lost in the pre-dawn darkness. Except for the swishing of automatic sprinklers, and the clear trills of the early morning birds, all was still. Sitting in the driver's seat, I did one last review of what I had with me.

The folder? Where was the swim evaluation folder with all my information?

I ran back into the house, grabbed it off the kitchen table and darted back out again. A deep breath, a drink of water and a nibble of a cracker and I backed out of the driveway, keeping the headlights off until I reached the street. I was on my way heading about 90 miles south to Santa Cruz, the location of the next open water swim.

———

Fifteen college-age lifeguards, dressed in wetsuits, were gathered in a circle in the fog on the beach next to the Santa Cruz boardwalk, a classic seaside amusement park that dates back over a hundred years. They listened intently to each point of the safety briefing being given by the event director dressed in a warm stadium jacket and knit cap.

"We're expecting about 350-400 swimmers, including about 50 kids under 18," he said. "Some are completely comfortable with cold ocean swimming. For others, this will be a shock. Today's water temperature is not quite 60° and the sun won't be out until about noon. We could have some hypothermic swimmers, especially those not wearing wetsuits."

The director carefully went over where the rescue paddlers would be stationed along the course and what to do if a swimmer wanted out of the chilly water. I listened from a few feet away. Impressed with the depth of knowledge and planning, I checked off one box on the swim evaluation—pre-race briefing for safety personnel.

Surrounding the circle of guards were their 10-foot long bright red rescue paddle boards and their red rescue tubes. I pulled out my camera. The black wetsuits and red rescue boards contrasted sharply with the molten grey sky and matching grey ocean. The makings for a good photo.

On the other side of the pier, swimmers were lined up on the sandy beach almost back to the sidewalk, waiting to register and pick up their swim caps and timing chips. This was not the typical California beach scene advertised on billboards. Instead, swimmers looked like they were dressed for a 49ers football game in December: gloves, warm hats, snug boots, fleece jackets and pants.

I walked around the crowd and stood behind the volunteers registering the swimmers to hear what they were saying.

"Identification? Do you have your membership card? Did you sign the liability release?"

Pretty smooth, I thought, but they could add another volunteer or two to help with registration. That would speed up the process. I looked at the evaluation checklist and took off one point for "ease of registration" and added a note as explanation.

Off to one side, a group of swimmers caught my attention when they all started to laugh. In the middle was Mike Menton, his arms stretched over his head, straight as an arrow, one hand on top of the other. The small woman in a wetsuit who had collapsed at the Lake Joseph swim, stood off to one side, talking to a group of men. To Menton's right, sitting in the sand and bundled up under a blanket, was his daughter. Where was the nerdy boyfriend I wondered? As if on cue, he walked up to the girl carrying a cup of hot chocolate.

When the crowd around Mike broke up, I slowly walked over.

"Different conditions from last week," I said to him.

"Yeah, almost ten degrees cooler," he said. "You swimming?"

"No, I'm Trish. I work at the Nor Cal Swimming Association office. Just started. You left a message there this week."

"Oh, right," he said. "Waddell. How tragic."

"Do you have a couple of minutes? I'm new to this world and have some questions about the open water scene."

"Sorry, I don't have the time," he said looking past me, maybe at some swimmers at the other side of the beach. "There's nothing to say. I don't know anything about his death. Besides, I can't talk now. I'm in pre-race mode and trying to stay warm. All I wanted when I called was Waddell's address."

With that he quickly moved away from me. No glance back. Just walked off.

I looked at the daughter and her boyfriend at my feet. "Are you Daisy?"

She stared at me.

"Didn't I talk with you earlier this week? I tried to leave a message."

"No, not me. Must have been someone else." And she turned her back, pulling the blanket up over her shoulders.

"Great family," I thought as I walked away.

From the center of the beach, the event director used a bullhorn to call the swimmers together for pre-race instructions. Although most were familiar with the generalities of the open water instructions, each swim was different and they crowded close to hear.

"Water temperature today is 58°. At the end of the pier, it could reach a balmy 60° in spots." There was a collective groan from the swimmers, most not wearing wetsuits. "I asked for warmer water but I guess nobody was listening," he said.

The crowd smiled and the speaker continued. As he described the course and the procedures for requesting help in the water, I checked off boxes right and left; so far, so good.

"Although the water is calm, not much in the way of current or swell, there are breaking waves right at the shoreline where you finish." He pointed to the water's edge and right on cue, a powerful four-foot wave seemed to appear out of nowhere and crash on the beach. Another groan from the crowd.

"So once you stand up, look behind you. There could be a wave ready to break and knock you over. That's it, folks. Have a good swim."

Then the swimmers began to move along the beach to the starting line. They passed under a pier that smelled of rotting seaweed, heading for a lifeguard tower about five minutes away. Some swimmers trotted through the numbing water, trying to get at least a small part of their body acclimated. Others ran into the ocean, ducked down, gasped, ducked down again, then made their way back to the beach.

I recognized the man walking right in front of me. I tapped him on the shoulder.

"Excuse me, I saw you at the Lake Joseph swim. You're Cody Stephenson, Dick Waddell's coach, aren't you?"

"I was," he said. "Terrible accident. He was a gifted athlete."

I introduced myself.

"We spoke earlier this week at the Nor Cal swim office. I took your message."

Cody nodded.

Well, he died doing what he loved," I said.

That sounded so inadequate. But I didn't know what else to say.

"Do you think that is true?"

"What, that he was doing something that he loved? Yeah, I do. He loved it and honestly, I think he feared it. He changed from when he first came to the pool."

"How so?"

There was a long pause as a group of swimmers walked by us.

"The only word I can think of is 'desperate.' Have you ever worked with an exceptional athlete?"

"Not me. I hardly do any sports at all."

"Well, some don't have the best social skills. They have spent their life practicing and competing. Making friends, having a comfortable family life often comes second. When Richard saw that the one thing in life that he did extremely well was gradually— and I do mean gradually—beginning to fade, he panicked. He was still faster than 99% of the men in his age group, but that wasn't enough. Not only did he hate to lose, he had to be first. He was compelled to be first."

"How could he enjoy swimming if that's how he felt?"

"That's what I'm getting at. I don't think he could. On the surface, he tried to give the impression of being laid back, relaxed. The cowpoke from Texas. But it was a cover up. Look, this is between you and me, okay? It's only a theory. He was a good man. I'll miss him."

We walked toward two red flags stuck into the sand that marked the starting line. The swimmers positioned themselves as close to the invisible line as they could get, but not be over it. Santa Cruz boardwalk was in full 'go' mode behind the athletes. Kids screaming on the Hurricane, a roller coaster with neck-popping turns and the Double Shot, a 125' tower that plummets riders to the ground like a diving airplane without an engine.

"I don't know what I'd rather not do more," I said to Cody. "The roller coaster or go into that cold water."

He was just about to give me his take on the choice, when the bullhorn gave an ear-shattering blast and hundreds of swimmers ran down the beach yelling, jumped into the chilly Pacific Ocean and started swimming. They were headed for the end of the pier. I managed to get a few photos of the first group plunging into the water. Cody disappeared in the crowd of onlookers at the water's edge.

"Where do they finish?" I asked a man standing next to me carrying a stadium jacket and a pair of boots that belonged to a swimmer who probably wished he was still wearing them.

"They round the pier and finish on the other side, where the briefing was held," he said. "The fastest swimmers are out of the water in about 20 – 21 minutes."

We started the walk back. Under the pier, I could hear sea lions barking and smell the rotting kelp.

"Don't tell me there are sea lions out on the course?" I asked.

"They hang out right next to the pier toward the end and are very territorial. This is their way of saying, 'I'm bigger than you and can swim faster than you. My ocean...get lost.'"

"Charming. Why do people do this? The water is so cold. There are things—living things that bite—in the water."

"Guess you're not an open water swimmer? It's fun, really, and it gives us all something to talk about," he laughed. "I'm Justin, by the way. Justin Rosencastle. I'm usually out there with them, but I have shoulder problems. Can't swim. I came to support one of my teammates. I also have a booth at these swims that gives out after race refreshments."

I must have done a double-take.

"What?" he asked looking at me. "When I said my name, you seemed to recognize it. Do we know each other?"

"No...I...ah...knew a Justin Rosen in high school...the names are similar."

He was a medium-sized man and the afro from his high school team photo was long gone. His head was shaved. He had a short well-trimmed goatee, broad face, pale eyebrows above light blue eyes—eyes that sometimes looked surprisingly vacant. His nose had been broken a time or two. By the time we reached the other side of the pier, the lead swimmers were heading for the finish line and the beach.

"This race is over before it begins," I said. I pulled out the camera and walked over to the finish chute, ready to snap the first swimmers approaching the beach. Justin followed me.

"You the official photog?" he asked.

"No. I'm the evaluator for the swim."

"All right. Good for you. Hey, what happened last week? With Waddell? Was it a heart attack?"

I shrugged my shoulders. The water was now covered with swimmers heading this way.

"I knew him."

So I've heard, I thought.

"Right," I said, peering through the viewfinder of the camera.

"No, I mean I knew him before."

"Before what?" I put the camera down and looked at Justin.

"Before he came to California. Before he went to college in Texas. When he was growing up in Nevada. Hey, gotta go. Here comes my swimmer."

He just confirmed what Pamela and Spencer had said. With that, he walked to the end of the finish chute, to wait for his teammate, probably a human popsicle by now.

Swimmers started piling out of the water and swarming up the beach. I walked through the crowd taking photos and ended up at one of the booths giving out free drinks guaranteed to replenish, refuel, and reload the depleted swimmers. Behind the counter were Menton's daughter, Daisy, and the nerd. They were getting ready to pass out samples of the revitalizing drink.

"Hi again," I said to Daisy.

"Hey," she mumbled and moved out among the swimmers, grateful for some nourishment.

Once the results were up and the awards distributed, the warm sun finally pierced through the fog. I saw Mike Menton again. This time his arm was around the small woman with the dark hair from the Lake Joseph swim. The black tight fitting wetsuit that hugged her curves was pulled down to her waist, exposing a purple bikini top. I thought she was connected with Dick Waddell. Now it was Menton. Quite a looker. Rubenesque. Not your typical long lean swimmer's build.

Her damp hair clung to her forehead and neck. With wide, deep dark eyes and a sultry smile, she looked more like a potential Playboy of the Month than a swimmer. She and Mike were posing for photos for a friend, each holding up their medals.

Maybe he'd be more open to a conversation since the swim was over. I waved and tried to get his attention. He looked over in my direction but didn't see me. I inched a little closer and snapped a picture. Maybe he'd talk to me if I offered him a photo.

"Hey, Mike," I called and waved again. With that, a smile froze on his face and he walked over to me, took my elbow and forcibly pulled me down the beach.

"Look, I'm not going to talk to you."

"But, I...."

"No, listen to me. I don't want the attention. You want to ask me questions about Waddell; so does everyone else. I wasn't involved. Understand? The guy died; I'm sorry about that. But I had nothing to do with it. So leave me alone and don't take any more pictures of me."

With that he gave my elbow a tight squeeze and then let go, turning to walk back toward the raven-haired swimmer, now surrounded by a number of men.

My camera dangled from the strap on my wrist.

"Welcome to the world of Mike Menton," said Justin from right behind me. I jumped at the sound of his voice. I almost dropped the evaluation folder.

"What was that all about? All I wanted to do was talk to him?"

"He's a turf specialist type of guy."

"A what?"

"Turf specialist. His turf. You're not special enough…get it?

"Okay. Who's the woman?"

"Jacqueline…Jackie for short…Gibson."

"Lovely, isn't she?" I said glancing at her as Menton now took hold of her arm.

"Yes. The Cleopatra of the swim set," Justin said.

"Excuse me?"

"Let's just say, she bestows her favors on the fastest swimmers."

"You are not talking about swimming tips, are you?"

"Nope. She was the apex of the Waddell/Menton triangle."

"Really? Didn't know there was a triangle. Guess there is a lot I don't know. Ah…would you be able to talk with me before you leave? I won't take much of your time. I've been around open water swimming before, but not like this. It is different. I have to finish up the evaluation first. Could we talk in about a half hour?"

Justin agreed to stay around. He suggested we meet at a small Mexican restaurant about two blocks away.

The swimmers were beginning to leave the beach and head for their cars, maybe to a restaurant or even to the rides on the Santa Cruz boardwalk. My evaluation sheet was filled with checks and detailed notes about the swim. I'd taken a lot of photographs of the swimmers following the race: sitting on the sand, at the refreshment booths, getting awards. A successful first outing, I thought as I walked over to the event director, introduced myself and congratulated him out loud and me—to myself—on a job well done.

I watched Mike Menton and Jackie move across the sand toward the beach boardwalk. The daughter and weirdo boyfriend were nowhere to be seen.

7

"Lucky, that's what Waddell's dad used to be called," said Justin. "Although the way I see it, most people nicknamed Lucky rarely are."

Justin and I were sitting in La Casa de las Playas, not far from the beach. The Giants game was on the television over the bar and we were working our way through a bowl of tortilla chips and eye-watering salsa.

"I worked on his family's ranch growing up and Dick and I were on the high school swim team. He rarely talked to me when he moved here. Putting the past behind him, I guess."

"What kind of past are you talking about?" I asked.

"His dad was something else. Always in trouble. Involved with some bad people. Once, he and a buddy stole some guns, held up a convenience store and took a highway patrolman hostage. Not the brightest thing to do. He spent a lot of years in prison after that. Dick told me he would send out Christmas cards saying 'Wish you were here.' It didn't matter what Lucky did, Waddell idolized him. But when he left Nevada for college in Texas, he never looked back."

"What about his mother?" I asked.

"A quiet lady. Had enough inner strength to manage the ranch when Lucky went to prison. She put up with a lot. Not sure if Dick kept in touch with her. She passed a few years ago."

A cheer erupted from the crowd around the bar and then settled into a groan. The new Giants shortstop, Ricky Ferguson, had just thrown a bullet to home plate. But it was high. "Safe," Justin and I said simultaneously.

We looked at each other and laughed.

"Baseball fan?" Justin asked.

"Giants fan," I said. "The new shortstop isn't bad for a rookie."

Justin smiled. "We have a lot to talk about."

The waitress started to put down a wood bowl of mixed nuts. I touched her arm.

"Please don't. I'm allergic."

"Consider them gone," she said and took them away.

"Hope you don't mind. Everyone in my family has some sort of nut allergy, some worse than others."

"No worries," said Justin.

I picked up my bottle of cold beer and started to peel off the label, strip by strip.

"So tell me more about Nevada. I've never been there."

"Well, it gets real cold in the winter, real cold. Lots of snow. Too difficult to get to school. Waddell's family had an apartment in town during the school year and he and his sister would live there with their mom."

"Is that unusual?"

"No, not really. There wasn't much other way to get an education. My mom lived in town, so that wasn't a real concern for me. Our high school had an Olympic size indoor pool. So while it was minus 15° outside with snow up to your eyeballs, we were working up a sweat in 80° chlorine-filled water."

"What was Dick like?"

"A real pain in the ass. No one could touch him in the water. But no one wanted to talk to him out of the water. Except the girls. He had it all figured out. Each week—or so it seems—there was a different girl. It started out with him giving the week's winner—that's what the rest of us guys called them—a rose. A week or so later, that girl was walking through the halls of our high school, head down, crying her eyes out. And he was on to the next one, and the next one and the next one. Kind of like a conveyor belt Casanova."

"Not a very sensitive guy."

"About as sensitive as a can of paint."

"So, he eventually moved to the Bay area?"

"Yeah, not that long ago."

"And made a name for himself locally in the open water world."

"That's right."

"I don't understand why winning these swims or being named overall winner is so important. There's no money involved. Or endorsements. They don't become worldwide celebrities, right?"

"Yes and no. You won't find a Masters swimmer on the Wheaties box if that's what you're asking. I take that back. Some of the swimmers on past Olympic teams have swum at Masters meets so that could be a possibility. The most well-known swimmers are sponsored by companies. That means they get free swimsuits. They show up at an open water event in one of those suits and other swimmers pay attention. And they really are celebrities within the open water swim community. Big celebrities."

Justin glanced down at his watch. "Hey, I gotta go. Things to do. Maybe we'll get a chance to talk again."

"Thanks. Good information. One more thing," I said as he stood up.

Justin turned around. "Yeah?"

"Back to Dick Waddell. Did you two swim against each other?"

Justin nodded. "Yeah, we did. But he was always too fast for me. It didn't matter. He was older by a little, so I had my chance to shine when he graduated."

———

After Justin left, I sat there for a while in the restaurant and slowly drank my beer. The Giants game droned on over the bar. Richard Waddell was an interesting character. Swimming seemed to be his whole life. He was good at it, but lacked social skills big time. Sounds like he might have been dragging a number of enemies behind him. From Nevada to Texas to the San Francisco Bay area. His death, as the email had suggested earlier this week, might be questionable. There were probably plenty of people around who would have liked to remove him from this planet, as well as any body of water.

And this guy, Mike Menton. Justin didn't have much nice to say about him. Or his dopey daughter. Don't know why he wouldn't talk to me. I wasn't going to accuse him of anything. Yet. All I wanted was some simple conversation—ask a couple of questions.

I switched on my digital camera and previewed the pictures from the swim. There it all was. Shots of the swimmers galloping down the beach to the ocean. Galloping out of the ocean at the finish line. Menton and Jackie were in the last few photos. He looked happy. She looked bored. Next photo was the drink booth behind them. There was Justin. And there was Daisy Menton and her boyfriend. Justin was handing something to Jackie. Daisy and friend were handing out white paper cups filled with the replenishment drink Justin told me about. The rest of the pictures documented the work of the lifeguards paddling the course, and the awards ceremony—good background material I could use to supplement my evaluation.

Grabbing my backpack, I walked through the dark bar, now filled with many swimmers from the Cold Water Clash. I headed into the glaring noontime sunshine for the car. A quiet sense of satisfaction drifted over me. Out of nowhere, I had an almost full-time job. Okay, the job was temporary and it wasn't exactly what I planned to do (I didn't really know what I planned to do), but it would bring in money. And this swim evaluation part was more than interesting. It was a rare chance to go behind the scenes to see how events like this were put on.

Justin seemed like a nice guy, even if he didn't come highly recommended by Pamela or Spencer. There are always two sides to a story. And I'd find out his. Anyway, he was someone I could tap for the background info on swims and swimmers. And he liked baseball.

8

I decided to take the coast route back to the San Francisco Bay area. Sure, it might add about 15 – 20 minutes to the trip, but driving next to the ocean, seeing the coastline, the Montara lighthouse, the waves crashing into the rocks sounded more enjoyable than a mad dash up the freeway.

I pointed the car north, enjoying the brashness of the Northern California coast. Not far from the small coastal community of Casitas Cove, I could see many flashing red, yellow, white, and blue lights. Up ahead were one, two, maybe even three emergency vehicles. Traffic slowed down and then stopped. I rolled down the window. The wind had picked up, blowing off the ocean. Long wispy strands of fog were drifting in. It was already 10 to 15 degrees cooler than Santa Cruz. The air smelled of salt—salt and waves that had flowed over long distances to reach the shores of Northern California.

Slowly, traffic began to move along the narrow two-lane road. On one side was a sheer granite cliff with almost no shoulder where a car could stop; on the other side, the ocean side, was a sharp 30-foot drop to the beach. Sandwiched between the two, I inched along, past fire trucks, an ambulance, police cars and a tow truck. It looked like someone or something had driven off the edge of the cliff. Glancing down at the ocean, I could see a car upside-down on its smashed roof in the shallow cold water.

Tragic. Whoever it was was probably out for a nice afternoon drive along the ocean and lost control of the car.

After a quick look at the emergency personnel down on the sand surrounding the car, I knew I had to stop, turn around and go back to the parking lot for the beach. Even from a hundred yards away, I could identify Mike Menton standing next to the overturned car.

———

By the time I pulled into the long narrow parking lot, the crowds gawking at the accident from both the road above and the beach had doubled. How did Mike manage to drive off the road? I grabbed my phone, my camera, climbed down the rocky path and ran toward him.

Normally, the explosion of the surf crashing at the water's edge and the whistle of the wind off the ocean dampens any beach noise. But not today. In between the crash of the shore waves, for a brief second, each sound was crystal clear. I heard the crackle and scratchy echo of the radios on the emergency vehicles. The wind blew the loud voices of the rescue personnel toward me. One voice didn't have the controlled calm of the others. It was Mike's.

"Jackie, Jackie…get her out of the car," he yelled.

He lunged toward the overturned car again and again, only to be held back by a standing brick wall, a San Mateo County deputy sheriff, from the Moss Beach substation.

"Step back, sir. We'll get her out."

I grabbed Mike's arm. "What happened?"

"What are you doing here?" he asked. He pushed my arm away.

"I was driving home and saw you on the beach. Were you in the car?"

"No. It's Jackie."

He moved closer to the deputy sheriff again. Once again he was told to move back.

The grey fog was now a thick impenetrable wall only a hundred yards off shore. It inched toward the beach. Above, the gloomy threads of vapor intertwined and completely blocked out the sun. Rescue personnel had little time to get Jackie out of the car and on her way to a hospital before the weather became another factor in the rescue.

The damp air was raw. Was it from the smothering fog and the chilling breeze off the ocean or was it the sight of Jackie that caused me to shiver? I moved toward the automobile and started to take some pictures.

She was upside down, sandwiched between the airbag, her seat and the collapsed roof of the car. The driver's side door was caved in. The windshield was cracked into thousands of tiny pieces. Jackie was conscious, but barely. There was blood, a lot of blood on her face. Ocean water was moving in and out of her window.

"My god, if the impact didn't kill her, she could drown," I said.

"Ma'am, please step back," said an officer blocking my view of the wreck. I walked back to Mike who was now talking to a different deputy sheriff.

"She was behind me most of the way. But her driving seemed erratic, slowing down, pulling off to the side, weaving across the solid yellow line."

"Had she been drinking?" asked the deputy sheriff.

"No, we just came from an open water swim in Santa Cruz. She had something to drink after the swim, but no alcohol. We were going to have lunch here," said Mike, looking out at the ocean, the same flat dull grey as the horizon and the sky above it.

While Mike continued talking, I stood to the side, close enough to hear what he was saying but with a good view of the overturned car. Seven firefighters moved around the vehicle, assessing the damage. Soon Mike was beside me. The firefighters, sometimes up to their knees in water, stabilized the car with thick metal struts.

"Got the tool," said one firefighter, referring to the large hydraulic rescue spreaders, commonly called the Jaws of Life. It was wedged into a collapsed corner of the door near the roof. Watching intently, I saw the dark green metal of the automobile separate against the pressure of the spreaders.

A firefighter climbed into the opening of the car and placed a white cervical collar around Jackie's neck. He eased her out of the car and helped secure her to a blue spineboard. Jackie's eyes flickered slowly to the men working around her.

Mike's face was ashen and his eyes large and glassy. He still wore the blue tee shirt given out to swimmers of the Cold Water Clash. He seemed unaware of the chilling wind blowing off the ocean and the drizzling fog, but his arms had goose bumps.

"Something was wrong with either her car or her driving," he said as he looked at Jackie, now lying still on the spine board. "She couldn't keep up with me. Once, I pulled over to the side and called her to see if she was having car problems. She made a comment about the car being hot and the windows steaming up. Then, she said she was feeling dizzy and sick to her stomach.

"I pulled into the parking lot and expected her to do the same. Except that she drove past. I saw her look back over her shoulder at me. Then she slowed down even more and tried to make a U turn. I thought for sure another car would be coming from the other direction around the corner by the cliff and hit her. But instead, she accelerated and drove right off the cliff. A swan dive. The bumper hit the sand and the car flipped over on its roof, then flipped again onto its side, her side, the driver's side. It skidded along the beach and when it hit the water, it was pushed back on its roof again. Then it slipped into the ocean."

I could hear the deep 'thup, thup, thup' of a helicopter moving toward the accident scene. It was an air ambulance and it had found a very wide stretch of beach not far from the parking lot. Jackie was quickly transported away from her twisted and crumpled car to the medical copter.

"Where are they taking her?" Mike asked one of the EMTs standing close to him.

"SF Memorial."

"There's no place closer?" he asked.

"Sure, but some of the hospitals don't have helipads or don't specialize in trauma victims, people who have been seriously hurt, like this. SF Memorial has both."

With that he joined a firefighter and an EMT and they jogged toward the copter. Police had stopped traffic in both directions and had cordoned off much of the beach. The helicopter started up again. The noise was deafening and the power of the rotors tossed the beach sand in every direction. It lifted straight up into the sky through the fog and disappeared.

It was an eerie sight.

Up on the cliff, near Highway 1, the onlookers were starting to get back in their cars. In less than fifteen minutes, the fog would erase everything around us.

"Are you okay?" I said to Mike.

"I'm going home," was all he said.

Not me, I thought. I'm going to San Francisco Memorial.

9

On the drive back, I punched in Terrel's phone number at the hospital.

"Hey, girl, really can't talk now. On my way in to see an injured nine-year-old soccer player."

"Look, a swimmer's been hurt. She's being helicoptered in."

"Who is it? What happened?"

"Long story. I'll tell you when I get to the hospital. Should be there in about forty-five minutes."

I hung up, and turned off on a feeder road that would lead me away from the coast to Highway 280 and a faster route.

———

By the time I reached the ER, Jackie was in an operating room, the young soccer patient had gone home with a blue and yellow cast and Terrel was out in the hall talking to the lab technician.

Terrel glanced up at me as I trotted down the hall toward him and the tech.

"You didn't tell me your swimmer was in a car accident," he said. "I was expecting something completely different."

"Sorry about that."

"The EMTs said that she drove off a cliff. How'd that happen?"

I explained what I knew, which wasn't all that much.

"The only thing that seemed odd was Mike's description of her following him up the coast. She kept slowing down and when Mike called to check on her, she mentioned something about the car being hot, her windows steaming up and that she felt nauseous."

"Maybe she had wet things in her car, a wetsuit and some towels. If they were thrown over the front seat, there might be condensation on the window. But that is easy to take care of," said Terrel.

"Right, just open the window or put on the defroster," I said.

"Let's continue this in a minute, I need to finish up here," Terrel said, turning back to the lab tech.

While the two men were talking, a colorful collage of children's drawings in a display case by the door to the ER caught my eye. Very clever, the triangular-shaped display was in layers, each layer smaller than the one below it. It cheerfully displayed generations of families. At the top, the pinnacle of the triangle, was one picture of a boy and a girl holding hands.

Cute, I thought. Wait a minute…who was just talking about triangles? Somebody. It was Justin Rosencastle, the guy I met at the Santa Cruz swim. He said that Jackie was the apex of the romantic triangle with Dick Waddell and Mike Menton.

"Terrel, do you think that Waddell's death and Jackie's accident might be related…maybe caused by the same thing?"

"It crossed my mind when I got your call. I've asked the lab to run some tests. I should know more later."

———

I stayed at the hospital for a few hours waiting for test results. But, eventually I left without them and came home to a dark house.

Lena was asleep. For that I was grateful; I didn't want to talk about yet another accident. I was hoping that the long drive to and from Santa Cruz, and the time at the hospital would be enough to keep me asleep all night. No such luck. I was up at 2:00 a.m.

Accompanied by the hamster running track on his revolving wheel in my head, I walked into the living room and stared at the one family picture my sister had displayed on the dark end table. Dad and Mom connected. In the photo, you could see it in the look in their eyes and their smiles in as they glanced at each other, but kept a death grip on each of us. It was taken at the Marin County Fair years ago by one of their friends. I was eating cotton candy and pulling away from Dad's outstretched hand. I must have been about 10-years-old. Mom had hold of the back of Lena's tee shirt as she tried to go in the opposite direction. Just two years old, Lena had the determination of an angel running from hell. We stood in front of a Ferris wheel. Mom and Dad were enjoying each other, the fair and us.

I picked the photo up and carried it over to the couch. Holding it was comforting. There were good times—once. None of us in that picture knew that the next five years would change everything.

I looked at the photo for a long time, then I put it back on the table, walked back to my room and fell into a deep quiet sleep.

In the morning, I could hear Lena banging pots around in the kitchen—not the 'Hey, I'm busy enjoying myself cooking' kind of banging, but rather, the 'I'm going to knock the shit out of this pan' kind of banging.

Something was clearly wrong.

"Lena?" I stood in the doorway. "What is the matter?"

"You. You're the matter."

"Excuse me. I'm the matter? What does that mean?"

"Just the other night—you drop this comment that you've been involved with the police somehow. What happened?"

"It's none of your business."

"I've been thinking of all the things you could have done. Each one gets worse than the rest. Tell me. You couldn't have been drinking and driving…you barely drink. I can't believe you hurt anyone."

"No, I didn't."

"Then what?"

"Okay." I sat down at the kitchen table and motioned for her to do the same.

"Before Brad walked out, we spent a lot of our evenings at the sports bars close by our house."

"But…"

"Let me finish. Brad seemed so restless. He would go to bars without me. I didn't like that. So I went with him and we drank together—a big happy family or rather a small drunk unhappy family.

"One night I was the designated driver. I ran into two parked cars and did extensive damage."

"Trish."

"There's more. When Brad left, I continued drinking, mostly at home. I picked up another DUI. I actually spent some time in the county jail."

"No…not you."

"Yes, me. The judge sentenced me to attend AA meetings. I wasn't crazy about the idea, but I went. It wasn't so bad and things began to change. I have to tell you, though, when I see a police car, I get very nervous. I want to stay as far away from the law as possible."

Lena looked stunned. "I don't know what to say."

She stood up and walked out the backdoor, heading for her garden. Picking up a hand rake, she attacked the few straggly weeds growing next to her tomato plants. Then she tossed the small garden tool as hard as she could at the tall wooden fence.

With a sigh, I headed for the front door. What would she say if she knew about my part in the local burglaries so many years ago?

The tree-lined streets were quiet, except for a few joggers out before the sun shut down their exercise. I thought about Jackie. Was she afraid when her car left the road and dropped toward the ocean? What about Dick Waddell? Did he panic when he realized he was too sick to reach the floating dock? My gut told me these two accidents were connected. I wanted it to stop this—whatever it was—before more people were hurt.

I took out my cell phone and punched in Terrel's phone number.

"Hey Trish," he answered. "What's going on?"

"Did you get any of Jackie's tests back yet?"

"Can't talk about it, Trish. You know that. Privacy laws."

"Understand. I get it. Can you tell me anything?"

"She's alive."

"Good."

"And there's something else. Remember the new street drug I was telling you about? I have a friend, Dr. Tariq Kapoor, who is one of the head docs at the Turk Street Community Clinic. He told me that High Test has morphed into something called HT2. It is an amphetamine. It can be injected, snorted, dissolved or swallowed in a capsule. Users develop heart palpitations, as well as shortness of breath, dizziness, sweating, anxiety and nausea."

"Charming."

"There's more. Some of his patients on this drug hear voices, see things and can be violent—like meth addicts."

"What does this have to do with Jackie?"

"Nothing yet. Tariq has seen people who have combined HT2 and High Test for a higher high and the results were fatal. Then, I got to thinking about the other swimmer who had the accident?"

"Waddell?"

"Yeah, Waddell. I did some research about swimming deaths in triathlons. You know, more people die in the swimming leg of a triathlon, than in the biking or running leg. I found a research letter that talks about it in JAMA, the American Medical Association Journal. It's by some folks at the Minneapolis Heart Institute Foundation."

"Did they say why?"

"Crowds, being bumped, kicked, maybe swum over. Add that to inexperience and you end up with distress."

"You mean panic. The starts for some open water swims can be brutal, from what I've heard. But Masters swims aren't that bad. I've seen them. And Waddell was very used to the open water starts, turns, finishes. Everything."

"They also mention that some of the swimmers that died had cardiovascular abnormalities. So if you combine the stress of a race, underlying heart problems and HT2 or something similar...see where I'm going with this? It is something to think about," said T and he clicked off.

I didn't think my boss would like Terrel's theory. But it was time to tell him about Jackie. I left a message on Bill's cell phone that there was yet another accident involving an open water swimmer.

10

Early Monday morning, I was on the road toward the Golden Gate Bridge and the swim office. I wanted to write up the open water swim evaluation, and have a chance to look it over before I gave it to Bill.

It was not quite 7:00 a.m. when I pulled into the almost empty parking lot at Fort Mason. There was no wind and rare early morning sunshine warmed this side of San Francisco Bay. But right down the middle, between the City and Marin County, a streak of dense thick fog from the Golden Gate Bridge all the way to the Berkeley Marina, wiped out everything, including the island of Alcatraz.

No one had been in the building yet, so I used my key to open the heavy front door and climbed the three flights of stairs. The office was quiet, peaceful, but the blinking lights on the phone indicated that there were calls waiting. Nothing unusual there. This was a much busier office than I ever suspected.

I punched in the numbers to hear the playback.

"You have six messages," said the robotic woman from her tin can recording studio.

"First message. Sent Saturday, at 1:30pm."

"Hey Bill, call me. It's Mike Menton. Jackie had an accident. Can't believe it. Just can't believe it." His voice was calm.

Did he sound overly unbelieving? Maybe.

In the background, I could hear the drone of a police radio, male voices and something about a tow truck. Then the line went dead. I pressed 'save' and then 'repeat.'

I listened to Mike's message again. Then the next message came on. This time it was a distraught Mike Menton.

"Bill, call me. Jackie drove off a cliff off Highway 1."

I know. I know.

The next call was an abrupt message from the Santa Cruz event director, the man I'd seen in the warm-up jacket and knit cap, prepping the life guards before the swim. "Bill, it's Randy. Call me as soon as you get in."

The rest of the messages were routine. Swimmers wanted to know about results, lost gear and how the end of the season points were tallied. In other words, nothing that was out of the ordinary.

Except for the last message. It was for me.

"Hi, Tricia. This is Justin. We met on Saturday at the Santa Cruz swim. I know you like baseball. And, uh, I have some free time this afternoon. Not enough to watch a whole game, but I'm going to stop by the Port Walk, the free viewing area at AT&T Park, across from McCovey Cove. Why, uh, don't you stop by? I'll be there around 1:00 p.m."

I smiled while I hit the delete button. Justin sounded nervous. Would this be considered a date? No, we would be two people hanging out at a ballpark. If we didn't have anything to say to one another, we could at least watch some of the game.

I'm going, I thought. But I had to finish the final version of the swim evaluation first. I read it over a few times, started to think about Justin, and the events of the past two weeks. They were more than puzzling.

I pulled a pack of 3 x 5 cards out of the desk and jotted down notes about the two incidents. I'd been told that no one died at these swims. Waddell's death had been the first for the organization in thirty years. Yet, here were two incidents a weekend apart. According to Justin, Jackie, Waddell and Menton were all connected. Could it really be coincidental?

This wasn't making any sense. I needed a cup of coffee from that expensive espresso bar in the next building—a fancy cup of coffee that takes almost five minutes to order—and maybe a sugary morning bun to go with it. I was bent over the bottom drawer of the desk pulling out my wallet, when a dark haired security officer from the National Park Service police knocked on the door and stepped into the office.

"Yes?" I said dropping the wallet and standing straight up.

"Sorry. Didn't mean to startle you," he said. "I'm not used to seeing anyone in the buildings so early, so I thought I'd better check."

I sat back down and let out a deep breath. "I'm fine. Have a little work I need to get out the way. It's easier to do when everything is quiet and the phones haven't started to ring yet."

"Got it," he said and smiled. "Just one more thing. When you leave the office, even for a minute or two, be sure and lock your doors. There's been a rash of burglaries—mostly purses, laptops. Nothing dangerous that we have seen. But you don't want to lose money and your ID."

"Thanks for letting me know."

"We don't really have a description of the thief, but some of the victims thought they saw a man wearing a dark sweatshirt with a hood."

"I see a lot of guys around here who fit that description," I said.

"I understand. But if you see someone like that, call security," he said. The officer walked down the hall to the next office and knocked. When nobody answered, he turned around, waved at me as he walked past and headed for the steps.

"Hey wait," I called after him. "I'll walk with you. I'm going for a cup of coffee." This time I picked up the keys to the office, my wallet and walked to the door, shutting and locking it behind me.

"My name's Jonathan Angel. Just call me Jon," he said, holding out a hand.

His handshake was solid, confident.

"Jonathan Angel, really. Do they call you Johnny Angel?" I said referring to the sixties pop tune.

"Jon is just fine," he said with a slight smile.

He held the large heavy front door open and we walked out into the early morning sunshine.

"You a swimmer?"

"No, not me. My sister is. I needed a job and this kind of fell into my lap."

"You know about Fort Mason?"

"Not really. I drive by it all the time, but…"

"Okay. Here's the five cent history tour." With that, Jon told me that in 1776, while the founding fathers were working on the Declaration of Independence on the East Coast, the Spanish were building Fort Mason on the West Coast. During the Civil War, one of its many uses was a defense point, in case of a water attack by the Confederates.

He described the museums, theaters and restaurants housed here. When he started in on the sporting events, in particular the curling matches, I said, "Enough, thank you."

I I

You wouldn't call Bill Rutherford, the chair of Nor Cal Swimming, a laid back type of person. Just the opposite. Everything was a big deal to him. When I walked back in the office with my cup of coffee, he was already there, headset in place, pacing the floor, shaking his head and waving his arms around like a mad man.

"Look, Randy, this was an accident. It had nothing to do with the swim. Sounds like she was going to meet Menton and drove off the cliff. It was a mistake. A terrible mistake. Maybe the accelerator stuck or something like that. But you and your team aren't liable. Our liability—the organization's and yours—ends when the swimmer leaves the parking lot. She was way out of the parking lot. As I understand it, Jackie left the swim almost thirty or forty minutes before."

There was a pause.

"I know. I understand. Look, I'll check with our insurance carrier. Maybe you should, too."

The call ended and Bill glanced over to me.

"Thanks for the call about the accident," he said to me.

"You know, I was there, driving home, up the coast road and I saw the car. I talked with Mike Menton at the crash site. This isn't normal, is it? Two accidents in two weeks?"

"No, not at all. Trisha, I can't explain why these two...uh... events happened, one right after the other. I know that Jackie's accident must have been upsetting and you were kind to go to the hospital and check up on her. But, and it is a big but, your job as an assistant in this office—even a temporary one—is to let me know immediately when things out of the ordinary happen. Mike Menton tracked me down from his car before he left Casitas Cove. I was very surprised when he said you had just left and then he asked 'hadn't she called' to let me know?"

"Sorry. My fault. I'll do better with the communication."

I walked to my desk and sat down. Bill was right. He needed to be informed. I had let him down.

"Bill, do you think it at all possible that Waddell's death and Jackie's accident are related?"

"No, I don't. They aren't. They couldn't be."

"What about Mike Menton? He seems to be connected to both Dick Waddell and Jackie. Do you think he is involved with these events in some way?"

"This has nothing to do with him. They were accidents. Mike's an okay guy. A little intense, but so are many of the swimmers."

I changed the subject. "The evaluation."

"What?"

"The evaluation for the Cold Water Clash. Remember? I was doing the evaluation?"

"Oh, yeah."

"I'll have it to you later today. Before I leave."

Bill glanced up at me.

"Bet you didn't expect all this to happen in your first few weeks of work," he said with a slight smile. "Like in Waddell's case, don't talk about Jackie's accident. You can say that she is alive and what hospital she is in. Other than that, be polite and vague. Got it?"

I nodded. "Right. Lawyers."

"Let's send Jackie some flowers," I said.

Bill gave me the office credit card and I called Green Street Flowers in the Marina District and ordered a cheery get-well bouquet.

"I'll pick them up," I said to the florist. "Around noon."

They suggested I text them as I was leaving the office and they'd wait outside of the shop with the flowers.

———

"I can't believe it."

I was standing in the large parking lot just outside my office at Fort Mason, looking at what was left of my car's windshield. Glass was scattered everywhere. Shards of it glittered like cold hard ice chips on the Honda's front seat.

"Who would throw a brick at my car?" I said out loud.

"Oh no." My hands went up to my mouth. "My car doors. They've been keyed."

I walked around the car and ran my hands along the deep scratches etched into the side panels. This car was the one thing that I owned completely. I was proud of it. It was mine. Now it was damaged and I had no money to repair it.

I called upstairs to Bill and told him what happened. In a few minutes, he was by my side walking around the car.

"What a mess. Who'd you piss off?" he asked.

"Nobody. I haven't worked here long enough to piss off anyone."

Jon Angel pulled up in a NPS car. "What happened here?"

"Some jerk ruined my sole possession in life."

"Did you see anyone around your car?" he asked.

"No. It was okay when we walked by to get coffee this morning. I haven't been outside since."

"Well, I'll need to make out a report."

Jon pulled out a small black notebook and looked at me. I wasn't paying attention, that much was obvious to him and the small crowd that had gathered around the car.

"Tell you what," he said, looking around at the gawkers, "let's call your insurance company and report this. Then, we can talk in your office."

"I was on my way to pick up some flowers, then go to SF Memorial. How am I supposed to do that? How am I supposed to drive home?"

How am I supposed to get to AT&T Park? I thought.

"We've got a small storage garage between the buildings by our headquarters. Maybe we can move your car there until you figure out what you want to do. Give me your keys. I'll meet you upstairs."

I threw the keys to Jon and followed Bill back up the three flights, mumbling to myself with each step.

"Randomness, that's what it is. Pure randomness," he said.

"I don't know about that." I gave the door to the office a good solid kick and it flew open and bounced back, almost closing in our faces.

"You want to use my car this afternoon. I'm not going anywhere for a change," he said.

"Thanks, that would work. I'll call my sister and get her to pick me up later."

It took about fifteen minutes before I heard Jon's footsteps in the hall.

"This belong to you?" he asked. He was holding a large red brick with some kind of paper wrapped around it.

"No," I said.

"It was on the floor of the passenger side in the front."

"What is it?" asked Bill. He walked over and took the brick from Jon. He turned it around and around in his hands. "Someone sent you a note."

A wrinkled piece of paper with a three word message was duct-taped to the brick. "Stay out of it."

"What does that mean?" asked Bill.

"Stay out of what?" asked Jon.

"I have no idea," I said. "Maybe it's a mistake...someone got the wrong car."

Or did they, I wondered. Instead of a mistake, it could be a warning. Who would know that I was interested in both Dick Waddell's and Jackie Gibson's accidents? The only name that came to mind was Mike Menton.

Jon and I sat down and we filled out the accident report. He included the wording of the note. When we finished, he gave me a strange look.

"You can keep your car in the NPS storage garage."

Bill handed over the keys to his car. "Be careful, okay?" All that was left was for me to deliver the flowers to Jackie.

I nodded and headed for the door, still talking to myself about the idiot who damaged my car.

12

Green Street was packed with the lunch crowd. The sun was like a magnet for pedestrians. The warmer it was, the more they headed outside their offices. They clogged the sidewalks and streets. I held down the horn trying to get them to move a little faster. It didn't help much.

As promised, there was a clerk in a bright green apron waiting in front of the shop. With a 'Hi, I'm really happy to see you' smile pasted on her face, she opened the trunk and carefully wedged in the flowers.

I wish I was in my own car, I thought. How much would the repairs cost me? Whatever the amount, I don't have it.

The streets surrounding the hospital were just as crowded as in the Marina District. I pulled into the hospital parking lot, took out the flowers and walked in. The hallway on the second floor that led to Intensive Care was surprisingly empty. By the double doors leading into the IC unit, there was a security desk; but the guard was nowhere to be seen. I pressed the automatic door opener and walked in, no questions asked.

The air was filled with a quiet hum. No loud talking; no heavy bass from a radio—just subdued voices. I walked by nurses checking computer screens outside each room. Most of the patient's doors were shut.

The hospital rooms formed a circle around a nurse's station where three staff members sat. They looked up briefly when I walked by, but then went back to their work. I stopped one nurse checking a computer screen outside a patient's door and asked where Jackie was. She pointed farther down the corridor and I continued walking.

Jackie was in a large airy room. She was hooked up to a number of machines that blinked and pushed out ever-changing numbers, monitoring her blood pressure and heart rate. The spikes and valleys of an electrocardiogram kept track of her heart's electrical activity. Her eyes were closed. One arm and a leg were in a cast.

My flowers were not the first. In fact, I had to make room on top of a table for my bouquet. I wondered how many of these were from men. Most of the cards were signed by names I didn't recognize, but some looked familiar. There was a spray of roses from Mike M. Next to that was one from an anonymous admirer. It was only signed 'Your almost Saturday night date.'

That's provocative.

There was even a bouquet from her swim team in Pacifica. And another with a card that said, 'I'll be there to help you recover. Xoxoxo Sis.'

The computer with her medical records had been moved inside the room almost next to the bed. Her nurse must have just left, since test results were still on the screen. Looking around first and making sure that the hospital door was shut, I clicked through them. For the most part, I didn't understand a word. But, I quickly jotted down the tests marked positive on the back of an envelope I had crammed into a pocket. Maybe Terrel could interpret what I was looking at.

I walked out and went to the nurse's station. "How is she doing?" I asked the fifty-something nurse sitting behind the desk.

"And you are?" she said.

"I'm with the organization that she swims with. As a group, we are all very concerned about her."

"You're not supposed to be in here," the nurse said. "This is Intensive Care, normally just family members." She stood up and pointed toward the door.

"Sorry. I wanted to drop off some flowers from the office. It doesn't look like she has any family close by. I only saw one get-well bouquet from a sister, but no one else. Are her mom and dad around?"

"You'll have to leave."

She pushed the automatic door opener and nodded to the guard now sitting at the door. He moved toward me at a quick pace. I politely thanked the nurse and walked out with him.

"Thanks for the escort. I know my way from here," I said, as I walked to the elevators and pushed the down button. Maybe Dr. T was in the Emergency Room.

———

Walking through the double doors to the ER waiting room, I approached the main desk. The same nurse that was on duty when I was here yesterday had just finished registering a patient.

"Is Dr. Robinson, Terrel Robinson, on this shift?" I asked him. The nurse had tattoos running up and down his arms.

"I'm a close friend," I said, since I could tell he was about to ask for every piece of ID that I was carrying. "Just wanted to say "Hi.""

"Sorry. He's not. Want to leave a message?"

"No thanks, he's my sister's boyfriend. I'll see him in the next few days."

I was on my way out when I turned around. I had almost blown one chance in a million. "Weren't you here yesterday when Jackie Gibson was brought in?"

"Oh, yeah. Crash victim. Drove off a cliff somewhere south of Pacifica. Lucky she's alive."

"Remember me? I came in about forty-five minutes later and talked to Dr. Robinson then."

He shrugged. "This is a busy place. People are in and out all the time."

"Anyone know what happened to her? Was it a major car malfunction? Brakes failed?" I was pushing my luck here. The nurse wasn't supposed to talk about a case with anyone except the family.

"Could be drugs from what the preliminary tox screen showed."

"Really? Like what kind of drugs? From Terrel's conversation yesterday with the lab tech, I knew they were testing for something in particular."

"Maybe you'd better talk to him," the nurse said, clearly uncomfortable with the way the conversation was going. He nodded at me, then turned to the woman standing behind me. "Can I help you?" he said.

13

The hospital was on the same side of town as AT&T Park. It wouldn't take me too long to get there and meet up with Justin. A few innings of baseball should keep my mind off my car. There was nothing random about what happened. The message was clearer each time I thought about it. Cease and desist. My inquisitiveness into the Waddell death and Jackie's accident was considered ugly meddling by someone.

I walked past the Giants Dugout store toward McCovey Cove. The game against the LA Dodgers was already in the third inning. I didn't see Justin so I inched my way forward into the crowd until I was standing against the fence.

The big hot-headed right fielder, Eddie Martinez, was only 25 yards in front of me. If the Giants are in the field, and Eddie misses a ball, the crowd at the Port Walk can be vocal. At the beginning of his career with the Giants, Martinez was known to end an inning with his face pressed against the fence, shouting insults right back. But that 'I'm going to kick your ass' attitude had mellowed with time on the field. Today, the Port Walk crowd applauded him after he made a dive to catch a fly ball.

I felt a tap on my shoulder. "You made it."

I turned around. There was Justin.

"Have you been standing there long?" I asked.

"Just walked over. Glad you could spare some time."

I reluctantly moved away from the front of the crowd and the game. I followed Justin over to the railing overlooking McCovey Cove. There were at least 15 kayakers and paddleboarders drifting around in the cove, waiting patiently for a ball to be launched out of the ballpark into the water.

"Party in the Cove," said Justin, staring at the enthusiastic fans on the Bay.

"Well, I needed a little R&R." Then I told him about my car.

"That's too bad. Any idea who did it?"

"Not a clue. But I think it's a way of telling me to back off."

"Back off from what?" Justin asked.

"I don't know if you heard. Remember the woman that was hanging on Mike Menton's arm after the pier swim?"

"Jackie? Yeah. Why?"

"Well, she had an automobile accident on the way home. She drove off a cliff on Highway 1."

"No. Really? I didn't know. How is she doing?"

"Not so good. I just stopped by to visit her and drop off some flowers from the office. She's connected to all sorts of tubes and machines. She will be out of the water for a long time."

"Too bad."

"You know, I don't think it was an accident."

A roar went up from inside the ballpark. It took a minute or two until it quieted down. So we stood there, awkwardly and waited.

"Sure it was. What else could it be?" said Justin.

"This is going to sound strange. I want to show you something."

We walked over to a bench by the Marina entrance to the ball-park and sat down. I pulled out my pack of 3 x 5 cards.

"What are those?" Justin asked.

"Remember, two weeks ago when your pal Dick Waddell died? Well, I think his death and Jackie's accident are related. And I think the brick through my car window is part of the same story. Look, I put everything about the events on these cards."

I spread the cards out on the bench. There was a card for Waddell, one for Jackie, one for Mike Menton, one for his darling daughter, Daisy, one for the brother-in-law, Spencer and his wife, Pamela.

"Spencer? You know Spencer?" He picked up each card and read them. "I don't get it. What's this supposed to prove?"

"From what I can tell, the one common denominator is Mike Menton."

"Mike? You think he's connected with Dick's death, that he keyed your car, and somehow made Jackie crash at the Cove? What do you think he did... tamper with her brakes or something like that?"

"Granted, it sounds farfetched. He seems to be the connecting link. But that doesn't make him anything more than that...just a link."

"If you're looking for people who knew both of them, there are plenty of those. Me, for instance, and the whole open water swim community for starters."

"Maybe someone has a grudge against open water swimmers and wants to get rid of them or some of them. Maybe, he or she, doesn't want me asking questions."

Justin just stared at me in disbelief.

"Why? What's the reasoning? That makes no sense at all."

"I need to talk to Mike Menton. One conversation, that's all it would take. I'd get a sense of who he is and his involvement."

"Really?"

"Yeah. I'm pretty good at reading people, but he won't talk to me. You saw what happened at the swim. Maybe I should talk to Waddell's sister? Maybe she can tell me something about what was going on in his life."

"Pamela? I knew her back in high school, too. Look, she just suffered a tremendous loss. This would upset her even more. Besides, I told you all about Dick last weekend."

"You said you two hadn't been in touch very much since he moved here. Maybe Pamela can help me figure this out."

"Well, Pamela won't be able to help you."

"Why do you say that?"

"She…Look. You're trying to put two and two together and get four. But there is no two and two. There's no nothing. Take your cards," and he picked them up and handed them to me. "Now put them away or better yet, walk over to the railing and toss them into McCovey Cove."

I gave the cards one last look and put them back into my bag.

"You're not going to throw them away, are you?"

I shook my head. "If these accidents are connected, I'm going to find out. One brick is not going to stop me."

"I have an idea. To help calm that overactive mind of yours, how about coming to a baseball game on Saturday with me? I have field club level seats behind home plate. We'll be on TV."

As he said that, my conspiracy theory and bull dog determination evaporated like bay fog on a sunny day. I had been asked on a date. A real date. And to a baseball game to boot. I hadn't been asked out by anyone since before I was married, 10 years ago. You bet I was going to go.

"Sure. After what happened to my car, I need to look forward to something. Who do they play?"

"Would you say no if you didn't like the team?"

"Well, some teams are better than others."

"That's not quite the response I was looking for."

"Sorry. I'd love to go to a game with you no matter who they are playing. But I hope it's a good team."

I looked at my watch. "I need to get back to work. My lunch hour has been stretched a little too far."

As we started to walk toward King Street, a roar went up from inside the ballpark. We both looked up at the same time. Over the top of the right field brick wall flew a small white baseball, sailing toward San Francisco Bay. Inside the ballpark huge fountains of mist shot into the air and the deep rumble of fog horns blasted to celebrate the home run.

Looking like a comet speeding toward earth, the baseball landed with a splash in McCovey Cove and all the kayakers and board paddlers frantically stroked toward it. One guy in a wetsuit dove off his paddleboard and reached the ball first. He was quickly followed by a kayaker who managed to run him over, pushing him underwater. But the swimmer bobbed up on the other side of the boat, raised his hand in the air, clutching the baseball in a victory salute. A cheer went up from the makeshift flotilla in McCovey Cove.

"That's where your cards belong," said Justin.

"They're staying right where they are," I said.

14

As soon as I walked back in the office, Bill tossed me a set of car keys.

"You have a ride home. That doctor friend of yours from SF Memorial dropped off these. Guess his dad and uncle own a body shop in Pleasanton. They picked up your car and took it with them. Oh, this car he left you…he said it's yellow."

"Thanks. Can't wait to see what it is. Dr. T is an old school car fanatic, so are the men in his family. I can guarantee you that this will be a very hot car."

"Why don't you go home? It's quiet right now and I'm here for the rest of the day."

That's all it took. I headed for the door.

The round key ring had the license plate number written on a circular white tab. I walked up and down the rows of cars in the large outdoor parking lot in Fort Mason comparing plate numbers. I checked out about 50 cars parked in front of my building. No luck.

Out of the corner of my eye, I saw a bright yellow vehicle parked close to the lot entrance.

"Oh no, this can't be it." I walked over and compared plates. I would be driving home in a completely restored 1978 Checker Cab, bright yellow, with trademark checkerboard black trim. It even had its original Checker top light on the roof.

I climbed into the big boxy car and ran my hand along the brown supple leather. The dashboard was flat, perfectly vertical. The back seat with its two jump seats was spacious.

"I could fit 12 people in here."

This would be a very interesting ride home.

Terrel was on the phone with his father discussing cars when I walked in the house.

"No, Pop. I don't want those wheels. Just tell me the best place to buy tires for the Charger up here in Marin County? (Pause) Yes, she's here. She just walked through the door. I'm sure she loves the car."

I rolled my eyes and Terrel smiled.

"I'll tell her. Now, please answer the question. Where do I go for the tires, Pop? The tires. Remember, the tires. Petaluma Swap meet? Yes, finally. Thank you."

Terrel clicked off the phone. "Talking to my father is exhausting. So what do you think? Great ride, isn't it? It's Pop's pride and joy. He just said that if you pick up any fares, you need to split with him."

"Not so funny," I said. "Two guys tried to get in the cab when I stopped for a red light on Lombard. They finally went away when I said I was off duty."

"Okay, you're set. Question for you. Have you learned anything more about the swimmer that might have had a heart attack a week ago?"

"Besides that he died? Well, I found some capsules in his swim-bag, so I suggested to his sister they have them tested. I was even going to volunteer your help."

"Have they done an autopsy?"

"His sister has requested one. Why?"

"The accident victim, the woman who drove off a cliff south of Half Moon Bay."

"Jackie Gibson?"

"Yeah, that's the one. Her preliminary tox screen came back. Let's just say it isn't what I expected."

"She tested positive for some type of drug, didn't she?"

"Do you think this has anything to do with the Waddell death?" asked Lena, walking into the room.

"Couldn't tell you without more information. Right now, the only connection is that they were both swimmers and they knew each other."

"Well, I think they are related and I am sure that the brick through my car window was a warning. And somehow Mike Menton is involved. I came by to see you today. Well, actually, it wasn't you. Our office gave flowers to Jackie. I...uh...had a chance to look at her test results. They had been left on the computer screen by her bed."

Terrel shook his head. "That's not supposed to happen. Go ahead. What else?"

I pulled out the envelope with the results I jotted down. Terrel looked at it.

"This tells the story of a woman whose judgment was impaired because of something she ingested. She shouldn't have been driving. You know the old, 'don't operate heavy machinery' on the medication warning labels. Her car didn't malfunction. She did. Jackie had a very bad reaction to something, probably drugs. Her whole nervous system went haywire. My guess is that this is what caused her to have the accident."

"Could it have been some form of performance enhancing drugs, steroids?"

"I could get in trouble for talking about this—privacy laws and all—but she tested positive for a crystalline tropane alkaloid."

"A what?"

"She tested positive for cocaine, or at a bare minimum, a substance made primarily of cocaine. This is a very powerful stimulant of the nervous system. If you're an athlete, you're going to feel in the zone, like you can conquer anything. It's possible that this is HT2, the drug that Kapoor talked about the other day."

I sat back and looked at T.

"Cocaine?"

"Yes," said Terrel. "I'm afraid so. There's more. It looks like the cocaine was cut with some sort of amphetamine, probably meth."

Lena had gone back into the kitchen and came back in with a handful of grapes. She threw one at me and one at T.

"What are you two deep in discussion about now?"

"Jackie's accident might not have been so much of an accident." Lena was interested.

"Terrel thinks she might have had a bad reaction to a drug."

"One of your designer street drugs, right?" Lena said.

"Unfortunately, yes. One that was made up of cocaine and meth," he said.

"I don't believe it. I flat out don't believe it. From what I heard, Jackie was a femme fatale, not a junkie," Lena said. "She didn't care if she finished in the top five or the top 50. She used those open water swims as a trolling ground for men. So why would she take any drugs at all? Didn't we have this same conversation about Dick Waddell a few weekends ago?"

"That was only speculation. At the time, I didn't think that Waddell's' death was anything more than cardiac arrest. This isn't speculation, I'm afraid. I have the test results, and now so does your sister."

15

Saturday evening, I was standing next to McCovey Cove once again at AT&T Park waiting for Justin.

"Where is he?" I wondered, looking at the crowd streaming into ballpark. As a concession to my safety-conscious sister, I took the Giants ferry in from Larkspur Landing. She thought this date was a big mistake. She brought up our conversation with Pamela, Waddell's sister, and her less than enthusiastic expression when we asked about the guy with the Afro in the swim team photo.

"He's a bona fide weirdo," said Lena.

I had a return ticket just in case things didn't work out.

Dressed in my best SF Giants World Series tee shirt and orange and black ball cap, I waited by the ferry exit, the spot we had agreed upon. No Justin. The crowd began to thin. I could hear the sounds of the national anthem being played.

Am I being stood up? I started to walk back to the Port Walk. At least I could watch the first three innings for free. Then, I didn't know what I'd do for the next two hours until I could get back on the ferry and go home.

My phone pinged. A text from Lena. "Everything okay?"

"He's a no show," I typed back. I checked my messages. Nothing from Justin.

"Jerk—him, not you," Lena sent back.

I tried calling him. It went right to "You know what to do. Here comes the beep." I hit redial. Same response. "Justin, where are you? The game is starting," I said into the phone.

Baseball, in general; this game, in particular, had lost its luster. All that cheering and frenzied excitement were like yesterday's garlic fries stuck to the floor in the bleachers. What was I expecting? Still looking for the prince charming who liked baseball, to sweep me off my feet and take me to an endless series of games? Guess I won't be on TV tonight.

I sat down on the bench we had sat on a few days ago, pulled out my 3 x 5 cards and leafed through them absently. Why do I care what happened to these people? They weren't family. Originally, I felt a kinship because of my own thoughts about death. That was until one of them messed with my car.

I shuffled the cards and looked at the associations once again, who connected with whom. They reminded me of a DNA molecule; there were different ways they fit together. But the results were still the same. One person was dead, another was seriously injured.

I pulled out two blank cards. Someone else connected with each person. That was Justin. I wrote his name on the card, underlined it. On the second card, I wrote the words "my car" and walked back to the entrance to the ferry, sat on a nearby bench with my chin in my hands and waited for the game to be over.

———

It was near midnight when I walked off the ferry at Larkspur Terminal. I couldn't get away from that boat fast enough. A Giants win meant a happy crowd. This was a very happy crowd. I heard the low rumble of Dr. T's Charger before I saw the black car. Terrel had come to pick me up.

"Trish. Over here," he called.

Inside, the car was meticulously clean. I thought about the dirt on my shoes and what it would do to the passenger's side rug pad.

"You okay?" he asked.

"Sure."

"Forget him. He's not worth your time or energy."

"I don't want to talk about it."

We rode in silence for a while.

"I called the medical examiner at Lake Joseph's hospital to discuss Dick Waddell. They sent the results of his preliminary toxicology screen to the sister."

"And?"

"They are identical to Jackie Gibson's. Cocaine, meth. Only Waddell had a much higher drug count in his system. The ME is going to call me with final results from the toxicological screen and the autopsy when they come back.

"Trish, someone is selling dangerous drugs to swimmers in the open water world. This combination—cocaine and meth—it's lethal."

I looked out the car window into the black night.

"At first, I wanted to help, I really did. I felt such compassion for Waddell's family. I tried to make sense of it before, but now I don't know. If they want to take drugs and drive off cliffs, what am I supposed to do about it?"

"You've had a tough couple of days...your car...Justin not showing up."

Terrel kept his eyes on the road as we headed up Highway 101 toward San Rafael.

"I'm worried about Lena," he said.

"She doesn't take drugs. You know that."

"She could end up a victim."

"The last thing Lena is, is a victim. She's tougher than an old rawhide whip."

"You and people connected to you could be in danger. Someone destroyed your windshield and the side panels of your car. Coming up, I learned a lot about the justice of the streets, revenge and displaced respect. To get you to stop doing whatever you've been doing, they may target something or someone else you care about."

"Lena?"

"Maybe. Anyway, keep an eye on her at the swims."

"I do that already."

I looked over at Terrel. "Consider this scenario. According to my very limited research, the victims, Dick and Jackie, were an item. Mike Menton and Jackie were an item. Maybe Mike wanted Dick out of the way. People do crazy things for love."

"That's where your theory falls apart. With Dick out of the way, Mike had free access to Jackie. Why would he hurt her?"

"Mike is pretty tightly wound from what I've seen. If Jackie goes through men—men swimmers, unless she is into other sports as well—she might have had another guy on the back burner. You know, a main man and a backup...always making sure that there is someone waiting in the wings."

"You think he'd hurt her because he is about to get dumped? It doesn't make sense. Anyway, you can talk to Menton and find out about Jackie."

"I tried that. I called him from work. I chased him down at the Cold Water Clash and he made it clear he didn't want to talk to me."

"What about Jackie?"

"She is in no condition to talk to anyone. You know that."

"She must have friends. Someone on her swim team, maybe. Her coach. Bet they know a lot about her."

"I'm not sure this will do anything but get me in trouble."

"Seriously, all you have to do is have a conversation with someone. You've got the connections now through work. And the phone numbers. Trish, people are getting hurt. One died, one almost died. I care most about Lena and you, but this could affect anyone who comes in contact with the killer."

"Killer? A killer?"

"Yes. I think you were right in the first place. None of this is a coincidence."

T pulled into our driveway. I got out and stood by the car.

"You're not coming in?"

"No, I have the next shift at the hospital. Lena knows. Consider what we talked about, okay?"

"I'll think about it."

———

Lena had fallen asleep in front of the TV. On the screen was the classic fight between good and evil. In this case, good was a sheriff at a coastal town in New England who was terrified of water. Bad was a really big shark who was dining on the local residents while they played in the water. I watched for a while considering the plight of the reluctant hero facing an angry town who didn't want their beach shut down over a holiday weekend and a frightening shark with a span of teeth broader than a double wide trailer.

At least he was a sheriff, I thought to myself. He had some idea of what he was doing. Maybe T was right, but who was going to listen to me? I can't even get a guy to show up for a date.

I tried to call Justin one more time. No response. With that, I picked up a blanket, threw it over my sleeping sister, switched off the television and made my way through the dark house to my bedroom. I sat down on the edge of my bed looking at the shadows outside the window.

Not tonight. Not this time. If I wasn't able to sleep, I had a place where I needed to go. I picked up my backpack and headed outside to the Checker cab.

It was 2:00 a.m. when I parked around the corner from Richard Waddell's empty house in Martinez. Except for a few outside porch lights, the neighborhood was dim and hushed. A light blanket of fog rubbed out the stars and shrouded the thin slice of moon.

I walked quickly down the path to Waddell's backyard, unlatched the gate and slipped in. Once again, I climbed up on a garden chair next to the kitchen window. Luck was with me; the plastic window lock had not been replaced. Pushing the window open, I pulled myself inside the dark kitchen. The small flashlight attached to my key ring threw just enough light to lead me through the house to Waddell's bedroom.

I stood there quietly, listening. No sounds, except the dull thud of my heartbeat in my ears and my unsteady breathing. I was alone. Harsh deep shadows hugged the slim beam of light as it panned around the room. Moving slowly, soundlessly toward the closet, I stopped and held my breath when a skittering ' thump, thump, thump' bounced across the roof. The noise stilled, then started again. Probably a squirrel. More important to me, it was an alarm. Don't screw around. Get what you came for and leave.

Waddell's closet was deep. His shirts, pants and suits were hung on both sides. I had seen Spencer throw the swim bag back behind the racks of shoes. I knew exactly where it was. Make that, exactly where it should have been. It wasn't there.

I needed to find the swim bag. I needed to get that small plastic baggie with the empty capsules. The narrow ray of light flitted across the bedroom…nothing…under the bed…nothing. I pulled open the tall chest of drawers and did a quick look…nothing.

I sat down on the bed and looked around. What had I missed? Swim bags aren't big, but they aren't small either. If it was here, I should be able to see it.

Someone…probably Spencer, maybe even Pamela, had taken it.

I glanced at the night table by the bedside. The small drawer of the night stand opened easily. Not much there. Two pens, a crossword puzzle book, an old address book, condoms, and a point and shoot digital camera. I slipped the address book and camera into my pocket and headed back for the kitchen. I shimmied through the window to the backyard. Stopped and listened. No sounds at all except the shooop, shooop of the sprinklers in the yard. I silently lifted the latch and headed up the sidewalk to the Checker.

16

I followed Terrel's suggestion and called Jackie's coach under the pretext of writing something about her for the upcoming swimming newsletter. The coach told me to show up after morning practice to meet Theresa Renoit, one of Jackie's lanemates. So now I was standing in the parking lot outside a swimming pool in Pacifica at 7:30 a.m. on a Tuesday and I was cold. Heavy mist hung like a damp curtain from the saturated grey sky.

When the swimmers started to roll out the door, dressed for work, carrying swim bags and soggy towels, I asked one man in a three-piece suit to point out Theresa.

"Here she comes," he said nodding toward a tall lanky woman, about 5'10", clutching a knee length blue warm-up parka with one hand and pulling a swim bag on wheels with the other.

"Hey, Theresa. I'm Trisha Carson from the Nor Cal Swim office. Your coach said you might be able to help me."

Theresa said a few words to the women she was walking with and came over. She had a quick smile and bright blue eyes. Her straight brown hair brushed her chin. She smelled of chlorine and jasmine shampoo.

"Yeah, Coach mentioned that you might be here this morning. What's up?"

"Can I buy you a cup of coffee, maybe something to eat while we talk?"

"Food? You have my undivided attention. During the last half hour of workout, my stomach was growling. All I could think about was food."

———

We sat in comfortable easy chairs next to a fireplace at the coffee shop. The warm rich aroma of coffee filled the air. Soft jazz could be heard underneath the low early morning conversations going on around us. I picked up my café mocha and the cup warmed my hands. It might be summer everywhere else in the Bay Area, but this morning it was still middle of winter in Pacifica.

"So what is this all about?" Theresa asked.

"Jackie Gibson."

"Unbelievable accident. Our team sent her flowers and we're filling out a card for her. She came so close to dying."

"The office was thinking of featuring her in the newsletter. It was suggested that I talk to you."

"Perfect. Well, she's been on the team for about six years. Good swimmer, good lanemate." Theresa stopped.

"I need a bit more information."

"She does the open water swim circuit. She doesn't compete much in pool meets."

"Yeah?" I nodded, encouraging her to keep going.

"Not for publication—but she's not the best swimmer in the world. Well, her swimming isn't that bad. But she doesn't work at it very much. Spends her time talking a lot before she gets in the water. Cuts the workout short. Doesn't show up that much to get better, if you know what I mean. You gotta put time in the water to improve."

"Wouldn't think of publishing any of this. I saw her at the Cold Water Clash. She is very pretty."

"That's part of her problem. She's a major flirt and the guys fall all over her. Not the best atmosphere sometimes, but the coach keeps it under control during practice. Most of the time, our heads are in the water."

"Just curious…did Jackie have a particular boyfriend? Or were they all her boyfriends?"

"She was a pro at handling men. Somehow, they all thought she was interested in each and everyone of them. The rest of the women on the team would watch in amazement. Sometimes we'd tease her about it in the locker room, but she never said much."

"Was there a current guy she was seeing?"

"She spent a lot of time with Dick Waddell. You know, the swimmer from Texas who just died at the open water swim a few weeks ago?"

I nodded.

"She liked him. Really liked him or that's how it looked. But you never know with her. She also talked about Mike Menton. But it was different somehow. I once overheard a cell phone conversation with Mike. She kept saying 'no' to whatever he was asking. He seemed pretty pushy. She eventually agreed to do whatever he wanted. That came as a surprise to me."

"Why?"

"Normally, nobody could force Jackie into doing anything she didn't want to do."

"Mike, Dick…the lady had her hands full. Was there anyone else?"

"Always—there was always someone else. She mentioned that she was having dinner with someone after the Clash but was thinking of cancelling it."

"Do you know who that was?"

"No. She didn't say. But it sounded like another swimmer or someone involved with the open water scene. Hey, I have to go pick up my kids and get them to daycare. My husband is probably wondering where I am so he can go to work."

"Just one more question. Was Jackie taking any medications, drugs, vitamins, that kind of thing?"

"I wouldn't know. Why would you need information like that for your story?"

"I don't. Not really."

I thanked Theresa and watched her go out the door into the drippy fog. I pulled out my cards, reached for a clean one and wrote a bunch of question marks on it. Underneath that I wrote "Jackie's newest."

17

My boss had taken a few days off. When there was a free weekend, meaning no results from pool meets or open water swims to worry about, he told me that he would disappear for a day or two.

However, this week we would be experimenting with something different. A midweek, early evening swim on the Russian River, near the picturesque town of Healdsburg. There were two distances half mile and one mile. Both swims started at the same time. This was a low key event and less than 70 swimmers were expected. Bill had left me a hastily scribbled note saying, "You're in charge. Let me know how it goes…if we should add it to our schedule next year."

I wouldn't say the added responsibility made me unhappy. I was glad he thought I could handle this. But I was apprehensive after the experience at the last two swims. Would this event go off without anyone getting hurt?

The office was very quiet. Probably the lack of Masters swimming activity over the weekend was the reason for the silent phones. Outside, San Francisco Bay had all but disappeared—once again—due to the thick gloomy fog. Could have been the end of the earth, as I looked into a wall of smothering grayness that was planted over the water. The fog erased everything. The Golden Gate Bridge was missing. Angel Island was missing and so was the rest of the Marin shoreline. It was just me standing in an office at Fort Mason looking out the window and not much else in the world.

Back at my desk, I picked up an envelope with my name on it. The return address was Nor Cal Swim Association.

"My first check." Not much of a first check, but money nonetheless. "Halfway back to normal," thinking back to the other half—Saturday's ball game date fiasco.

I began to jot down what I would do with my newly found limited wealth. Had to pay Lena back the loan she fronted me to get from Colorado to California. Chip in for food and work out a payment plan with T's father for the repairs to my car. There wouldn't be much left.

Next to the check was a small oblong white box with office business cards. They didn't have my name on them. But it seemed like a positive step forward to making this a permanent job. I stuck a few of the crisp white cards with black lettering in my wallet and put the box in a desk drawer.

I was starting to answer a few of the emails when there was a quiet knock on the office door.

There was Justin.

"Hey," he said.

"Bill's not here." I stared at him and then shifted my gaze back to the computer screen. My heartbeat jerked from 75 to 165 in less than a second. I could feel a warm flush creep up my neck to my face. My fingers, poised to type something on the keyboard, were shaking. But still I kept my glance on the monitor.

"I screwed up. I know it," he said.

I didn't look up.

"It was a misunderstanding," he said.

"Really." He had my attention now. "A misunderstanding? You asked me to go with you to a ball game. We talked about where we would meet and what time. Tell me exactly what I misunderstood."

"Not you. The guy I was buying the tickets from. I was hosed. He sold them to someone else and didn't tell me. Probably got more money."

"That doesn't make sense."

"I didn't want to look stupid. I tried to pick up other tickets but it didn't work out."

"That is one of the lamest excuses I have ever heard. Why didn't you call me and tell me? I called you. Twice from AT&T Park, once when I got home. You never called me back. I was left standing by the ferry dock checking my phone."

"No excuse there. Just wasn't thinking," he said.

"Why are you here? To see Bill? He's out for a day or two. Write him a note and I'll put it on his desk. Better yet, turn around walk down the steps, and then call and leave a message for him."

"Trisha, you're killing me. I'm here to see you. Look, I'm sorry."

"You invited me to a game you didn't have tickets for. Nothing major there. But you didn't tell me you didn't have tickets and I never heard from you. I felt ridiculous standing there. I had to hang around until the game was over before I could get on the ferry and go home."

"I'm here to apologize."

"I'm not interested."

"Let's try again. I don't want it to end like this."

"End? There is nothing to end. Nothing ever got started."

I stood up and walked toward the door with every intention of closing it in his face. I could hear a NPS security guard making his morning rounds, coming up the stairs. The heavy thud of his boots echoed through the stairwell.

"Just leave. I have work to do," I said lowering my voice.

"Okay, but I want to make one more offer. Consider it, okay? Meet me after work. We could grab a quick dinner at El Oriente Salvaje. It's in the heart of the Mission District. Do you like Salvadoran food?"

"Go," I said, my voice rising.

"They make great papusas. The real thing. Came here from El Salvador in '84 to get away from the war in their country…"

"I don't want a Central America history lesson. Just go."

"Everything okay here?" said the security guard as he walked closer to the office door. It was Jon Angel. He stopped and looked hard at Justin, then at me.

"No problem, buddy," said Justin, backing away from the door.

"Consider it, please. I'll be there at 5:30 p.m. I hope, really hope you'll come," he said as he headed for the stairwell.

"Think I'll walk him out," said the guard, glancing after Justin.

"Don't waste your time. He's not a threat. Just a guy that stood me up."

"Think I'll take a walk anyway," he said as he turned around and headed for the stairs.

My mind was about as fogged over as the Bay. I shut the office door and sat back down at my desk. I bent over my knees, head hanging toward the floor and took some long deep breaths. In slow and out slow.

There was a knock on the door.

"Hey, hey there, Trisha. "You still here?"

The door opened slowly. It was Jon holding a to-go cup. I could smell the heavy rich chocolate from the white container and see soft whipped cream oozing through the slit on the lid.

"Thought you might like this," he said and handed me the drink.

"That guy come back again—you let me know."

He looked around, taking in the swimming photos, ribbons, plaques hanging on the wall, much as I did when I first walked in the office.

"Nice view, I bet, when the fog's outta the way."

"Yeah, it is."

He sat down in the straight-back chair by the door, tapping his hand on his knee. He was a big solid guy and his body overwhelmed the chair. It disappeared underneath him.

There was a long awkward silence.

"What are those?" he said pointing to the 3 x 5 cards sitting on the corner of my desk.

"A puzzle I'm trying to figure out. Two open water swimmers have had accidents recently. One died and one is hospitalized. These are the people who are connected to both of them."

When I explained what had happened to Waddell and Jackie, he was all business again.

"Considering the attack on your car, I'd say something is going on. Don't mess with this. Go to the police."

"Well, you're the police."

"We deal with crimes on National Park property. Not general crimes taking place in the Bay Area."

"What do you think?"

"You didn't hear me, did you? I think you should talk to the SF police and keep your door shut and locked."

———

Lena checked in about an hour later talking so fast she was hard to understand.

"Traffic is terrible...I have been condemned to the tenth circle of hell that Dante never wrote about—driving through road construction...Do you have to evaluate the swim this Wednesday? The new one in the evening? Of course you do, that's your job. Well, we may be taking another passenger...Terrel wants to come...Do you believe it?...Would I love to see him in the water!...Hah, what a sight that would be...I won't be home for dinner...We're doing a practice swim off McNears Beach in the Bay...wanna come?"

There was a long pause as Lena caught her breath.

"I'll probably hang out here for a while. Maybe I'll stop at McNears on the way home."

"Okay. Trisha, I hope you're not still thinking about that lowlife from the ball game."

"No, not really," and I hung up quickly.

The day stayed surprisingly quiet. Maybe because nobody died or got hurt over the past weekend. Maybe this is how the office normally is.

I walked over to Bill's desk to drop off a team's proposal for another new open water swim. It would be a 10K, a little over six miles, which to me was a long way to swim. But some swimmers were clamoring for one.

On the corner of the desk was the Dick Waddell file. It looked much the same as the first time I saw it. There was a new phone number with the initials ME next to it. Bet that's the medical examiner. He will have the autopsy information. I copied down the number, planning to put it with my Waddell case file. I couldn't find any folder at all on Jackie Gibson.

Guess you need to die to merit a folder of your own.

Bill's phone was blinking. The red on and off light told me that someone had used his back line to get into his voicemail. I dialed the number to retrieve the call.

"Yo, Bill. Dude, it's Chris. Lovin' it here in the Northwest wing of our spectacular country. But I have to come back to the Bay area. More expensive than I thought it would be. Cash is running low. Went fast. I know you understand, dude. Handling money has never been my strong point. Is my job still there? Buddy, I won't walk out this time. Word, brother."

The line went dead.

Great. Laid back drifter Chris is ready to give up on his quest to find nirvana because he needed a paycheck. It only took him a month to go broke. Now, he wanted his old job that is now my job. I glanced over at the paycheck still sitting on my desk. I needed that money. A moral dilemma stood in front of me—to delete or not delete, that was the question.

A ringing phone pushed the decision out of mind.

"Nor Cal Swim Association," I said.

A familiar high pitched voice on the other end of the line asked, "Is this Trisha?"

"Yes."

"This is Daisy, Daisy Menton? I'm…uh…like.. Mike Menton's daughter?"

Every sentence she uttered in her squeaky voice ended with a question mark.

"Yes, I remember you from the swims. What's going on?"

"I think I know who hurt that swimmer a few weeks ago."

"Richard Waddell?"

"Yeah, the old guy. I don't think he meant it. I think he was trying to help. But it didn't work and the guy got sick in the water."

"Wait a minute. Slow down. Trying to help, how?"

"Giving him stuff to take."

"You mean like drugs?"

"Of course I mean drugs."

"Were the drugs supposed to help or hurt him?"

"Help. No, hurt. It depends what you're talking about."

This girl was not making sense.

"Have you spoken to your father about this?"

"No. He'd get mad at me."

"If it was a mistake, all he has to do is tell someone. Even if it was a drug and he offered it to Waddell, then he, Dick, has some responsibility in this."

"But that's just it. I don't think Waddell knew."

"Knew what exactly?"

"Knew what he was taking."

"Wasn't Richard Waddell one of your father's big competitors?"

"Sure was. Dad called him DickWad. Pretty funny, uh? I often heard him talk about him like that to his friends. Dad really thought he would win his age group this season. Then he'd get to go to the Open Water Nationals in Maryland. He's going to go now, for sure."

"Look, if you think that your father has done something that might have hurt Richard, we need to tell someone. Even if he…"

"My father? I'm not talking about my father."

"You're not? Then who are you talking about?"

"Nick. He's the one, my boyfriend."

I stared at the phone in complete bewilderment.

"Your boyfriend? The pale kid who looks like he never gets outside? What is he, 16, maybe? How could he possibly do anything to hurt Richard and why would he want to?"

"You don't get anything do you? He knew winning was a big deal for my dad. And if it's a big deal for Dad, it's a big deal for me. When DickWad showed up this season, well, it wasn't like it was a sure thing anymore. I used to talk to Nick about it, I'd go, 'Dad is so pissed. He lost today to the new guy.' And he'd go, 'yeah?' and I'd go 'yeah.' He wanted to make me happy and he knew that I wanted to make my dad happy. So it just makes sense to me, about Nick, that is."

"Do you really think he would hurt someone?"

"All the time, he goes, 'I'll do anything for you.'"

"Do you have any idea where the drugs came from?"

"So easy...school, off course. It doesn't take much to get anything you want. Just ask the right people, that's all. I thought you knew all about it. That's why you were calling the house and wanting to talk to Dad at the Clash. I figured I'd better tell you."

"Tell me about Nick."

"He likes science stuff, chemicals and computers."

"Maybe we need to talk to your dad."

"No. You can't. You don't understand. He wouldn't let me see Nick anymore. And he's the only guy I know who has a car that my Dad thinks is okay."

"Do you think Nick had anything to do with Jackie's accident?"

"Jac Kay" she said emphasizing each syllable, "is a skanky bea-atch."

"The woman almost died. She drove off a cliff."

"BFD. She is a total slut. I heard her and my dad fighting. She was dating DickWad and my dad at the same time. Dad didn't like that. I really wished he would dump her. I'll run away if she ends up my stepmother, I swear."

This conversation was more than strange. I actually thought that her father was somehow involved with Waddell's accident that ultimately took his life. But what about Jackie? And my car? Could Nick and maybe some of his friends be involved, like Daisy said?

"Daisy, you better speak to your father. Have you talked to Nick about this?"

"I got to go."

"One more thing. What does your father do?"

"He sells stuff."

"Stuff? Like shoes, computers?"

"Airplanes, jumbo jets, that kind of thing."

"You sell things like that out of an office?"

"He works mostly from home."

Her voice dropped to a whisper. "Dad just came home" and the line went dead.

———

As 4:30 p.m. came around, I considered leaving early, shutting the office down and heading home. Daisy's call was unsettling; so was Justin's visit. Was he as sorry as he said? I have a feeling that if I asked that question to my immediate circle—Lena, Dr. T, my NPS security pal, and probably even ditzy Daisy Menton—they would all stand in front of me, stick out their right arm, and give a unanimous thumbs down.

18

I changed my mind at least four times after I slipped into the driver's seat of the Checker cab. But I was now parked down the street from El Oriente Salvaje, in the Mission District. And I was early.

The Mission is a high-strung neighborhood with an active pulse. The sidewalks were packed—people rushing out of the BART station, San Francisco's subway, coming home from work, families stopping into taquerias to pick up dinner, and young teenagers in tight black jeans skateboarding around parked cars. I'd do the 'one Mississippi' thing a few times. If I didn't see Justin go in, I was on my way home.

I was on the ninth 'one Mississippi' when I saw him walk through the restaurant's front door. A combination of dread and relief flushed over me. Okay, I was going in.

But first, I texted Lena and asked her to call my cell in about an hour. A quick look in the flip down mirror showed that I looked... like me. No miracle change. Just the same dark brown eyes stared back at me that have stared at me my whole life. I took my hair out of the ponytail and ran a comb through it. Lena was lucky. She had the bouncy curly hair that always looked good. Mine was reddish brown, fine and straight.

"This is as good as it gets," I said, and headed for the front door.

The restaurant appeared closed. I could barely see the small twinkling lights through the thick blackish-grey window shades. I walked slowly toward the front door. Just as I pushed it open, an older Latina pulled up one of the shades.

"Hola," she said smiling.

It was like walking across the border. Outside, horns honking, motors running, the starkness of concrete sidewalks and streets, graffiti and too many hurrying people. Inside, I found myself in a warm family restaurant. Wider than it was long, the kitchen where the abuelitas—the grandmothers—were preparing the food, was at the back. Couples and families with small children sat at tables topped by Formica. The walls were covered with black and white photographs of a dusty rural El Salvador. Laughter and chit chat were mostly in Spanish. Some people stood at the back counter picking up food to go.

Justin sat at a corner booth talking with a short olive-skinned woman, in her early thirties with round deep brown eyes, and long dark hair pulled back and up, held in place by two combs of golden sunflowers. Even from the front door, I could hear the music and joy in her laughter.

He saw me when I walked in and waved me over.

"Nancy, this is a good friend of mine, Trisha. Nancy is one of the owners."

"Hello, very nice to meet you," she smiled a warm gracious greeting. "Ever eaten Salvadoran food?"

I shook my head. "No."

"Very tasty. My mother, Patricia—see back there—she runs the kitchen. You are a friend of Justin's. Then special papusas for you."

With that she walked toward the kitchen behind the bar and started rattling off a mile a minute in Spanish. "Si, si," said Patricia, holding a large dark frying pan in her hand over the stove. She looked up at me, smiled and called out, "You will like."

I sat down across from Justin.

"You came. I didn't think you would. I'm not sure I would have."

He's right, I thought. Anyone with common sense would have stayed away. My 3 x 5 cards came to mind. I could see his name on one of them. Why exactly had he invited me? Was it really to apologize again? Or was it something else?

"I don't know what I'm doing here," I said.

I glanced up at him. His shoulders sagged and he rarely met my eyes. Every now and then, he gave me a tentative and lopsided smile. Basically, Justin was non-descript—you wouldn't even look up when he walked by, but there was an undeniable undercurrent, a low voltage of electricity, running through him.

On the side of his neck, he had a tattoo of a clock with no hands in blue ink. When his hands were on the table, I could see the remnants of tattoos right above his knuckles. Above that was a faint spider web.

"You said yourself that you probably wouldn't have come."

"So why did you?"

"I'm not all that sure. But, I believe that people can make mistakes. I know I've made my share."

"So we're cool?"

"I'm not ready to go that far yet, but I'm still here."

"Nancy and Patricia are cooking just for you. I don't want to disappoint them. After we've eaten, if you want to leave, well... that's the way it will be."

Nancy brought over a plate of papusas, thick corn tortillas filled with melted cheese, pork and beans. With it came curtido, a simple tangy cabbage salad. It looked good and smelled great. I have to say that the food kept me in the restaurant more than Justin. For a few minutes, I did nothing but revel in the gooey cheesiness.

Patricia had come out from the kitchen, wiping her hands on a white apron. Like her daughter, she had a lilt in her high-pitched voice. She sounded happy no matter what she said. "Justin, he is one of my favorites." She patted him on the cheek. "You like?"

"Es bueno," said Justin.

"It's beyond bueno. Delicioso," I said, using my limited Spanish. Patricia smiled. Her waist length dark hair had a streak of grey that began at her left temple and stretched to its end. It was pulled back in a ponytail and wrapped into a circle on the back of her head. She continued to walk around the small room, stopping at tables and chatting in Spanish. If Nancy and Patricia liked Justin, maybe he was more than the jerk I thought he was.

But I still had no idea what to say to him. Where to start? So I said the only thing that came to mind.

"You like tattoos?"

"So-so. Why do you ask?"

I tapped the faint markings on his knuckles and pointed to the clock with no hands on the side of his neck.

"When you're young you do stupid things." He dipped his head. "Well maybe, when you're older too. Anyway, I had these tats done a while ago. Now I'm getting them undone. Not cheap."

"Does it hurt?"

"Getting inked or de-inked?"

"Both, I guess."

"Yes, to both."

Justin's cell phone rang. He looked at the screen. "Sorry, but I have to take this."

Turning sideways, he spoke quietly into the phone.

"Yes. Now. This is the time. Okay."

He hung up and looked at me with a sad smile. "Sorry about that. Business gets in the way of everything sometimes."

"Do you know when you'll be able to swim again?" I asked, trying to fill up the dead air floating between us.

"The doctor says a few more weeks. I miss it. You swim, don't you?"

"No, well yes, but not like you and my sister. I just float around. I like the water. For me, it's relaxing."

"Your sister swims?"

"Yeah, Lena Shriver is my sister. She competed in high school and college. Now it's mostly for fun, to stay in shape. She likes the open water swims and I usually end up driving her."

"What does she do?"

"Website designer. She's good at it, too."

"Maybe I'll check her out. My business could use a more sophisticated site."

He glanced over at Patricia in the kitchen, then looked back at me. "So how's the job?"

"You know what surprises me about it? The accidents. I never expected people would get hurt."

"That's right. You were showing me your cards. Girl detective. Do you still think someone is after open water swimmers?"

"Yes, I do. But I don't know why and I don't know who."

"Although you couldn't really classify open water swimming as an extreme sport, it has definite dangers. This community here has been accident-free for years. Maybe it's just time. Still have your cards and your clues?"

"No clues. I'm just trying to connect the dots. See who is related to who."

"A genealogy for the accidents?"

"Sort of. Hey, when we first met, you mentioned that you had something to do with the food booths that are at the swims. What exactly do you do?"

"I started a company with a friend. We make this product called RazzleD. We develop nutritional supplements for athletes. We're fairly new, but we have a pretty good foothold in the local open water swimming community. We're branching out and hitting the national swims. We're in talks now with the triathlon head honchos to see if we could get a spot at their events. There's a lot of money there. Thousands of triathletes compete in a season—pure gold for us."

"How'd you get involved with that?"

"Well, I'm trained as a chemist. You wouldn't believe that, would you? I've been interested in how nutrition and nutritional supplements can help performance. And I'm a swimmer, been one since as far back as I can remember. I have two partners, one is silent, gives us money and looks over our shoulders. The other is a big wheeler-dealer, entrepreneur-type. I'm the grunt worker, coming up with the formulas. You've seen the booths then?"

"At the Cold Water Clash, I saw some teenagers giving out drinks from a booth. Was that your booth?"

"Yeah. Do you remember seeing the name of the product?"

"Sorry, no."

"Mmm, well. That's interesting. We need to do something to get more name recognition. Maybe your sister could help with that."

Nancy stopped by the table. "Anything else you'd like?"

The papusas had been filling, but I had seen Nancy carry out a wonderful looking dish that looked like bananas.

"What is that?" I asked Nancy, pointing to a nearby table.

"Fried plantains with crème. Usually you have it before a meal or maybe breakfast. But it's sweet, so people in this country eat them for dessert."

"We'll share an order," Justin said.

Like the rest of the food, the fried plantains were very tasty. Again, we were quiet for a while as we ate.

"How do you know Nancy and Patricia?"

"I know Nancy's brother, Roberto."

"Is he working behind the counter...one of those guys back there?"

"No. He comes in later. Guy's been in and out of trouble. Sad story, wonderful family, but a sad story. That's enough. Let's finish up and get out of here," he said, calling over Nancy for the check.

I felt like a door had closed. Was asking about Roberto taboo? Or was it something else? I was just about to ease into some questions about Jackie and Dick. What was going on?

"Let's head back to my office," he said. "You can try out some of our products."

Don't think so, I thought. I'm not ready to be alone with you.

Just then my phone rang. It was Lena. I'd forgotten that I asked her to call.

"Yes?"

"Well, here I am," said my sister. "I'm still at Stinson, but the group is getting ready to leave. It will be dark soon."

"I didn't know that."

"You didn't know what? Trish, what's this all about? Are you okay?"

"Yes, not a problem. But I'll be there. I'll leave now."

"Trish, where are you?"

"Still in San Francisco. I'll be there soon," I said and put the phone back in my bag.

"I better be going," I said.

———

As we stood outside the restaurant, Justin kept looking around. When a car backfired on Mission Street, he jumped and backed up closer to the front window of the restaurant.

"We'll do the office thing some other time," he said, looking over my shoulder to the sidewalk across the street. I saw him nod. I turned to see who he was looking at, but there was nobody that I could see, just a woman walking down the street holding her son's hand, two twenty-somethings in the middle of an animated conversation and three men all in sweatshirts gathered around an ATM machine.

"Sure, it was fun. Food was great."

Before I finished my sentence, he had started to walk away, quickly turned the corner and vanished.

19

Instead of heading for the Golden Gate Bridge, I drove to the swim office in Fort Mason. I wanted a few minutes to myself before I went home. Even though Justin took off as if I had a contagious disease, I enjoyed the dinner, not just the food, but his company. Interesting man.

Pulling into the parking lot, I saw NPS security drive by. At the wheel was my friend, Jon Angel. He stopped when he saw me and slid down his window.

"Too nice to be working, but I'm here," he said, looking over the Bay, shimmering in the evening sunlight. "Did you forget something?"

"I think I left the copier on. This will only take a minute."

I walked quickly to the front door of the building. With Jon out there, I wouldn't have all that much time to sit and think over my dinner with Justin. If I didn't reappear in fifteen minutes, he'd come looking for me.

The door was still unlocked, but it felt so heavy to push open. Too many papusas. The automatic lights in the hall switched on as I walked into the building and climbed up the three flights of stairs. Not a soul was around. My footsteps echoed through the empty stairwell.

Stopping in front of the door to the Swimming Association office, I dug in my backpack for the keys. The rush of adrenaline that I felt before dinner was draining away. I rested my head against the door, beginning to feel pleasantly tired. The weight of my head pushed the door open slightly. I had closed and locked it when I left, I was sure. I always do.

Could someone be in there? I thought of Jon in the parking lot. Should I go get him? I held my breath and listened. Nothing, no noise, no sounds. All I could hear was the echo of my heartbeat in my ears. The darkness of the hallway closed in around me. Maybe the cleaning people had been there and forgot to shut the door.

I quietly placed my hand on the door and gave a small push. It opened a few inches. I stopped and listened. Nothing. I pushed again and then, "Hello, is anyone here?" All I heard was my own tentative voice. I gave one big push and stepped back quickly against the wall in the hallway. The door widened and hit the chair just inside the office. I reached in, searched for the light switch on the wall and turned it on. The office was empty, just as I left it a few hours ago.

With an audible sigh, I walked in and sat down at my desk. The red light was blinking on the phone, but the calls could wait. I walked over to the window and stared out. The pulsing navigation lights on Alcatraz could be seen. The sun was low in the west, a huge orange ball drifting down toward the ocean outside the Golden Gate. It turned the waters of the Bay a deep, bottomless blue-black.

I walked into hall heading for the storage room with the space-age copier. The automatic hallway light had switched off and it was dark. For some reason, it didn't go back on again when I stepped out of my office.

Hard to find the right key in this darkness. I squinted at each one in the dim light. Three flights down, I heard the front door to the building open. "Hello?" I called. There was no answer. "Jon, is that you?" Then I heard a door open and close. Somebody else must be working late.

Unlocking the storage room, I flipped on the light switch, shut the door behind me and looked at the copier. I really had left it on. Wanting to get a head start on the next day's work, I grabbed a few packages of paper and filled the paper trays of the copier. I tested the machine and then powered it down and off.

Okay...exit stage right. Time to go home.

I walked out of the storage room. The light from the office across the hall created a yellow angular shadow on the black floor. I looked into the darkness, but saw nothing.

"This is creepy. Why doesn't the light go on?"

I took a few steps forward and pushed open the door. Standing at my desk, was a thin man, about 5'8". He was wearing a dark blue knit cap pulled low to his eyes, a black hoody, old Levi's and Converse sneakers. He had my backpack in his hand.

"Put that down. Now," I yelled. "Now, leave. Go, go."

The backpack dropped to the floor. Like a football player running down a field, the thief stuck one arm straight out, pushed me out of the way and sprinted out the door, heading for the steps. I picked up the office phone and called the security guard number pasted on the wall.

"NPS Security."

"There was someone in my office. I scared him. He almost took my backpack."

"We'll be right there. Are you all right?"

"Yes."

"Lock your door. Someone will be there immediately."

Within a few minutes—what felt like a very long few minutes—there was a knock.

"Trisha, are you in there?"

"Yes."

"Open the door. It's okay. It's me, Jon."

"I don't want to."

"Trisha, please. I need to talk to you. I need a description of the man you found in your office."

I opened the door a few inches. It really was Jon.

"He was trying to steal my backpack. I yelled at him to get out."

"Not the best of moves. You could have been hurt. Next time, either go back into the storage room and lock it or run out of the building. You're okay?"

"Just a little shaken up. I thought all he wanted was my backpack. But look over there at Bill's side of the office. His files. They are all over the place."

I walked over to Bill's desk and started picking up the files on the floor. Jon came over and crouched down besides me. He picked up a manila folder and handed it to me.

"Why would someone be looking through the files?"

"I don't know."

For the next few minutes, Jon asked me questions about the thief's description and radioed my answers to other guards in the area.

"Did anybody know that you were coming back to the office?"

"No, I wasn't supposed to be here."

Jon's radio buzzed. The NPS security had stopped someone matching the description I gave. He was near Hyde Street Pier.

"Want to take a ride and see if this is your guy?"

"Not my guy," I said as I securely locked the door behind me and followed Jon down the steps.

———

I sat in the passenger side of the security car as we headed down Bay Street toward the popular tourist attractions near Ghirardelli Square.

"What were you doing back here? Did you stop to have a drink with some friends…go to a movie…what?"

"Why does it matter?"

"Well, if someone knew where you were and that the office was empty…?"

"Okay, I was having dinner with someone."

"Did that someone have any connection with Nor Cal Swimming Association?"

"No…well…maybe. Kind of, I guess. It was the guy I was talking to earlier today."

Jon never batted an eye.

"What is his association with your office?"

"Not much. He has a booth at the open water swims for nutritional products, mostly rehydration drinks."

"Did he know that Bill was out of town?"

"I think I mentioned that to him."

We crossed the cable car tracks at Hyde Street. Then, at the corner of North Point and Leavenworth, we turned left heading toward the Bay and the historic waterfront. July is the middle of tourist season in San Francisco and it is usually very chilly, especially by the water. But tonight was a rarity in the city, a warm summer night. By warm, I mean high sixties. Not a whisper of wind. The streets were jammed with visitors.

How could I pick someone out in a crowd like this.

Turning left on Jefferson, we slowed down. A block from the cable car turnaround, an NPS security guard was outside his car. Standing next to him, leaning against a bike, was a tall lanky man wearing a dark knit cap, black hoody, old Levi's and Converse tennis shoes. The cyclist stared off into space.

We drove slowly by him and continued past the entrances to the South End Rowing Club and Dolphin Club, two swim clubs that encouraged Bay swimming. The narrow street near Aquatic Park was a dead end. We turned around and drove by slowly again so I could see his face.

"Nope, not him," I said. "Right clothes, but wrong guy."

Jon radioed the other guard. "Not our suspect. Let him go."

With that, he turned right up Hyde Street past the crowd of tourists standing in line for the cable car and drove me back to the parking lot in Fort Mason.

"It's none of my business, but you didn't seem too happy to see that fellow earlier today. And didn't you say, he stood you up? You sure this is a man you want to have dinner with?"

I didn't answer. As soon as he parked the car, I jumped out.

"I need to do one last check on the office. Make sure everything is turned off, really turned off, and locked up."

I trotted over toward the front door.

"Let's get you safely in and out of here," Jon said, following me.

"What's that?" he said, looking at the tall green prickly shrubs that bordered the front door. I followed his gaze and saw some folders caught in the bushes. He pushed his hand through the greenery and picked up about three crumpled manila folders.

"Just a guess. Since these weren't here earlier today, do they belong to your office?"

The tab on one folder said 'Accident File, Richard Waddell.' I opened it up but all the papers were gone. The other folders were labeled 'Open Water Schedule' and 'Pool Meet Schedule.'

"Are you sure there aren't any more papers stuck back behind the hedges?"

We both bent over the shrubs and poked our arms around. Jon turned on his flashlight. All we found were candy wrappers and a few empty soda cans.

"The thief took the insurance forms plus a few pages of notes. He wanted information about the Waddell accident. My backpack was just the cherry on top of the sundae. An unexpected bonus."

Jon looked at the Waddell folder. "Can I have that? I'd like to show it to my supervisor." He looked at me closely. "Did you ever talk to the SF police about your suspicions regarding the two accidents and your cards?"

"Not really."

"Does that mean 'no'"?

"That means 'no, I didn't.' It seemed silly."

"It's not silly any more. This doesn't fit the profile of the burglar who has been hitting the Fort Mason buildings during the day, and running out with purses, jackets, wallets, even laptops. Snatch and run. Like the damage done to your car, this is much more deliberate. There's a specific intent here. This is getting serious and you and anyone working in the office could get hurt. I'm going to talk with the neighborhood police and alert them. Someone, either the

SF cops or the NPS security guys will stop in tomorrow to talk to you."

When we walked into the building, the automatic lights didn't turn on. Jon walked over to the switch on the whitewashed wall. It had been unscrewed and pulled out. The switch plate was on the floor. The wires were cut and dangling from the wall.

Jon picked up his radio and called for another guard to come to the building. He kept his flashlight on and we walked up the steps.

"I feel like I'm walking in a dark closet," I said.

I unlocked the door once again, picked up my backpack resting on the desk, and switched off the light. Jon held his flashlight on the door while I locked it. Then he walked me back down and out to my car.

"You okay to drive?"

"I guess. Thank you."

He nodded as I got in my car.

"Lock it," he said. When he heard the door lock, he nodded again and watched me drive to the exit of the parking lot.

––––––

The drive back home over the Golden Gate Bridge is normally the highlight of my day. Tonight the huge blazing sun was about to explode. It dropped behind a thin layer of fog. Sun above the fog; sun below the fog—an enormous ball cut in half. Then the top half sank into the thick grayness. When it emerged, the vibrating orange ball began to melt into the ocean. It was hard to make out the color of the water, as inch by inch it swallowed up the sinking sun.

I watched it and felt nothing. I wanted to be off the Bridge and home.

It was after 9:30 p.m. when I walked in the quiet house. I headed for the kitchen, sat down and pulled out the 3 x 5 cards from my backpack. I started a new one. Thief—male, late twenties, thin, watch cap, black hoodie, jeans, and Converse tennies.

I pulled out the card for Justin. I added, 'Chemist, RazzleD. Friend of restaurant owners.'

20

I stared into the mirror.

I looked like a human radio communication satellite ready to be launched. The small pieces of tinfoil wrapped around sections of my hair stood straight out or straight up.

After last night's scare, I felt I deserved a little me time. I took the next afternoon off and was in downtown San Rafael. Just around the corner from Fourth Street, the main shopping street was Mandraka's Salon. I passed it almost daily, going and coming to the west end of San Rafael. The name had always intrigued me. This time, I parked down the street across from the San Rafael Fire Station, walked in, looked at the woman behind the reception desk and said, 'Is it possible to help this?' and I held my hair out with both hands.

Mirana, the owner of Mandraka's, looked up at me, threw back her head and laughed. Her chocolate skin was deeply oiled and it glistened under her short-sleeved white blouse. And when she smiled, her full oval face lit up like a Hollywood spot light.

The beauty parlor was small and narrow, just four stations, two on one side of a long mirror and two on the other side. Shades of rosy red and green dominated the room. I slipped a lightweight robe on over my clothes and she went to work on my lifeless hair. I was now in the holding pattern all women experience when they are having a color boost. It would take 20-30 minutes for the color to set.

With nothing to do, I dug around in my backpack looking for my phone. Instead, I pulled out Waddell's old address book. I had forgotten all about it. It had to be at least 10 years old. Many of the area codes were from Dallas, Texas. I started calling numbers. Most were disconnected. Some went to businesses. Others went to message machines. Those that did pick up said they never heard of a Dick Waddell.

I was about to put the address book away when I saw a receipt from a fast food restaurant taped to the last page. I carefully pulled it off. That day, Dick had bought two orders of burgers, fries and two chocolate milkshakes. Why would he keep this? The location of the restaurant was Fresno, California.

I turned the receipt over. On the back was written "Jeremy Reid," and two phone numbers. I punched in the first number. A little boy answered the phone.

"Is your daddy there?" I asked.

"No."

"Is his name Jeremy?"

"Mom," called out the small voice.

I hung up. I had no idea what I was going to say if 'daddy' was Jeremy and he came to the phone. Then I dialed the second number.

"You have reached University High School, located on the campus of California State University, Fresno." The recorded message continued. I listened absent-mindedly then clicked off. So, Waddell had friends in Fresno. No crime in that.

Lena's picture came up on the screen of my phone. I punched the talk button.

"Hey."

Lena was at full throttle.

"New client. I have a new client and I have you to thank for it. So thank you, thank you, thank you."

"Me? I don't remember recommending you to anyone…not that I wouldn't, of course."

"Doesn't matter. Maybe it was someone who knew you or knew me. Anyway, they liked my work on the Nor Cal Swim website."

"What's the name of this company?"

"Don't remember, but their products have something to do with health and fitness. I have it written down somewhere."

I could hear her shuffling through papers. Lena chatted on while I adjusted the tin foil flaps on my head so I could position my cell phone and hear better.

"They want me to come in on Monday to talk to them, get a feel for their products and their company. Then I have a few weeks to develop a formal plan."

She paused for a split-second and I jumped in, telling her about last night.

For one of the few times in her life, she was speechless.

"You have to get out of there…too dangerous…much too dangerous. Need to change the subject for a minute. Will you be home soon?"

"In a few hours, why?"

"Can you help me pick out what I'm going to wear for this meeting with the new clients? I have to meet all the partners and I want them to like not just my work, but me, too. Maybe they can become my main client. Put me on retainer. With a guaranteed monthly income. Then you can quit your job at the Swim Association. You shouldn't work there anymore. You can look for something you really like."

"Right now, that dangerous job is my only source of money. Wait…did you say all the partners? How many are there?"

"Three, I think."

"Look, Ms. Dress for Success, why don't you pull out a few things that you are thinking of wearing. I'll see you at home."

Mirana looked at me or rather my tinfoil flaps. She undid one, studied the color. It must have been to her liking because she said, "Okay. We're ready. Time to wash."

I followed her back to a small rinsing station with two sinks, sat in the chair and rested the back of my neck on the edge of the deep sink. She pulled out the foil and clips and rinsed my hair with warm water. Then she wrapped my head in a towel and we walked back to her station.

While she was taking out her scissors and combs from a small drawer, I pulled out my cards and looked them over.

Mirana glanced at me through the large mirror.

"Flash cards? You are a student?"

"No. Just trying to figure something out."

Holding up a damp section of newly darkened hair, she asked, "What do we want to do?"

"I have no idea. Whatever you think would look best on me, I'm for."

Mirana put her hands on her hips and stared at my reflection.

"Okay, I have an idea." She began to comb and snip.

"Your cards. They are a puzzle?" she asked as she kept her eyes on my hair and her comb.

"Kind of. Each card represents someone or something that is related to two accidents. In one, someone died."

Mirana looked at me through the mirror with raised eyebrows, "Died?"

The chatter in the rest of the beauty salon came to an abrupt halt. Everyone was listening.

"Yes, died. I think the accidents are related and someone in this pack of cards did it."

I put down the cards of Jackie and Dick Waddell on the counter.

I explained to Mirana what had happened to both of them. Then I pushed back the cans of hair spray, containers of gels and mousse and laid out the remaining cards in a circle around the two middle cards on the counter. Aina, the other stylist in the shop, walked over and looked at each card for a moment and picked one up.

"This person, Pamela. I think it is her. She did it."

"Why would you say that?" I asked.

"Look. She kills her brother. Now, brother is dead. He has no other family but her. She gets everything he owns. But to make sure it all comes to her, she gets rid of girlfriend. Simple. Now she is rich."

"Possibly. I met her. She doesn't seem like a killer to me."

"This is about love, isn't it? These two people were lovers, yes?" asked Marina.

I nodded.

"There are all kinds of love. Love between a man and a woman. Love in a family, mother child, father child. Love of money. Love of self."

The customer whom Aina was combing out, left her chair to come over and look at the cards. "Love of self. That's my husband. He doesn't need anyone else in our marriage. Not sure what I'm doing there." Everyone chuckled. "That's right" and "Amen" were heard in the little shop.

Mirana continued, "Hate is not very far from love. You agree? I look at these names and think, these are probably good people. Maybe some better than others. Why would a good person do something bad to someone else? Maybe jealousy or revenge.

"In Madagascar, my country, we say 'To be two things like a bat: flying it's a bird, resting it's a mouse.'"

"I don't understand."

"Think about this…the person who did these bad things is not what he or she appears to be. Because they have two sides. You are only seeing the mouse side of them. That is the side they want you to see."

Aina's client looked at me. "The whole picture, sweetie. You have to see the whole picture."

"Easier said than done," I said. "Everyone wants to look good."

Mirana smiled. "I think the answer is right here in front of you," and she reached over, picked up my cards and handed them back to me.

"You mean, if I find the 'other' side, I'll find the killer?"

"Could be. You will figure it out, I'm sure."

Mirana hummed as she snipped away. I actually felt lighter. She picked up a black blow dryer and a round large bristle brush and spent the next 10 minutes rearranging my hair. The shape of my face began to change right in front of me. Was this the other side Mirana was talking about? Could you change your insides, by changing your outside?

Then she looked at me through the mirror. "So, what do you think?" My hair was a rich reddish-brown with golden streaks running through it. It looked like I'd spent afternoons at the beach.

Mirana had created a simple but elegant style, easy to care for and nice to look at.

"Much better," she said.

I couldn't believe my eyes. I looked like a different person. I felt like a different person.

"I'm speechless. It looks great."

I thanked her, wrote a check and was walking to the door when she called out to me.

"One more thing—in Madagascar we say, 'the rolling stone…'"

"Gathers no moss," I added.

"No, in Madagascar, 'the rolling stone never stops till it reaches the bottom.'"

"I get it. The person responsible for these accidents—he or she—will not stop until they're caught."

———

As I headed down Fourth Street, I kept thinking about that rolling stone. Was the person behind all this done? My gut said, 'no.'

Tall sycamore and maple trees lined both sides of the street, shading shoppers as they visited the many restaurants, jewelers, dress shops, coffee shops and florists. I walked past the restored Art Deco Film Center and the tables and chairs outside the Rafael Coffee café next to it. As I passed a glass storefront I couldn't help but look in at my reflection.

"Not bad," I said quietly. "Not bad at all."

"I agree," said a young woman who had stopped to look at the display in the window. "I would love to surprise my boyfriend wearing one of those."

I hadn't realized it, but I was standing in front of a lingerie shop. On display were lacy bras and panties. The faceless manikin was wearing a black garter belt. I hadn't seen a garter belt since I was in high school. And they sure didn't look like what I was currently staring at.

"Do people still wear those?" I asked the girl next to me.

"Oh yes. They do. They most certainly do."

"Maybe I need to check this out." I opened the door to Sweet Nothings and walked in.

————

"Well, look at you," Lena said as I entered the house. "Your hair, I love it."

She walked in a circle around me, nodding her head.

"Very nice." She glanced down at the pink and black shopping bag in my hand with the stylized initial SN in gold on either side.

"What's in the bag? You went to Sweet Nothings, didn't you?"

She reached for the bag. I tried to pull it away from her, but she was too quick. She grabbed the shopping bag from me and dug through the pink tissue paper.

"Let me see. What did you….well, well, what do we have here? New undies and just not your usual cotton undies. Do you have something planned with someone I don't know about?"

"Give those back to me."

She laughed and moved away, holding up a white lace bra and matching white bikini panties.

"New hair, lacy underthings. Sister, congratulations. You are back in the world of the living."

————

Lena had two different outfits laid out on the bed. She reached down for the straight pencil black skirt, stepped into it, and pulled on a wraparound printed jersey and slipped on high, high heels.

"What do you think?"

"Don't like it."

"Why not? What's wrong with it. It says professional, stylish but casual."

"You look like a TV version of an executive assistant on the prowl. There is nothing about it that says creative. 'I am creative.'"

"I don't know why I'm asking you. Your fashion IQ is about 14."

Lena turned this way and that, looking at herself in the full length mirror on the back of her door, then started to peel off the clothes.

"Did you ever remember the name of the company that you're interviewing with?"

Lena reached down to a pile of papers scattered on the floor and picked up a notepad. "Yeah, it's a very non-descript name. JL, Inc."

Next, Lena stepped into a pair of tailored trousers and put on a snow white blouse and a pair of ankle length rock star boots.

"I like. Wear that artsy necklace you have from Italy and you're ready to go. You still haven't said what it is they make?"

"The only thing I could find on their website was a drink, a hydrator for athletes."

"Aren't there enough of those already? I would think the market is saturated. No pun intended."

I picked up the deep red and burnt-orange necklace I had suggested from her dresser and draped it around her neck.

"There, that looks good."

We both stared at her reflection in the mirror and nodded our heads in unison.

"From the brief conversation I had on the phone, they think their product is really unique and that athletes will see a tremendous difference in their performance and that their recovery time will be cut in half."

"Well, be careful of their claims. They have to make sure they are true, which means they have to be tested," I said. "I'm guessing the product hasn't been introduced yet. At the office we get all these emails promoting new nutritional supplements and drinks for swimmers. I haven't seen anything that says JL."

"That's not the name of the drink. That's only the name of the company. Their first product was announced a few months ago. There's a pre-competition and post-competition drink. It's called RazzleD."

"You're kidding, RazzleD?"

"Yeah. Have you heard of it? You may have seen it at the open water swims."

"Lena, who called you to set up the appointment?"

"The admin for someone named Matthews. Why?"

"Matthews? Was it Spencer Matthews—Dick Waddell's brother-in-law?"

"I can't remember his first name."

"I bet it is. That means he and Justin Rosencastle are partners."

"You mean the 'Let's go to a Giants game and I won't show up' Justin?"

"Yeah, that's the one."

Lena came over and sat down on the bed next to me.

"And how would you know this?"

"I might have mentioned to Justin that you were a web designer when he was talking about his company."

"You talked to him? Really, I thought he was a done deal. And why did you bring me up?"

I stood up and walked over to the window.

"Trisha? You, me, both of us, said the guy was a jerk."

"Those were your words."

"Those were your words, too."

She stared at me. "Do you have something to tell me?"

"I had dinner with him last night."

She started to interrupt me.

"No, now just listen. He came by the office to apologize. Said that he was embarrassed that he really didn't have the tickets when he asked me to the game. I realize that it is a dumb excuse. However, he wanted to make it up to me and invited me to dinner. I went. It was nice. He was nice. That's it. That's all. Go to the interview."

"Maybe he wants to impress you so he set up this appointment with me. But he has no thought of really hiring me."

"Maybe it's as simple as he and his company needs a designer."

Then, she started to smile. "It all makes sense now—the new hair style, the sexy undies—staying late at work—you've got something more on your mind than just baseball."

"Maybe," I said as I walked out of her bedroom.

But, I was puzzled. Why hadn't Justin mentioned that Spencer was his partner? He had the opportunity. Odd, that's what it was. Odd.

21

Bill had been right. The new Russian River swim was small. Only fifty swimmers showed up. Maybe the rest didn't want to battle their way north through the sprawl of Santa Rosa, a well-known traffic stopper. Lena and I decided to drive separately since I had to be there early. I was the fifth car in the large shaded parking lot. I walked across the lawn to the steep sandy beach and watched the timing crew plug in their computers and printers and inflate the yellow finish arch. Although this was a small low key swim, the timers wanted to try out some new equipment. They thought this would be the perfect venue.

The air was still warm, 85°, and the sun was hanging low in the deep blue cloudless sky. According to the swimmers getting out of the river after a quick dip, the water temperature was in the low 70's. A perfect combination for the laid back group on shore.

I sat down at a picnic table and looked over the notes Bill had left me. Everything was straight forward. There was only one thing out of the ordinary.

No businesses promoting their products at this swim.

Okay—got it.

The check-in table was ready to go. About ten yards away, volunteers were cutting up bananas, slicing watermelon and filling the large water coolers with sports drinks for after the swim.

As athletes began to trickle in, I heard, rather than saw, Terrel's black Charger pull into the parking lot. Then hand in hand, Lena and T walked past the changing rooms toward the grassy area where swimmers were spread out on beach chairs and towels. Terrel rarely came to a swim. Today's exception was obvious. He was here to watch over my sister.

"Hey, Lena," I called.

She gave me her typical floppy wrist wave and Terrel nodded his head. He walked over when Lena stopped to talk with some friends.

"You didn't think I could take care of her?" I asked.

"You're busy during these events. You can't see everything."

Terrel had a point. If I was doing my job, I wouldn't have time to keep an eye on my sister.

Since a half mile swim, which is a relatively short distance, was planned, quite a few swimmers new to open water had signed up. They nervously paced back and forth on the cool grass, sometimes walking down to the river's edge, wading up to their knees, and then out again. I had my evaluation sheet and was halfheartedly going down the list. This was more an observation than an eagle eye approach to what they did right or wrong.

In thirty minutes, the event director and his crew were ready to start.

"Time for the pre-race briefing. Everyone gather round," he said through a bullhorn.

That soft summer evening air and warm sun were coma-inducing. No one wanted to move. Then slowly, the swimmers stretched, left their beach towels, and walked over to the event director. As they crowded around him, I saw Mike Menton, directly opposite. He looked at me without recognition. Beside him was Daisy's boyfriend, the scrawny, pale Nick.

The director described the course and urged the athletes to head for the yellow buoys. The water level was down and the river was shallow. If they strayed too much off course, they would actually be able to stand up and walk. The new swimmers, crammed as close to the director as possible, seemed to breathe out in unison. Not so bad. They could take a break if needed.

The winding course would lead the pack under a bridge.

"Stay away from the bridge piers. And don't, let me repeat myself, don't cut the corners on the return leg. Limbs of trees and shrubs are underwater, right off the shoreline ready to snag anyone looking for a shortcut to the beach," he said.

While talking, he pointed to the bridge and the shoreline in the distance. As the eyes of the swimmers followed the announcer's arm in the direction of the water, I saw Terrel get into a kayak with another paddler. So much for keeping an eye on his girlfriend.

I walked over to Lena. "That's a first," I said gesturing toward Terrel who even from 500 yards away looked extremely uncomfortable.

"I'm not sure he knows how to paddle," she said as she handed a water bottle back to the swimmer standing next to her. "I don't know why he's doing that. All he said was that he wanted to see what went on at these swims."

The announcer gave the five minute warning and the crowd pulled on their caps and goggles and headed into the river. This was an in-water start and it was divided into two waves—under 40-year-olds were first; the over 40's were in the second wave. The first group waded into the roped-off swim area that was used during the day. They ducked under the water and the long line of blue and white buoys and swam toward the start line.

The river glistened like a polished green mirror. Sharp edges of the pine trees reflected perfectly. Then, there was a piercing blast from the starting horn, and the green mirror shattered as the group sprinted away, kicking up water. I could see Terrel in the head kayak next to the lead swimmers. He had already given up paddling, leaving that chore to the other kayaker. His paddle was resting on his knees as he scanned the swimmers. Somewhere in that group was Lena. And if I knew Terrel, he had already spotted her.

The second group moved into starting position, treading water until the starting gun fired. After seeing a swim from an evaluator's point of view, I knew everything was on track. I walked over to the first aid tent. There were two well-padded cots, an extensive first aid kit and two nurses who were swim team members. No ambulance today.

"Are you expecting anything out of the ordinary?"

"Not really," said the nurse with a ponytail. "I've done swims here before. We might get some scratches from underwater branches; occasionally, someone will step on something sharp at the water's edge, but this should be fairly tame."

"Let's hope," said the other nurse, pushing up her sleeves. She walked with me as I headed toward the director, a tall well built older man with a grey mustache. He was standing on the beach watching the disappearing swimmers through a pair of field glasses.

We listened to the scratchy voices of the lifeguards over the radio, checking in around the course.

"The first wave has rounded the first buoy and is on their way to the second," said a man's voice.

"Here they come," said a girl's voice. "Looking good."

"I'm at the back with the last swimmers," said another voice. "No problems."

I looked at the race director. "Piece of cake," I said.

With the sun dipping lower in the sky, the water took on a silver sheen. Birds flew overhead, soaring from one side of the river to the other. A peaceful early evening quiet settled over the water.

I heard the metallic click of the radio again and hollow static. "I've got a swimmer waving her arms. We have a paddler going to get her out the pack and bring her to the rescue boat."

"Can you tell what's wrong?" asked the director. He sounded calm but alert.

"Not sure. She was one of the slower swimmers. Maybe the distance was too much for her. I can see her better now. She looks okay. She climbed onto the rescue boat under her own steam, so she's probably fine."

I stood next to the event director. We couldn't see the swimmers. They were at the other end of the course around a point of land. All we could do was stare in that direction.

The rescue boat checked in.

"We have a swimmer on board, race number 342, female. She was in the second start. Said that both her legs cramped up. I'm going to bring her back to shore. Rescue Boat Two will take my place."

Within five minutes, the power boat came into view.

"I'll get her and walk her into the first aid tent," said the nurse.

"Is it okay if I go back out with the boat?" I asked.

"Sure," said the director.

I jogged down the steep sandy beach and caught up with the nurse. We waded into the warm knee-deep water. The boat pulled into the shallows and the nurse and I reached up, took hold of the swimmer's damp arms and guided her out of the boat.

"I'm so embarrassed," she said, grabbing onto to us. "When I felt both legs cramp up, I didn't know what to do. It took my breath away. I started to panic and swallow water. I've never been pulled before."

The nurse reassured her as they walked up the beach toward the first aid tent.

I introduced myself to the two-man crew when I climbed onboard.

"I'm from the Nor Cal Swim office. If it's okay with you, I'd like to see the rest of the swim from the water."

"Fine. Let's go."

A dark, cool shadow from the bridge above fell across the boat as we headed for the pack of swimmers at the far end of the river. One lifeguard standing next to the boat driver picked up a pair of binoculars from the seat and scanned the water, checking out the placement of the paddlers and the athletes.

"Leg cramps, like what that girl had, sounds like a normal occurrence...nothing out of the ordinary. Right?"

"It happens. With a little more experience, she'll realize how to handle the panic and the cramp. Next time, she'll be fine," the boat driver said.

I could see the lead pack of swimmers heading toward us and a kayak close by. Probably Terrel. Off to the other side of the course was Rescue Boat Two.

The radio crackled again.

"We have another swimmer who needs help. A paddler is on his way...wait a minute. Two more swimmers are waving their arms. Now a fourth."

"What's going on?" said the director over the radio. His voice had risen an octave.

"I can't tell right now," said the voice. "Paddlers are on their way."

The lifeguard with the binoculars glanced from swimmer to swimmer in the distance waving their arms. "What is happening?" he said quietly.

"Can you see a kayak?" I asked.

He handed me another pair of field glasses. Further down the river, I located three of the swimmers in trouble. Two were hanging off one paddle board, a third had just been given a red rescue tube.

And the fourth—the fourth was Lena. My view shrank to a half dollar sized circle and a struggling Lena was right in the middle. Waving one arm, she seemed to be breathing heavily, gasping almost. Small waves rolled over her shoulders. She tried to float on her back to relax. Then her body went vertical in the glittering water. She was sinking.

An arm moved across my field of vision and grabbed her. It was Terrel on the kayak. He pulled her close to the side of his small boat and held onto both of her arms. His face was calm as he talked to her. She tried to respond, but I could tell he didn't understand what she was saying. The other kayaker picked up his paddle and waved it frantically back and forth.

"Oh…that's my sister. She's in trouble. You've got to get her."

Our rescue boat bolted forward, picking up speed. The driver flipped on the boat's lights and siren as we accelerated toward Lena and Terrel.

"We have a Code 3," he said into the radio.

Through the binoculars, I saw a paddler come up beside Lena and slip a rescue tube under her arms. She slumped over the thick red tube laying her face on it. It took us three long minutes before we reached the lifeguard holding onto my sister. She was gasping for air as she was lifted onto our boat. Terrel was right behind and climbed on board, keeping his eyes pinned on her.

"Lena, what happened?" I asked.

"Can't breathe. No air," she wheezed.

Her lips were swelling, her eyes were almost swollen shut. Her face was frighteningly pale.

"Terrel, what's wrong with her?"

"Does she have asthma?" asked the guard.

"No," I said.

"It's an anaphylactic reaction, a severe allergic reaction. Get her to shore," said Terrel. A voice from the other boat came over the radio. "We have three swimmers on board. All seem to be having trouble breathing."

"I'm an ER doctor in San Francisco. Let me have the radio," said Terrel. "We have four swimmers who are having severe allergic reactions. Please have four ambulances dispatched. This is high priority."

He placed his fingers on the inside of her wrist.

"Her heart beat is irregular."

The lifeguard pulled out the boat's oxygen kit from a backpack and slipped a mask over her face.

"Lena, we're almost there. Try and breathe normally," he said. I heard a soft "haah."

She gasped again as she tried to breathe in.

"Slowly, breathe slowly. Out. Relax. In, slowly. Relax."

The wail of one ambulance, then three more could be heard in the distance as they raced to the park. Growing louder by the moment was the deep bellow of a fire truck siren and air horn, blasting through the air.

The other rescue boat reached the shore first. The three swimmers were met by the ambulance crews waiting near the water's edge. All but one were walking unaided. The paramedics pulled their oxygen kits from the back of their rigs, but only one swimmer seemed to need it. The other two were okay.

"My sister needs help. She can't breathe," I yelled.

An emergency worker quickly waded into the water and climbed on board the boat. Terrel briefed him. Without hesitation, the paramedic gave Terrel an Epi-Pen and Dr. Robinson injected epinephrine into Lena's thigh.

Soon, Lena's color returned and the swelling began to go down around her eyes and her lips. She seemed to be breathing more easily. Terrel and I helped her off the boat. Two of the paramedics took her arms and supported her as they walked to the ambulance parked on the sand.

"Just breathe naturally," one said to her. "That's it. You're doing fine."

Most of the racers were back on shore and heading for the outside shower. They glanced over at the boats, the ambulances, the fire truck and the sick swimmers. There were no smiles; no high fives. The jubilant laid back mood before the start was gone.

"This is getting too dangerous to do anymore," one man said, draping a towel over his shoulders as he watched the medics. There was concern in his eyes.

I looked at Terrel. "What happened to her? What happened to them?" I asked looking at the other three swimmers.

"A very serious reaction to something. It closed up her airways. She could have died. She's allergic to nuts, isn't she?"

"Yes, the whole family is, in varying degrees. But there aren't any peanuts or cashews, any nuts at all here. And what about the other three swimmers, could they all be allergic to the same thing?"

"I don't know. It's worth checking out. This ambulance is going to take Lena to the ER at Healdsburg General Hospital. I'm going with them."

"Me, too," I said.

"Why don't you finish up here," Terrel said. "She's going to be fine, now. Has she ever had a reaction like this before?"

"I think once when she was little. It was after she took a few bites of her first peanut butter and jelly sandwich. She was in the Emergency Room twenty minutes later. That was so long ago. But I remember the whole thing. Mom came home from the hospital and tore the cupboards apart, reading ingredients on everything. If it had nuts in it, even the smallest amount, it was thrown away."

"I'll call you later. Try not to worry. I'm sure she'll be home tonight."

I watched as the doors of the ambulance were shut and it headed out of the parking lot.

———

I sat down on the grass, pulled out my phone and punched in Bill's personal cell phone number.

"Bill, there was another incident at the swim today, the mid-week Russian River one. Four people, including my sister, had an allergic reaction to something and had to be pulled from the water. Lena's been taken to the hospital. There were four ambulances here and a fire truck. Someone is out to hurt our swimmers and shut down the open water season…maybe for good. I'm still at the swim. Got to talk to the event director now."

There, done. He knows as much as I do.

The director was standing in front of the food table trying to give out ribbons to the first, second and third place winners.

Unfortunately, he was talking to a very small impatient crowd. Most people had left.

I walked over to the first aid tent. Both nurses were there.

"Do you have any idea what happened? Is there some sort of insect in the water that would cause an allergic reaction like this?"

"Not that I know of. We sometimes get cases of swimmer's itch. But I have never seen it affect someone's breathing," said the woman with the ponytail.

"How's your sister?"

"She'll be okay."

"Did she say anything?"

"She could hardly breathe. Maybe later tonight, she and I can talk about it."

"Of the four people, two were related. Brothers," said the nurse with the ponytail.

"Could you give me their names and phone numbers? The office will want to check on them," I said.

"Sure, I plan on calling them tonight, too, to see how they are," said the other nurse. She looked at her intake log and copied the names and phone numbers for me.

———

The beach was now empty, except for the timers who were packing up. Standing alone by the changing rooms, the event director was looking at a clipboard. He was subdued.

"Not sure I want to do this again," he said.

"Well, if it matters, your swim went well. Everything happened like it was supposed to, except for...you know what I mean," I said.

He nodded.

"Water rescues were efficient. These swimmers had excellent care waiting for them when they reached the shore. I'll pass that information along and recommend that this swim be put on the schedule."

The man nodded absently again. He was clearly preoccupied. I patted him on the arm and walked across the grass. I punched in Terrel's number on my cell.

"How is she?" I asked.

"She says her teeth itch."

"Her teeth?"

"Probably means her gums. It is not an uncommon reaction. She is going to be fine. They want to keep her for a few more hours, for observation. It will give me a chance to pick up my car and get back here. See you at home."

My eyes filled up with tears. Knowing that she was going to recover was a relief. Both Terrel and I had been as close to her as you can get to any swimmer, and still something happened. This had to stop. I walked out to the parking lot, eyes down, lost in thought.

"Hey, Trisha."

Leaning against a van decorated with the large red, yellow and blue graphics of RazzleD bottles, was Justin Rosencastle.

"You okay? You looked like you were a thousand miles away."

"What are you doing here? Bill said there were no promotions at this swim."

"Just a misunderstanding. We worked it out. Everything's fine now. What happened? All those ambulances and a fire truck?"

"Some swimmers, including my sister, had a very bad reaction to something in the water. When did you get here?"

Justin was putting his table, the RazzleD samples, and two large banners into the back of the van.

"About forty-five minutes before the swim. Want a drink?" he said, holding out a bottle.

"No, thanks."

He stared at me.

"What?"

"You look different. Not sure what. But something's different. Looking good. You...uh...want to hang out sometime? Maybe another Salvadoran dinner?"

"Sure. I'd like that." I smiled. He could be disarming when he wanted to be.

"I'll give you a call. Go take care of your sister."

He climbed into the van, waved and headed for the park entrance.

I watched the van turn out of the park and head west. I was puzzled. Maybe Bill wrote the note to me about the swim before he talked with Justin. Maybe he forgot to update me. That was not impossible, but not like Bill. I'd have to ask him.

———

Lena and Terrel arrived home two hours after I did. Lena's face was still a little puffy, but other than being tired, she seemed okay. Now she was asleep.

Terrel and I sat in the kitchen.

"Do you think someone was targeting Lena?" Terrel asked.

"Maybe. But what about the other swimmers? Why were they involved?"

"Smoke screen. Collateral damage, maybe. No one but you really knew about her nut allergy, if that's what it was. I don't think someone was trying to kill her. Scare her, maybe, but not kill her."

"Terrel, two of the four swimmers were related. But something happened to all of them. I need to find out what the connection is."

22

The door of the Nor Cal Swim office was wide open when I arrived the next morning. Two National Park Service police were there talking to Bill, who seemed more agitated than ever. He was pacing the floor, arms flailing in every direction. His fair skin was flushed to the top of his scalp.

"You've got to be kidding. Someone broke into this office. For what? Trisha, Trisha, did you know about this?"

"Actually, I did. I was here when it happened."

"They said you thought it was connected to a murder…a murder of one of our swimmers. When did that happen? What have you been telling these men?"

"Well, I think that Dick Waddell's death wasn't an accident. And I think the other events, including the one last night, are related."

"Hell of a mess. We had a swimmer that died of a heart attack at one of our open water swims. Even his family and the doctor at the hospital confirmed that. No murder here," he said holding the wrinkled folder that Jon and I had found in the shrubs.

I recognized one of the officers. He was the one leaning against his patrol car when Jon drove me by to identify the suspect.

"Why were you here in the evening?" Bill asked me.

"I was in the city and I couldn't remember if I had turned off the printer…like you always ask. I came back to the office."

"What about this folder? Where are the papers?"

The security guards looked at me.

"I don't know. We—that is, Jon, one of the NPS guys and I— found it outside of the building. There were actually three folders. The other two contained swim schedules. But I think the thief was really after the Waddell file, not my backpack that was sitting on my desk. To me, that says someone wants information on Dick Waddell's death."

Bill's face flashed from pink to red, like the change of a stop light. He turned to the officers.

"Trisha is new to the office. She's temporary help. Nothing sinister here. The Waddell event was tragic, but it was a heart attack. That's what the doctors said. That's all. That's enough, of course. The thief probably picked up the folders by accident when he picked up Trisha's backpack."

The comment about 'temporary help' stung. It was true, but it still hurt.

The officers and Bill chatted for a few minutes. They came over to my desk, asked me a few more questions about the thief and reminded me to keep the door locked when I wasn't in the office. Then they left.

Bill shut the door and walked toward me. His hands were shaking. He spoke in a slow, very controlled manner. "I'm very sorry you were involved with this—whatever it is—attempted burglary. And I'm glad you were not hurt. But…" and he emphasized 'but' so that the word bounced off the walls in our small office, "you do remember that I said not to get involved and not to talk about the Waddell incident? Don't you?"

Before I could answer, he continued.

"Everything is almost settled: insurance claims, family questions. I don't want it put back on anyone's radar. Let it just go away. It was our first death in open water swims in…"

"Thirty years. Yeah, I know, but…"

"But, stay out of it. There was no need to involve the NPS."

"Bill, this is more than my backpack almost walking out the door. I think the thief wanted the information in the folder. That's why all the papers are missing. Did you know that the Waddell family has requested an autopsy? Maybe that was the information he was looking for."

Bill took a step back. "I knew they were considering it. How did you know? Have you spoken to Waddell's sister?"

"No, the medical examiner told a friend of mine."

"The ER doctor? The one who lent you the Checker Cab?"

"Yes. Dr. Robinson thinks…"

"You are talking to people about the Waddell event. I told you. Do…not…do…that. Trisha. Think about it. Nothing in that folder was confidential. Someone could get all those names and numbers, even the medical information, with a little work."

"But maybe they wanted to know what you know?"

"Do you want to know what I know?"

First I shook my head yes; then no.

"I know this is none of your business. This has nothing to do with a murder," he said.

"Last night's swim is the third accident in about a month. It can't all be coincidental. First Dick; then Jackie, now four other swimmers, including Lena. At the very least, what do you think this will do to the rest of the open water season?"

"Why are you trying to make our organization look bad?"

"I'm not. It's just…"

"Focus on what I'm about to say, Trisha, regarding the Waddell death. Do not talk to anyone. Do not answer any questions."

"What about the other events?"

"They are not connected. There is nothing to say. Forget you ever heard about them. Am I clear?"

"Yes."

"Good."

Bill finally stopped moving and waving his arms. The crimson color on his cheeks began to fade. "Anything else happen while I was gone?"

I took a deep breath and launched into an update of calls and requests from different swim teams, skipping over the one from his past assistant, Chris. I couldn't remember if I had deleted his message. One way or another, I had a feeling that Chris was a step closer to getting his job back.

Bill didn't react when I left to drop some caps off at a swim club for an upcoming open water swim. He was probably glad to get me out of there.

————

The glass doors of the Emergency Room at SF Memorial glided open as I approached. Sitting at the reception desk was the same ER nurse who was there when I visited Jackie earlier the previous week.

"Hey," I said to the nurse with tats up and down his arm. "Remember me? I'm Dr. Robinson's friend. Is he around?"

"Oh yeah, you were asking questions about an automobile accident victim that had come in earlier. I think Dr. T just went to radiology. Take a seat and let me see if I can find him."

I took a seat in the waiting room. Next to me was a construction worker with his hand wrapped in white gauze. Two chairs down was a Latino family holding a small infant, no more than three months old. I wondered which one was the patient; the baby, the mom who looked exhausted, the worried father or the small girl sitting on her father's lap.

What a way to spend the afternoon.

I could feel my cell phone vibrate in my backpack resting next to my legs. A new message. I dug out the phone and glanced at the screen. The email was from a photo storage website. Nothing in the subject line, just three attachments. I opened the first. It was a photo of me and NPS guard, Jon, pulling folders out of the shrubbery at Fort Mason. My fingers stiffened and I almost dropped the phone.

The second was of Lena walking into the water at the Russian River. I'm standing beside her laughing. My arms began to tremble.

And the last photo, was me coming out of the backyard of the Waddell house in Martinez at 2:20 a.m. My mouth went dry.

I frantically looked around the waiting room, at the receptionist, at the glass entrance doors. Someone was following me, taking pictures. Were they here? For a few seconds, I didn't breathe. Then, I got up and moved to a chair where I could see anyone coming in or leaving. As if on cue, Terrel walked into the reception room.

"Hey, Dr. T. Someone to see you," said Robert sitting at the receptionist desk.

"Girl, what are you doing here?"

"Do you have a minute?"

"Don't tell me you're involved with another emergency?"

"I need my car back. Is it ready?"

"Is that why you came? I'll give Pop a call. Don't you like driving the cab?"

"Terrel, I've got to show you something. In private."

He led me back into the ER's break room.

"Look at these."

He whistled when he saw the photos. "Whose house is that? Where were you at 2:20 a.m.?"

"Dick Waddell's house."

"What? No. This isn't good."

"That cab is like a blinking neon light. I need my car."

"You need to go the police."

"And tell them what? I can't convince anyone, except you, that the heart attack theory is dead wrong. That Jackie's accident and the Russian River swim events are all related. Besides, I don't like dealing with the police."

"Trisha, you are a lifetime member of the hardheaded women's club. If my mama was here, she'd say 'you're as stubborn as a mule.' Lena told me all about your DUI's and your run-ins with the police. Things like that happen. This is very, very different. You and now Lena are in danger."

"Do you have the results of Waddel's autopsy?"

"Stop changing the subject. But, no, not yet."

"I'll come back tomorrow... we can meet for lunch. Maybe the results will be back by then and we can switch cars."

"Just give me a call to confirm. Please talk to the police. If you don't, I will. In the meantime, be careful, okay?"

He turned to walk away.

"Forgot to tell you. Your friend... Jackie. She's out of intensive care."

———

"She's here. I know she's still here," said the woman carrying a blue 'It's a boy' helium balloon, a teddy bear dressed in blue shorts and a potted plant.

The hospital receptionist at the front desk looked at her computer screen again, typed in the name of the new mother once more and then said, "Ah yes, here she is. Her name was spelled wrong. She is on the sixth floor."

The woman smiled and almost bounced down the hallway to the elevator.

"Yes?" said the receptionist.

"A colleague of mine, Jackie Gibson, was recently moved from intensive care to a step down unit. I'd like to visit her."

"Ninth floor, room 311."

It was lunchtime and the elevator was crammed with staff heading to and from the cafeteria. I shifted back as far as I could go. Each time the elevator door opened, some people got off and more got on, crowding me to the point of feeling claustrophobic. But at least, no one could take my picture here. When it reached the ninth floor, people parted like the red sea and I lunged for the door, glad to be out. A medical assistant at the reception desk pointed in the direction of Room 311.

"A friend of Jackie's?" she said.

"Yes, I work with her, kind of."

I gasped when I pushed open the door to her room and caught sight of what was a strikingly beautiful woman just a week ago. One side of her face was covered with bruises, eggplant purple and a sickly yellow. The top of her head was wrapped in snow white gauze. I couldn't tell for sure, but it seemed that some of her thick black wavy hair had been shaved off at the scalp. An IV bag hung by the side of her bed. Pain medication dripped slowly through the clear tubing connected to her lower arm. The other arm was in a cast. And so was a leg. There was a clip on one of her fingers, monitoring her heart rate. Next to the bed, the lines on the computer screens kept changing, as she breathed in and out.

She seemed to be sleeping, so I sat down next to her bed and reached out to touch her hand. To my surprise, her eyes fluttered open.

"Who are you?" she said in a faint voice. I had to lean forward to hear her words.

"I'm Trisha Carson. I work for the Nor Cal Swim Association. I just came over from the office to see how you were doing."

"Great," she said. "Just great. Can't you tell?"

"Well, you're out of intensive care, that's a good thing."

Jackie turned her face away from me.

"Lovely flowers," I said, gesturing to the many get well bouquets around the room. "I really hate to bother you about this, but do you remember what happened?"

She looked back at me.

"Not really. I was driving…coast road. I didn't feel well. My heart was racing, pounding. I felt hot and started to sweat. I was having trouble breathing. It felt like my throat was closing up on me. Couldn't concentrate. That's it. I woke up here, in this room, yesterday."

"Did you feel okay during the swim?"

She nodded. "The swim, yeah, right. I felt okay. Felt really thirsty after…I remember that."

"Did you get something to drink?"

"Mike had the kids fill up my water bottle."

"Do you remember posing for pictures with Mike Menton?"

"Yes."

"Is he your boyfriend?"

"What business is it of yours?" She grimaced in pain.

"I don't mean to pry, but is he?"

"No, just someone to have lunch with. Not my type. Bratty daughter. I don't have a boyfriend. Anymore…"

A nurse poked her head in the door. "Don't spend too much more time. She is still in the early phase of recovery and she needs her rest."

I smiled at the nurse. "I'll be out of here in a minute."

Jackie's eyes were closed.

"Can I ask one more question?"

No response.

"Was anybody mad or upset with you?"

Her eyes barely opened.

"No. Well, guys get upset with me sometimes. But they get over it."

She paused and closed her eyes, then opened them again.

"I was supposed to have dinner with someone the evening after the swim. I cancelled. No big deal."

"Who was that?"

"No one you'd know."

"Try me."

"It's none of your business."

"Do you think anything might have been put in your water bottle?"

"Sure, water."

"No, I mean something else."

She opened her eyes wider and for the first time, really focused on me.

"What is this? One of the doctors said I tested positive for cocaine and meth. Does that sound right to you? I don't need drugs to get what I want."

She tried to raise herself up in the bed and the heart monitor clipped to her finger slipped off, causing the computer to start beeping. At once a nurse was in the room.

"You'll have to leave now."

"Sorry, so sorry. Feel better, Jackie."

———

I slid into the front seat of the Checker Cab in the multi-tiered concrete hospital parking lot. I was parked on the third floor, the purple floor, as large squares of color indicated. Patients walked by on their way to the elevators, looked at the tank-sized bright yellow taxi and smiled. Normally, I would smile back and nod. But that didn't happen today. I was lost in thought.

Once again I opened my phone and flipped through the photos emailed to me. Then I looked around the parking lot, peering into the shadows partially hiding each car. Was someone there with a camera? The temperature seemed to dip inside the cab. The hairs stood up on my arms and the back of my neck as I glanced from parked car to parked car. There was a steady stream of automobiles driving up the circular parking ramp looking for empty spaces. Were their glances aimed at me or the cab? As each car passed, my breathing became more rapid.

I punched in some phone numbers and left a message for the three swimmers who had been pulled out of the water with breathing problems. I wanted to know what they had in common with each other and my sister. A dark sedan pulled up directly behind the Checker. The driver, a man with a full, round face and rusty colored goatee glared at me. I stared back, my mouth open. This was it. I knew it. This was the guy who had been taking pictures. I took a deep breath, and put my hand on the door handle. My plan was to open the cab door, stay low, and run across the parking lot for the elevator—screaming all the way.

"Lady, are you coming or going? I've driven up and down this ramp three times and you're still in the same place," he said. "Are you leaving or not?"

"Leaving," I said. My voice was weak; my knees were weak. I'm glad I didn't have to stand up. He backed up his car as I turned the key in the ignition, pulled out of the parking space, and headed for the exit.

23

The next morning, Bill was back at his usual place, talking into his headset, using his hands to punctuate a thought. He nodded as I walked in the door, mouthed 'pick up' and pointed to the phone.

"Trisha just walked in. I've asked her to join us. Trish, this is Richard Waddell's swim coach, Cody Stephenson. You've talked to him before, right?"

"Yes, at the Cold Water Clash."

"He is helping Richard's sister, Pamela, plan a memorial celebration of Waddell's life and I volunteered you to help."

"Okay," I said wondering how the 'Don't talk about it' rule was going to fit in.

"We want you to pull some of his past swim records and do a search on photos under his name. Plenty of material should come up."

"Glad for any help you can give me," said Cody.

In the background, I could hear voices talking, someone giving a countdown, then yelling 'Go' followed by loud splashes.

"I've got my hands full with both the adult and kids team, but I promised Pamela that I would help."

"Maybe we need to meet and figure out our next steps," I said.

"Great," said Cody. "I'm supervising an open water swim practice this afternoon for my Masters group at Shadow Cliffs in Pleasanton. Do you want to meet around lunchtime? Maybe after the meeting and before the swimmers arrive?"

Bill looked at me and nodded his head. "Yes."

"Sure thing," I said. "I've never been there."

"It's easy to find. Just look for the blue waterslides."

When we all hung up, Bill brought over a folder about Shadow Cliffs Recreational Area, which was once a gravel quarry and was now a 226 acre park with an 80-acre lake.

"It's a nice park, great place to swim. Don't get into your 'dead swimmer' theory. You are there to help develop a memorial program. That is all. Remember. Why don't you do a quick computer search on Waddell and take over what you find?"

"Will do."

Actually, already did, I said to myself. Right after Richard died, I downloaded page after page about him. My Waddell file was sitting in a folder in my desk.

––––––––

It was late morning when I left the office and climbed into the Checker. I locked the cab doors; then looked over my shoulder at the rows of parked cars. Was there someone with a camera here? In the parking lot? On the hills next to the building? Would I ever get into a car again and not feel a pair of eyes watching me?

As I drove down Van Ness Avenue, I kept glancing into my rear view mirror. A dark colored sedan had been a few cars behind me since I left Fort Mason. It looked like the car from the hospital parking lot. I stepped on the accelerator and buzzed through an intersection on a yellow light. The sedan stopped as the light turned red. I never saw it again.

"Not everyone and every car is following me," I said out loud. I switched on the radio and rolled down my window.

Bridges are a necessity here in the Bay Area. While the Golden Gate Bridge with its deep orange towers is perhaps the most photographed bridge in the world, I think of the long Bay Bridge with its two spans as the neighborhood workhorse. More than twice the number of vehicles use it each day than use the Golden Gate Bridge. The bridge fed into Highway 80 and I veered onto 580 on my way out to Pleasanton.

———

After pulling into the Shadow Cliffs parking lot, I walked past the snack bar and there it was. A lovely warm lake. Kids were playing at the water's edge, splashing and laughing with their mothers watching from the shore. A little farther out, three swimmers were following each other in the area set aside for lap swimming.

While San Francisco had been in the low 60's when I left the office, here it was about 80° and sunny. Cody said he'd meet me by the snack bar, so I sat on the concrete steps leading to the beach and waited. I stretched out, face toward the sun.

"Trisha?" a deep voice said.

I picked my head up. It was Cody. Carrying a clipboard, stopwatch and a bullhorn, he was ready for his team to show up.

"Let's sit over here." He motioned to a picnic table out of the sun.

As we sat down, I pulled out my file and turned on the laptop I had brought with me.

"So this is for a commemorative service for Richard Waddell, right?"

"Yes. As I mentioned to you before, this is a loss for our team. He'd been a member for less than a year. But he came to every workout, went to the pool meets, loved the open water swims. He was a real competitor. Before I forget, I told Pamela that you were working on this and she asked if you would stop by her house after we talk. You know Pamela, right?"

I nodded.

"She's not far from here. She says she has some pictures of Richard when he was young. Can you include those?"

"Will do. But let's start at the beginning. Are you looking for any particular type of tribute? Do you have something in mind?"

"Wish I did, but I haven't had the time to do more than agree to help with it. The idea actually came from Pamela. I said I'd spearhead it…don't know what I was thinking when I agreed to do that…but some of our swimmers are willing to help. One knew Richard pretty well. If you could put the photos in some kind of order and write simple copy, that would be a start. Maybe you can begin with his upbringing in Texas. He was very proud of being from that state. He only moved to Northern California to be close to his family."

"He wasn't from Texas originally," I said.

"Really?"

"He was from a small town in Nevada. We're not talking Las Vegas. He grew up on a cattle ranch."

Cody shook his head. "Well, I never heard that before. Are you sure?"

"Yes, I've seen his high school swim team picture. It was definitely Nevada," I said. "How about if I ask you some questions to get us started?"

"I can only really talk about the year that I've known him and that's pretty much been at the pool."

"Let's start there. What was he like at the pool?"

"Hard worker. Competitive. Very competitive. He pushed himself unlike anyone I've ever seen."

Cody stopped and stared down at the folder on the table.

"Yes?"

"He hated to lose. Even the fun relays we did during workout, you'd hear him complain if his team lost. Maybe you can reword that somehow."

"I will...no problem."

"His teammates were somewhat in awe of him. He came to the team after years of swimming at the very highest level. He was one of the fastest men in the pool, didn't matter what age they were. But he wasn't able to relax and enjoy himself."

"Doesn't sound like much fun to me."

I pulled out some of the pages I had downloaded with swimming statistics and showed them to Cody.

"Some of these need to be included, for sure."

On my laptop, I brought up the file with his photos. They dated back to his college swim days, through his attempt at making the Olympic team to his move into open water.

"That's what we're looking for, but you'll have to find someone else to talk about his past. I really haven't known him that long."

"Maybe Pamela could help with that. I also know a friend of his. They swam together in high school."

Cody waved to two women that had walked on to the beach. The swimmers dressed in shorts, tee shirts and flip flops, strolled over to our table. "Gonna get in some extra yardage before practice starts," said the dark haired woman.

"Good for you. This is Trisha from the NC Swim office. She's going to help with the memorial for Richard."

"So sad," they both said in unison. "But he died doing what he loved," said one woman. And they walked off.

"We had that conversation earlier, remember, about him doing what he loved? You had a different take on that, didn't you? You called him 'desperate.' What did he do for you to say that?" I asked.

"About eight months ago, he stopped by my office after workout. He wanted to ask me about nutritional supplements, what I thought would help him get that edge back. I remember him very distinctly saying, 'When it comes to swimming, I have had control over my body since I was about eight years old. It's not there any more, I can tell. I'm doing the same things but my times are slower.'

"I tried to talk about how important rest was, probably more so than any nutritional supplement, as well as body flexibility and core strength, especially as we age. He didn't want to hear it. He wanted more workouts, not less."

"So what happened?"

"He wasn't happy with our conversation. At the end, he said he was going to try some new vitamins. I joked and said, 'Are they legal?' He glared at me and said, 'nobody tests in Masters swimming. And besides, USMS has no rules against what I think you are talking about.' I remember looking at him and saying, 'Are you sure?' He said he was. He had checked. I didn't know what to say after that except, 'Richard, don't do it. It's not worth it.'"

"And?"

"He left. In a few months, his times began to drop. He got faster. His personality, which was never a strong point, was erratic. He reminded me of a junk yard dog, looking to attack. There were other telltale signs; he developed pimples on his back. What 50-year-old gets a case of acne? That blond wavy hair of his seemed to be falling out."

"Those are signs of what?"

"Classic signs of steroid use, probably testosterone."

"Do you think he died of a heart attack?"

"I don't know a lot about medicine. But for me, I'd call it an in-water drug overdose. I think he was using performance enhancing drugs of some kind, and that killed him."

"Any idea where he got them from?"

"I have some ideas."

"Yeah?"

"Sorry…not comfortable accusing someone unless I have specific proof. And I don't."

Off to the side, a lifeguard driving a small motorboat carrying two yellow round buoys headed out for the middle of the lake. He dropped one anchor line into the water, dumped the yellow buoy over the side, and repositioned it; then motored off to set the second buoy.

Cody was looking out at his swimmers on the lake and glancing over to the guard setting the buoys. "We can continue this conversation later, if you want. Better yet, I can have one of our team members who knew Waddell give you a call. Gotta go. Remember, none of this—especially the steroid part—is to show up in the memorial presentation."

"I understand."

He picked up the bullhorn, clicked it on and called out to the swimmers in the water. "Okay, everyone, let's do a warm up out to the first buoy and back." The swimmers slowly moved together as a group, about two or three abreast, each group following the other heading for the first yellow buoy.

I walked with Cody over to the water's edge. He stepped onto a small boat and took off, following the line of swimmers while they stroked gracefully up to the first buoy.

As I was walking out to the parking lot, my cell phone rang.

"Where are you?" said Terrel. He was clearly annoyed. "I thought you were coming by the hospital today at lunch."

"I forgot, sorry. I'm in Pleasanton for a work project, but I can drive back through the city and stop at the hospital if you'll still be there in about three hours."

"Seriously, Trisha, I thought you had an office job. You're on the road more than a Muni bus driver. I have your car. We can switch vehicles when you show up. By the way, you know that woman, Jackie Gibson? The nurses on her floor say she is pissed—P- I- S-S- E-D—pissed and wants to talk to you."

"Me? Why?"

"How am I supposed to know? Get here as soon as you can. I have something to show you you won't believe."

On the 15 minute drive to Pamela and Spencer Matthew's house, through the graceful golden brown hills of the Livermore Valley wine country, I thought about my conversations in the last week. Waddell's death had been blamed on Nick, a nerdy 16-year old. A hairdresser thought it was Waddell's sister, Pamela. And Cody hinted about someone else. What about Mike Menton? I thought he was the likely suspect. And his motive? Does winning an open water championship mean murdering your competition? I didn't know.

24

The Matthews lived in the exclusive gated community of Opal Valley. Their two story multi-million dollar hacienda bordered the Opal Valley Golf Club. I pulled into a circular driveway and parked the Checker by their three-car garage.

Pamela walked past the garage from the back of the spacious house and stopped while I got out of the cab. She was in work jeans with dirt on the knees, a pair of clogs on her feet and garden gloves still on her hands. Her blond hair was tucked under a broad brimmed straw hat. Frankly, I never pictured her living in a huge, very expensive house. She always seemed to be cleaning up. A home like this with its two story glass windows overlooking a golf course demanded that the woman of the house be dressed in designer casual clothes or expensive golf or tennis outfits. But she wore neither.

She left her clogs at the front door.

"Renata, that's one of our maids, hates it when I leave my shoes outside like this. Says it looks trashy. She's not here today, so I can get away with it. Come in. I pulled out some photos and a scrapbook full of clippings about Richard that you might be interested in. I think there might be more. I've seen boxes of medals, photos, and news stories at his house."

We walked through the spacious living room with a floor to ceiling stone fireplace, by a kitchen that was larger than my living room, past the family room which rivaled an intimate movie theater and stopped at the door of a wood-paneled study. The windows opened on to the fairways of the Ruby Hill golf course.

"How do you get any work done with a view like that," I asked.

"I don't even see it any more when I walk in here. On the desk, you'll find all the things that I put together for you. Sorry, but I won't be here much longer. I'm going back over to Richard's house to clean out his closets. But you can stay as long as you like. Spencer's home, but he is in his office, working upstairs."

"Cleaning up your brother's house, it must be difficult for you. I hope this doesn't sound impertinent, but couldn't you hire someone to do that? Wouldn't that be easier?"

"I suppose. I like to keep busy. Spencer doesn't want me to work. He says I don't have to; but Richard and I grew up on a small cattle ranch. When we weren't in school, we were up at dawn and worked with the ranch hands until dinner. We had to help out our mother to keep the ranch going. I always worked until I got married."

She told me to help myself to drinks and food in the kitchen and wrote down her cell phone number.

"Any results yet from the autopsy?" I asked.

A weary smile washed across her face.

"This has been very hard for me."

That's all she said as she walked out the front door. In my mind, I ran a line through Pamela's name as a potential suspect. The hairdresser from the Mandraka Salon was wrong. Pamela didn't need any more money. She had plenty. And she was following through with something that was extremely uncomfortable for her. She didn't kill her brother.

———

Much of the material in the folder on the desk consisted of clippings I had already downloaded. There were a few photos of her and Richard riding horses in deep snow surrounded by cattle. She looked about 10-years-old; he maybe 12, probably on their family's ranch. There were a few pictures of an eight-year-old skinny kid in swim trunks, still dripping wet, holding up a first place ribbon and a few photos of Richard as a teenager, standing next to a girl in a swimsuit. Both were smiling and holding out their first place ribbons. It took less than 10 minutes to go through the Waddell material. I was about to leave the study when I heard a door open upstairs and a voice speaking on a telephone.

"Well, thank you so much for coming in for the interview. Sorry I couldn't be there in person. I like your overall approach – our branding, our logo, our website. It all needs to be coordinated, I agree. (Pause) Any other questions? Our name, JL Associates? Sure. I'm a big Jack London fan. JL, the initials, it was a no brainer. And one more thing. Jack London's first boat was called the Razzle Dazzle. That's where RazzleD came from."

There was a silence. "Sure, thanks again. Justin, can you stay on the phone for a minute?" Another silence.

"Do whatever you want, I don't care. She seems capable. Look, we got to talk about something. Tip is unhappy. We're not getting enough of our inventory out on the streets. That's your job. (Pause) He doesn't care. This sports crap you are so big on doesn't bring in enough money. The audience you're pushing it on is too high and mighty or maybe too afraid to try it, so it's slow building. (Pause)

"Forget about it. Talk to your distributors; get them out on the streets. Go down to the warehouse in South San Francisco and make it clear. Do you hear me? They have got to do more... A recession? Give me a break. That's when we do our best. But it can't get to the suburbs until it is on the streets. Do your job. And Tip said no more monkeying with the formulas to help your friends. You're getting careless. People are starting to ask questions. Like your girlfriend from the swim office. No more of that stuff, understand?"

The voice became muffled as the door shut upstairs. Well, that was interesting. I had heard the end of Lena's interview with Justin and Spencer. They must work together. I thought they couldn't stand each other.

And the follow up conversation—was he talking about distributing RazzleD or their other nutritional products on the streets? Was RazzleD a cover for something else? My gut said that at least Justin from JL & Associates, maybe even Spencer and the third partner, Tip, could be manufacturing or supplying some type of street drugs that Terrel always talked about. I didn't believe that Justin was knowingly involved. Spencer's comments about the girlfriend asking questions—it was clearly me. And here I was in his house.

I had to get out of here and I wanted to call Lena. As I walked past the kitchen, I pulled out my cell phone. It dropped and clattered across the marble counter top.

"Pam? Thought you went to your brother's house" came the voice from upstairs. Spencer walked to the banister on the second floor and looked over. "What are you doing here?"

"Just gathering up some news articles and photos for Richard's memorial?" I picked up my phone and headed for the door.

"Wait. Come back."

Spencer started moving down the stairs and I backed away from the island in the kitchen, keeping my eyes on him.

"Need to go," I said. I opened the front door and quickly walked to the Checker.

Spencer stood with his cell phone to his ear at the front door and watched as I drove past him, down the circular driveway to Opal Valley Drive.

———

Driving toward 580, I punched in Lena's number and the speakerphone. "Pick up, please pick up." But it rolled over to voice mail. Then I tried Dr. T again.

"Terrel, call Lena. Get her out of that interview if she is still there."

25

It took me an hour to retrace the route back to San Francisco. Even though I was driving opposite commute traffic, cars were creeping along the top span of the Bay Bridge, heading west. Must be an accident or a stall ahead. I glanced into my rear view mirror. A few cars back was the dark sedan.

The turn signals on the Checker didn't work, so I stuck out my left arm and waved it. The other drivers ignored me. No one would let me in. I could only inch forward with all the other traffic into San Francisco. The Fifth Street off ramp was coming up. I steered the large grill of the Checker toward the car in the next lane. He honked at me, threw up his arms, but put his brakes on. I was one lane closer to the exit. One more 'get out of my way' lane change and I was traveling down the ramp off the freeway. The dark sedan missed it completely and passed by. I could see the driver's face. It was the man with the rusty colored goatee from the hospital parking lot.

———

I walked through the sliding glass doors of the Emergency Room and took a seat in the surprisingly empty waiting room. Terrel came out through a door behind the receptionist, nodded at me. "Taking a quick break," he said to her. "Page me if you need me."

As we walked out of the ER, he threw my car keys at me and told me where it was parked.

"Why did you want me to call Lena and tell her to leave the interview? Which I did and, by the way, I was not able to reach her. You sounded panicked."

"I overheard the last part of her interview at JL's; then I heard the interviewers talking, not about Lena, but about what I think might be drugs."

"How would you know this? You were off somewhere in Pleasanton. Her interview was here in the city."

I explained why I was visiting Pamela's house.

"I think I know who and maybe even what is involved in all this." Then I launched into a recap of my conversation with the swim coach and what I overheard at Pamela's house.

Terrel turned around and nodded to a pair of physicians walking by.

"One minute," he said to me as he pulled out his cell phone and punched in some numbers.

"Hey, Tariq, got a question. You ever hear of a JL Associates as it relates to...? Really? You're sure about that? Okay. Thanks."

Terrel looked at me. "It's commonly known in the city's health clinics that JL Associates is on the radar of the SF Police Drug Task Force. Just what have you gotten yourself and your sister into? Here's the problem...I have spent the better part of my life trying to distance myself from the shit that goes on in the neighborhood. And now you and your sister are involved with some kingpin dealers."

"I'm not involved with them. I didn't know who these people were. I've just been doing my job...well maybe a little more than only doing my job. But I was curious about...oh, it doesn't matter now."

"All right. All right. You have to stay away from them. We have police in this city. Their job is to go after the bad guys. Your connection with them, whoever they are is over, O–VER, got it."

I nodded.

"Now, I want you to meet someone." He led me to the back elevator used for transporting patients. We got off on the same floor that Jackie Gibson was on.

"Hey, Dr. T. How's it going," said a young African-American nurse sitting at the nurse's station. T nodded. "We're going to go visit Jane Doe."

"Room 367. Remember, she's sedated."

"Who is Jane Doe?"

We walked toward the closed door of a small hospital room at the end of the corridor. Terrel slowly pushed it open. The woman in the bed had stringy washed-out brown hair. She could have been forty, fifty or even sixty-years old. Her grayish skin contrasted starkly with the white sheets on her hospital bed and barely covered her angular collarbone. She looked old, tired and her face was badly bruised. Her eyes were closed. A small map of blue veins on her eyelids matched the color of the bruises on her face. She had an IV inserted into her left arm. Her right arm had the telltale tracks of a junkie.

"Trisha, meet Holly Waddell, Richard Waddell's wife."

I sipped the cup of hot coffee that Terrel got for me from the staff kitchen. We were sitting in an empty patient room right next to Holly Waddell's.

"I don't believe it. No one has mentioned a wife. Not his sister, brother-in-law or any of the newspaper clips that I've seen. Where did she come from? How did she get here?"

"A good Samaritan, from what I can tell. She's homeless and an addict. She was on her way here to the ER because she didn't feel well. Could have been a drug interaction. Because—drum roll, please—she has tested positive for the same drugs found in both Jackie and Waddell. However, it was more meth than cocaine. She was pushing her shopping cart and trying to maneuver it down a curb and around a car, when a cyclist hit her, knocked her down. She smashed up her face on the edge of her cart and the street."

"So, the cyclist brought her in?"

"He called 911 and stayed with her until an ambulance showed up. The EMTs brought her here at about 8:30 a.m. We had her as a 'Jane Doe' because she didn't have any ID on her and she was semi-conscious, couldn't answer any questions. About twenty minutes later, the guy with the bike walked into the ER pushing her cart."

"You're kidding?"

"The truth, I swear. So, I put on a pair of latex gloves and started shifting through the cart hoping to find some identification. In an envelope, I found a California ID and Medi-Cal card with the name Holly Waddell. Seriously, I thought it was a coincidence. But then I found two faded blue swim ribbons, you know the kind they give at swim meets?"

I nodded.

"They were from the 70's. There was also a very well-worn newspaper clipping from some small town paper in Nevada. It was the wedding announcement of Richard Waddell and Holly Worthington, from 1978."

I glanced over at Terrel.

"In the interviews I read about Richard Waddell, they said he moved to Northern California to be close to his family. I was thinking his sister. But maybe it was Holly. Pamela must have known about her. But she managed to skip over that part of his history," I said.

"You know, Holly's probably entitled to Richard's estate since she is his widow."

"Now hold on. You don't know if they were still married."

"I bet they are. Waddell never remarried. He had girlfriends. One of them happens to be on this same floor. Do you think I can talk to her when she wakes up?"

"Up to her. But, you've got other problems right now."

"Like what?"

"Room 925. Jackie Gibson."

————

Jackie Gibson was sitting up in bed with the television on. It droned quietly along, adding to the whirr and whoosh of the medical apparatus keeping track of her blood pressure and heart rate. But she wasn't watching it. She was glaring at the man sitting in a chair with his back to me.

"Thank you," she said. Her mouth was pinched into a straight line. "But I don't need to go to your home to recover. My sister's coming."

"But Jackie…," the man said. It was a deep voice and very familiar.

"Well, look who's here." Jackie spit out the words like bad tasting medicine. "The woman who thinks I'm a junkie."

The man turned around. It was Mike Menton.

"Talk to you later, Trish," said Terrel as he ducked out the door. "Stop by the ER before you leave."

"You're looking better," I said to the upset patient, whose facial bruises were now more of a sickly yellow.

"You're looking better," Jackie mimicked me. "I look like shit. I want to get out of here and go home."

"The nurses said you wanted to talk to me."

"I don't like you talking to my teammates and my friends." She nodded at Mike.

"What's she like? Is she your girlfriend?" She mimicked me again. "What business is it of yours what I do? Who I am?"

"Okay. I talked to people. I was trying to find out who might have wanted to hurt you."

"Hurt me? What are you talking about? I had a stupid accident."

"Only one week after Richard Waddell had a 'stupid accident' that killed him. And a week before 'a stupid accident' affected four swimmers at the Russian River."

"Are you saying that Dick's death was intentional and that someone or something caused my accident?"

"I think so."

"Who would do that?"

I looked over at Mike. If he was involved with this, I had just said too much. When will I learn to think before I open my mouth? He didn't react to my statement, but glanced at Jackie and then at me.

"Mike, I'd like to talk to Jackie alone. Could you wait outside for a bit?"

"I don't like this. You're saying that Dick's and Jackie's and the Russian River accidents could be related?"

"Possibly," I said. "But I need to talk to Jackie."

Mike got up and leaned over the bed to kiss Jackie on the forehead. "I'll be right outside in the waiting room."

Jackie and I were silent until the door quietly closed behind Mike. Then she picked up the remote and switched off the TV.

"What is going on?" Jackie asked.

"Like Mike said, I think that your accident and Dick's death are connected. I don't think Dick had a heart attack. I think it was a reaction to a drug and it was too much for his heart to take."

Jackie became very still. Instead of glaring at me, her gaze dropped down to the white sheets on her bed.

"Did Dick ever talk to you about wanting to improve his swimming?"

"All the time. A friend that he had was helping him get some nutritional…mmm…items…to keep him swimming fast."

"Did he ever mention the words High Test or HT2?"

"Yes, but I thought he was joking. He started taking some kind of capsule before open water swims and swim meets saying he was topping off his tank."

"Jackie, the drugs that you tested positive for have the same chemical make-up of this HT2."

"I don't do drugs. I told you that before."

"I know, but somehow they got into your body. Your judgment was impaired. I think it was the reason you drove off the cliff. And it could have caused Dick's heart attack in the water. Did Dick mention who supplied him with these nutritional supplements?"

"Not in so many words. But I got the feeling that there were a number of people involved."

"Did Dick ever talk about his past?"

"No. He wasn't that kind of guy. He talked about growing up in Texas, but that's about it."

"He wasn't from Texas. He was from Nevada originally."

"No. You're wrong. He was from Texas."

If that was hard for Jackie to believe, I could only imagine what she'd say if I told her Dick's wife was in a room down the hall.

"Were you and he serious?"

"I was. For the first time in a long time, I felt like I might have a future with someone. He knew I'd seen a lot of guys, but that didn't seem to bother him. We were beginning to talk about getting married. Well, maybe I was the one talking about getting married. He usually sidestepped the conversation, but he never said no."

"What about Mike? He seems to think you and he are...uh...together?"

"He doesn't get it. Sure, I went out with him a few times. And I was seeing Dick, too. So what? Mike didn't mean anything to me."

"Was there anyone else?"

"No, not really. Well, there was this one guy I kept running into at the open water swims. He wanted to get together, to hang out. We had dinner a few times, drinks. He was okay. Spent the night a few times, but he was pushy, too persistent. He started to call me three or four times a day. He'd show up at workout wanting to talk to me. I couldn't get him to stop.

"About a week before Dick died, I had lunch with him and told him that I wanted to move on. I try and do these things face to face, you know. It's more civilized that way. Anyway, he was extremely upset. Started talking about Dick and Mike—very unsettling. He said I really didn't know Dick at all...that he wasn't who he said he was. Mike, he just blew off as an overbearing idiot. He was making this big dramatic scene in a restaurant. I agreed to have dinner with him one more time so he would quiet down. I never planned on really going. I just needed to shut him up."

"When was the dinner planned for?"

"Well, we were supposed to meet after the Cold Water Clash. But then Dick died; Mike was coming on like a locomotive. I didn't want to worry while I was swimming about how I was going to dump this guy, so I told him I wasn't going to dinner—that I saw no point in going out with him again. That was before the race started."

"And this guy's name?"

"Justin Rosen-something or other."

"Justin Rosencastle?"

"Could be. I never got that part straight."

————

Each piece of the puzzle was slowly working its way into place. Unfortunately, Justin's name was coming up too often and not in a positive way.

Mike was leaning against the wall by the nurses' station.

"You want to explain this to me?"

"You know, this hospital has a healing garden. Let's go there."

The entrance to the garden was through two wide sliding glass doors between the side-by-side units that housed oncology patients. I hoped the openness and the visibility would be safe for me. Late afternoon meant sunshine in this microclimate of San Francisco. The vivid greenery and bright flowers were a welcome contrast to the dull green and blue of the hospital walls.

Mike started in on me as soon as we sat down. But first, he checked to see if anyone could hear us. No one could. I checked to see if we could be seen by patients, families and nurses walking by the entrance to the garden. We could. I felt as safe as possible in this situation.

"What exactly is going on here?" he asked.

"I think that Dick's death and Jackie's accident and the Russian River events are related and that if we don't find out who is at the bottom of this and why, other swimmers could get hurt. I also think this has something to do with performance enhancing drugs. From what I found out, Dick moved into this area right when you had one of the best chances you've ever had at going to the Open Water Nationals. And he also moved in on Jackie, someone you cared about."

"I hated the SOB, but not enough to kill him. By the end of the season last year, I was putting it all together...ended on a high note. Then super stud comes in with his Texas grin, down home accent and cowboy hat. I expected him to ride up to the swims on a fucking white horse."

"Let me backtrack," I cut in. "I was at the open water swim at Lake Joseph waiting for my sister to finish. Can you describe that swim to me?"

Mike took a deep breath, looked up at the blue sky and then off into space.

"Okay. I might as well. There were four waves of swimmers, about a hundred in each wave. At the start of our wave, we were treading water between two orange buoys. All of us were inching up to the invisible starting line, but trying not to be pushed across it by those behind us. I was surrounded by swimmers wearing orange and yellow caps.

"There's always a lot of laughter at a start, some nervous—some not. People call back and forth to one another, that kind of thing. I was behind DickWad—that's what I called him.

"I got so close I could read the black number on his upper arm. 254. His arms had goose bumps. I remember thinking 'big strong guy and you're cold in 68° water? Wimp.' While he was treading water, he turned around. You know what that asshole said to me? 'I'm on you like flies on shit. You won't get away from me. I'm going to win again.'

"Then, the starter on the sailboat at the far end of the line waved a green flag. An air horn blasted—Go! Arms, legs, splashing water everywhere. DickWad bolted forward. I remember thinking, 'Go ahead. Take it out fast. You'll die soon enough.'"

Mike gave an awkward smile. "Prophetic, huh? Anyway, swimmers were inches apart, trying to move forward, almost swimming on top of each other.

"Wad took off like he was chased by a shark. I tried to keep up with him. But I was breathless and it was less than five minutes into the race. I can't sprint for three miles, so I eased into a slower pace. Wad pulled ahead and the amount of space between us grew. He was in the lead pack. But then, that initial burst of energy was over and he began to fall slightly behind the first group of faster, younger swimmers. Soon I had caught up. I knew it was him because of the green lightning bolt on his swimsuit. I could see it underwater.

"I was swimming right at his hip, drafting, saving energy for when I wanted to pass him. He must have sensed someone was near by. Instead of breathing just to his right side, he began to breathe every other stroke, first to his right, then to his left, quickly looking around to see who was next to him. When he spotted me, he tried to push ahead faster. But he had used up so much energy at the start, he couldn't accelerate. Instead I moved up and slowly took over the lead. We were halfway into the race and I was ahead. Now all I had to do was stay there."

"So, from there on in, it was easy?"

"Never. He was driving me crazy. He was so close that he was touching my toes with each stroke. I kicked harder, but he was still there. I couldn't lose the guy. So, I threw in a couple of quick breaststroke kicks and could feel my feet connect with either his arms or even maybe his head. Must have been effective. Right after that, he didn't touch me again.

"That last leg of the swim was brutal. I could see the finish arch getting closer, growing larger. It was yellow, a little blurry, like I was looking through a thin layer of Vaseline. My lungs had shrunk to the size of walnuts, hard to bring air in and push it out. I remember hearing my breathing, like it was coming from someone else.

"I dug down for every last bit of energy I had. When my hand grazed the bottom of the lake, I stood up, lifted my knees high out of the shallow water—kind of like a drum major strutting down a football field—and sprinted through the finish arch. Once I crossed the timing pad, I was bent over, breathing hard. Then I turned around.

"DickWad wasn't right behind me. He wasn't swimming at all. He was floating face down in the water with rescue paddlers racing to his side and an ambulance pulling up at the lake's edge.

"That's the swim. That's what happened."

Mike looked down at the green lush ferns by the side of the bench.

"Him dying took the edge off."

"What do you mean?"

"Other swimmers wondered if I would have won if he had lived. If I really had it in me to beat him. I know I do. But people talk."

"So your winning has some question marks connected to it?"

"Not for me. I was the fastest that day."

"No one has said anything about a kick to the head. I don't think that had anything to do with his death," I said. "Do you know if Dick was taking any kind of medications, drugs, maybe PEDs?"

"I heard talk, but I never believed it. He seemed to thrive on being a clean athlete. I've never heard of anyone using drugs in Masters swimming, but I'm no expert."

"One more thing. Do you think that Nick, your daughter's friend, could be involved?"

"Nick? You've got to be kidding me. He is a grade A pussy. He doesn't have the balls to do anything illegal."

"Okay. Look, if you hear of anything or think of anything else, give me a call. Here's my card. I somehow think that anyone that was close to Dick or Jackie could be a potential victim."

"Are you saying that I might be next?"

"It's possible," I said.

———

I was sitting in my own car this time, in the hospital parking lot. Terrel's dad had left me a note on the passenger's seat. 'Good as new,' it said, signed 'Pops.' In the scheme of things, having my car repaired had been easy. But nothing else was. Justin Rosencastle was turning out to be bad news. He was probably selling drugs. And, he was interested in Jackie, obsessively interested in Jackie. I remembered the card by a vase of flowers in Jackie's room that was from her 'almost Saturday night date.' Must have been from Justin. I sure know how to pick them.

I went over Mike's version of the swim again in my mind. Nothing seemed out of the ordinary, not even the kick to the head. Lena has done that before to get someone off her toes. I pulled out my 3 x 5 cards with the names of everyone connected to the events.

I put a question mark by Mike's name on my list of suspects. I added a card for Holly Worthington-Waddell.

I wanted to go home. I was tired of Richard Waddell, Justin Rosencastle, swimming accidents and High Test.

———

Lena's car was in the driveway. I heard her say, "I'm fine" as I opened the front door. I dropped my backpack on the couch, reached for the remote to turn on the ballgame on, and sunk down with such a thud that I moved the couch about six inches backwards. I leaned forward, elbows on knees, remote held in both hands. The Giants were melting, self-destructing right before my eyes. It was like driving by a car crash. I couldn't not look.

"T, catch you later," Lena said and closed her phone. "What was the frantic call about?" Lena asked, sitting at the dining room table.

"I don't want to talk about it right now. I'm tired," I said, staring at the TV. She reached over, took the remote from my hand and turned it off. I kept looking at the screen for a few seconds.

"That's all you ever say. 'I don't want to talk about it.' You've got to talk about it. I get this call from you telling me to leave the interview immediately. Then I get three calls from Terrel asking me where I am. Everyone knew where I was. And you know I don't like to answer the phone—any phone—but especially when I'm with a potential client. So why were you and Terrel going into orbit?"

She walked over to the varnished rocking chair next to the couch and sat down. "In case anyone is interested," she said while looking around the room as if there were a crowd, "I was offered a contract with JL. And I'm being well paid, very well paid."

"Lena, I'm not sure it's such a good idea that you work for JL & Associates."

"What? Aren't you the one that gave them my name in the first place?"

She stood up and started pacing around the living room.

"Just listen to what I have to say. I've been trying to figure out who is responsible for Dick Waddell's death and everything else that's happened. I think JL & Associates is involved."

"Don't tell me you're still absorbed with Dick Waddell? You need help. You have to talk to someone. I'll pay for it."

"Lena, someone has been following me, taking pictures of me and you. I'm sure it's related to the Waddell death. And I'm almost positive that whoever murdered him is responsible for Jackie's accident, you going into shock at the Russian River, and Waddell's wife's meltdown."

Lena stared at me. "What did you just say?"

"Dick Waddell has or had—I don't know yet—a wife. Her name is Holly. It was Holly Worthington. She's one of those homeless people in San Francisco you see pushing grocery carts. All their belongings stuffed inside."

"And you know this, how?"

"Dr. T, your Dr. T, introduced us. She is currently sedated at SF Memorial, some kind of drug overdose. Sound like familiar symptoms? And guess what, she's on the same floor as Jackie, just a stone's throw down the hall."

"How convenient."

I gave Lena a blow by blow description of my day and why I was trying to reach her.

"So you heard the last part of my interview. That's weird. You know, the JL interview was nothing out of the ordinary. I met Justin—not bad looking, by the way—and I didn't mention that I thought he was a jerk for standing you up at the ball park. He said that he knew you but after that, it was all business. 'This is what we need; this is when we need it by.' Could it be possible that the 'product' you overheard them talking about was the stuff that they sell—like RazzleD—purely legal? Could you be reading too much into it?"

"Terrel checked with a doctor friend of his at a San Francisco clinic. The doc has connections with the police since he treats so many patients on drugs and found out that JL & Associates are being watched by the Drug Task Force in San Francisco."

Lena stared at me.

"I think it's time that you talked to the police."

"That's what everyone says. But, I don't like talking to the police. I told you that."

"What makes you so inflexible? Look, your association with the police was…was…I don't know. Anyway, that was then. This is now, something completely different."

"You sound like Terrel. What if I'm wrong?"

"What do you care? Let them figure that out. It's their job. But…but…I think, only for the next few days until you talk to the police, we continue doing what we are doing. If they are behind this, we can't act suspicious. I'm back in their office in the next day or two. I'm actually going to be working there. I'll look around. See what's in the file cabinets and on the computers."

"I can't believe Justin is involved," I said.

"You don't want to believe it."

"It's hard to think he would purposely hurt someone."

I thought of how apologetic and kind he had been at dinner, how approachable he seemed after the Russian River swim.

"I'm going to give him a call and come up with a reason to talk to him. Could be as simple as needing more information about

Waddell for the memorial presentation. We need to meet some place in the open. I know it is not a good idea to be alone with him. Maybe I can ask him to tell me more about RazzleD, because… because…the office wants to develop a business relationship with his company. How does that sound?"

"If he is dangerous, maybe you should do it over the phone?"

"No, that won't work. I want to see him, watch his reactions while I talk to him."

"We are in this only for a few days, right?"

I nodded.

"Don't tell Terrel," Lena said. Then she went into a full-on Terrel imitation, deep voice, complete with head bob. "Seriously, should you be involved with this? No…you… shouldn't."

26

I had just turned on my computer at the office, when the 'dude', that's the only word for him, walked in. Shaggy blond hair, dark grey hoodie, baggy shorts and sandals. I guessed right away. It was the wandering Chris.

"Hey, sistah," he said, looking quickly at me and then at Bill or rather Bill's empty desk. "Where's the head man?"

"Should be in shortly. You're Chris?"

"You got it."

It's the Peter Pan of surfers. I stared at his face. There were wrinkles around his eyes and off the corners of his mouth. He had to be in his early forties.

"You know I used to work here," he said, moving over to sit on a corner of Bill's desk.

"So I heard. I'm Trisha. It's my job now," I said with a 'Gee, I love you' smile that I didn't feel.

"For reals?"

"Yeah, for reals."

"Hmmm, no worries. I'm sure Bill will find you something else."

I felt like picking up my stapler and tossing it at his head. From down the hallway, I could hear Bill talking on his cell phone non-stop. He exploded through the door, Bluetooth blinking in his ear, both hands waving wildly in the air.

"Oh, holy shit, Chris. What are you doing here?" Bill said good naturedly. "I told you I had the job covered. 'Hey, Chris is in the office,'" he said into the cell phone, "Gotta go. Good to see you man." They went into an elaborate series of fist bumps. "You met Trisha. She's got your job, now."

"Bro, I wanna take you for some serious coffee. You up for that?" said Chris tugging Bill in the direction of the door he just came through.

"Love to." He glanced over at me with a 'what am I supposed to do' grin, shrugged his shoulders and walked out the door, not more than three minutes after he first came in.

"Hey Jon," Bill said as he passed the NPS security officer on his rounds in the hall.

Jon walked into the office. "Chris is back? Very likeable guy, not great on the business side, but fun to have around."

"Let's hope he's not back as in 'back at this job.' I need it."

"So tell me, Miss Marple, anything new with your case?"

It took ten minutes to fill him in.

"What is it going to take for you to involve the police? This is serious."

"That's what my sister says and her boyfriend. Look, all I'm doing is asking questions."

"Trish, by asking questions to the wrong people, even to the right people who pass along your interest to the wrong people, you put yourself and your sister in danger. But I bet you already know that."

He walked over to my desk, put both hands on the corner and leaned down to look me straight in the eyes. Very serious.

"Can you come down to the security office later this morning? I'm going to have someone from the San Francisco Police there. It's time you talked to them."

"I don't have that much to tell anyone."

"I'll call you later with the time."

When I walked into the NPS Security office that afternoon, there was a woman standing with her back to me. She was about 5'5", slim, wearing a long sleeve, dark blue sweater and dark blue slacks. She had thick, pure white hair that curled around her ears. Three officers were laughing at a comment she made.

How nice, someone's grandmother stopped by, I thought.

Jon looked over at me.

"Hey, Trisha."

On cue, the woman turned around. This was no grandmother. She was about my age, in her forties, with the deepest blue eyes I had ever seen. She wore her badge on a lanyard, hanging around her neck. On her left hip was a holster with a Sig 229 resting inside. Attached to her belt were handcuffs. She held out her hand.

"I'm Inspector Carolina Burrell with the San Francisco Narcotics Task Force, Investigations."

Inspector Burrell with her starkly white hair and ocean blue eyes was a knock out. But more than that, she exuded intelligence, cunning and toughness.

Two of the NPS security officers excused themselves and Jon led Inspector Burrell and me into a small conference room.

"Jon tells me you have had a break in at your office."

I nodded. "Yes, about two weeks ago."

"Anything since then?"

I shook my head. My vocal chords had turned to stone.

"Tell her about the swimmer who died," said Jon, leaning forward.

"This is awkward. My boss instructed me not to talk about it. He feels that it reflects badly on our organization if the death was not a heart attack. If the swimmer was actually, uh…"

"Murdered? Does he believe that the swimmer was murdered, but he isn't willing to talk about it?"

"No, I don't mean that at all. He thinks that the swimmer had a heart attack and that the incident and any accompanying publicity, should go away."

"What do you think?" she asked.

I glanced over at Jon. He nodded at me as if to say, "Go ahead."

"I disagree with him. I think even the swimmer's sister disagrees with him. Because of some test results, she requested an autopsy."

"What do the results say?" asked Inspector Burrell.

"As far as I know, they aren't back yet."

I pulled out my growing number of cards, laid them carefully on the table and explained who each person was and how they were related.

"So, we've got a death, two people in the hospital with the same drugs in their system, another swim where there were some adverse events—which may or may not be related—and a connection with JL & Associates. You've been busy. Do you compete at these events?"

"No. I just work for the Swim Association and I drive my sister to the swims."

"How did you learn about JL & Associates?"

"They make a sport nutritional drink, RazzleD and have a booth at some of our open water swims. I met one of the partners and he told me about the company."

"And who was that?"

"His name is Justin Rosencastle."

Jon shook his head.

"Do you know anyone else connected to JL?"

"Yeah, the brother-in-law of the swimmer who died. Spencer Matthews, that's his name. He is one of the partners, I think. Then, there is someone named Tip."

Carolina glanced up at Jon.

"You met Tip?"

"No, his name was mentioned in a phone call that I overheard."

It was time to explain more than what was on the cards. I gave a word for word recap of the phone call.

"T, my sister's boyfriend, said that JL & Associates were being watched by your Task Force? Is that right?"

"Who is T?"

"Dr. Terrel Robinson. He's an ER doctor at SF Memorial. He heard this from another doctor, one who works in a community clinic."

"You certainly have access to a lot of information. Anything more?"

"I think there are too many things happening to the swimmers for them not to be related."

"Thank you, Trisha. We'll take it from here. Call me if something else comes up." She handed me a card. "Or talk to Jon."

"Okay, I will."

I stood up and shook hands with her, nodded to Jon and walked to the door of the conference room. They both looked at me. It was obvious they were waiting for me to leave to continue the discussion.

"Yes?" she asked.

"Someone's been following me. A guy with a goatee in a dark colored car. And someone's been taking my picture and my sister's picture."

"Why don't you sit back down for a minute or two," Inspector Burrell said.

27

For the rest of the day, I helped Bill prepare for the Nor Cal Swimming Association board meeting. It was to take place this evening in a conference room one floor below the office. When I typed up the agenda, I noticed the first item under New Business was 'Accidents.' That would be interesting to hear. I wondered if any of the board members even suspected that the accidents were connected and planned. Guess I'd find out tomorrow.

I made sure there were thirty copies of everything: agenda, committee reports, schedules. I ordered dinner from a small Italian restaurant on Chestnut Street in the Marina.

On my way down to the room to check on the phone lines and internet connection, I ran into Cody Stephenson. With him was a man I'd seen before—short, squat with a full face, shaved head, and deep-set dark brown eyes, topped by a partial unibrow. Well developed upper arm muscles pressed against the sleeves of his black tee shirt. His neck was thick and wide.

"Trisha, this is Mario Rossi. He was a friend of Dick's. This is the guy I was telling you about."

"We met, remember? Lena introduced us at the Lake Joseph swim."

"You're right. Not good with faces."

Cody continued on up the steps to the office.

Mario stood in front of me, a wide stance, arms crossed in front of him. His biceps rested on his chest. He was a human wall; no one would get by him.

"So what do you want to know about Dick?"

"I need to set up the room for the meeting tonight. Why don't you come with me and we can talk."

He turned sideways and I had just enough room to squeeze by him.

Like many of the offices and meeting rooms in the building, this one had tall unadorned windows that faced San Francisco Bay. A graceful long oval table was in the middle of the room. To the side, against the wall, were two small tables, an easel with an oversized chart pad and a box of large multicolored markers.

"Kick ass view," Mario said.

"Give me a hand," I said, holding stacks of papers out to him. "This will go faster if you help me. Just put one stack at each place."

He worked his way around the table while I set up the multimedia projector or at least tried to.

"Are you still into body building?" I asked.

"Yeah," he mumbled as he meticulously lined up each packet, making sure every piece of paper was directly below the piece above it.

"Is that how you know about JL & Associates?"

Mario lifted his head and smiled. "I thought the questions were going to be about Dick? Material you could use for his memorial."

"I think I have enough for the memorial. How did you come to join a swim team? Kind of a strange jump."

"I was injured. I'm swimming as part of my rehab. You wanna know the truth, I sink like a stone. But I like the water; I never thought I would."

"Did you know that Dick and Spencer were brothers-in-law?"

"Dick talked about it from time to time."

"Did you know Spencer?"

"Oh, yeah. The bodybuilding guys were well-aware of the guys from JL."

I pulled out a chair and sat down at the long table.

"I know that body builders are big on nutritional supplements, creatine, things like that. Do you use them?"

"Everyone I know does. That stuff is legal. You can walk into a health food store and buy it over the counter. Even the illegal stuff is easy to get. Mention it to a buddy one week in the gym; the next week he hands you something in a paper bag."

"Did you think Dick was taking anything illegal?"

"I'd bet on it. One day in the locker room, he mentioned his brother-in-law's company. I'd heard the name before and I knew what they really manufactured. Later he asked me what I thought about High Test and HT2."

"Did you ever see him take this stuff?"

"Are you kidding? This is a hush-hush thing, very private. Lots of people do it, but they don't want anyone to know."

"So you think he got this from his brother-in-law?"

"I didn't say that. I never heard Spencer's name used in the same sentence with High Test. I have to believe, however, that his drugs came from JL & Associates."

I couldn't get the projector to recognize the connection to the laptop so nothing was showing up on the screen. I held the directions in my hand, absentmindedly drumming my fingers on the table and mumbling to myself.

"Hey, let me help."

"I would be forever grateful."

He turned some switch on and off, pressed a button I thought I had pressed and the screen lit up.

"Think you might want to work here?" I asked.

He laughed. "Nah, got my own job. Have to go track down Cody. I need to find him, then take off. Did you get your questions answered?"

"I guess. Did you ever hear of Mike Menton?"

"No, who's that?"

"Doesn't matter. Another swimmer. Big competitor."

"I don't do the competitive swimming thing. Sometimes, I'll swim an open water event. That's it."

I remembered a name from Waddell's old address book.

"You ever hear Dick say anything about someone named Jeremy Reid?"

"Yeah, he's a relative, I think. Teaches in Fresno."

I thanked Mario and showed him how to get to the office.

————

Later, Bill mentioned that I wouldn't be attending the meeting since I wasn't a permanent employee. But then, he looked at me and smiled. "Trisha, you're doing a good job. You've learned quickly and the swimmers, our clients, customers, whatever you want to call them, like working with you. Although you have been a little too concerned about the recent accidents, I'm going to tell the board tonight that I want to hire you permanently. Then, lucky you, you'll have to attend these meetings and the executive committee meetings all the time."

Even with the rambling Chris showing up on the scene, I still had my job. And it was going to be those wonderful words, 'permanent and full-time.' That meant a steady paycheck, benefits and health insurance. I could start thinking about my own apartment. Every inch of my body breathed a sigh of relief.

I stayed around to make sure any stragglers knew how to find the meeting room. Fifteen minutes later, I heard someone running up the steps, taking them two at a time. Justin came barreling through the office door.

"What are you doing here?" My hand reached for a nearby phone.

"The meeting. I'm late. Where is it? There's been a misunderstanding. I need to clear it up."

"You're not on the agenda."

"I am."

"Downstairs, in the conference room. Justin, I need to talk to you. About RazzleD and the swims. The office is thinking of..."

He cut me off.

"That's why I'm here." He turned around and was gone.

I picked up my cell phone and texted a message to Bill.

"Justin Rosencastle is on his way."

Something was up. The other day when I finally had a chance to give Bill a full recount of the Russian River swim, I mentioned that the RazzleD van had been there. He seemed unhappy with that news. He said that he specifically told 'that group' not to come to the swim.

I still had to wait in the office for about another hour. With not much to do, I dumped out my backpack on the desk. Time to get rid of the cookie crumbs stuck to the inside. There was Waddell's camera. I had forgotten about it.

I sat back in the chair, put my feet up on the desk and turned it on. Most of the photos were swim related—open water races, pool meets. I recognized some of the swimmers.

I flipped through them quickly. Boring, boring, boring. But then, I stopped. Here was a shot of Richard and a young man in his late twenties, early thirties. They stood side by side, not touching. Richard was smiling. The other man was biting his lower lip. They stood in front of a modern building. The faint letters UNI could be seen at the bottom left of the photo on a stone fence. It was the shouter from the Lake Joseph swim, the man who alerted the lifeguards to the swimmer in distress.

These two had to be relatives; their resemblance was striking. Maybe this was Jeremy Reid? But where did he fit in the family? Pamela and Spencer didn't have any children. Could be a distant younger cousin, maybe another part of the West Coast family he wanted to be close to. Strange though, the date stamp on the photo indicated it was taken three years before Waddell moved to California.

I turned the ringer on my phone and it vibrated, dancing around the desk, telling me there were messages waiting. The calls were from the racers pulled out of the Russian River. I had asked all of them if they had any allergies. I listened with disbelief. They were allergic to nuts. Just like Lena. But none of them had eaten any nuts before the swim. How did it get in their bodies? Maybe Terrel had an idea, because I didn't.

———

It was 8:00 p.m., when I left the office and headed for my car. Seeing Justin run in and out like that was unnerving. Add to that the pure joy and relief I felt about being made a permanent employee. I couldn't go home and I was too jazzed to sit still. Once again, I found myself looking for a parking spot in San Francisco's Mission District. I had driven past El Oriente Salvaje twice with no luck. I made a quick right turn and there it was, a rarity, a place to park. When I pushed open the front door, it was close to 9:00 p.m. and there were only two people sitting in a booth by the window. Nancy stood back by the cash register chatting with her mother.

"Hello," she said when she saw me. "No Justin?"

"No, not tonight. He's in a meeting. I just had some good news. So I guess you'd say, I'm celebrating."

"Felicitaciones."

"Thank you." I sat down at a table not far from the kitchen.

"Nancy, who is that back there? Is that your brother? He looks just like you."

But even from across the room, I could see he was missing Nancy's warmth and her easy smile.

"Yes, that is Roberto. He helps out in the evenings when we are about to close. The abuelitas working in the kitchen have gone home, so mama is making the last batch of papusas. I'll bring you some."

As she walked back toward the kitchen and called to her mother in Spanish, Patricia looked up, smiled and then nodded to me. Roberto glanced in my direction with a blank stare on his face. He ran a hand over the dark stubble on his chin. Then he moved back into the kitchen and I couldn't see him anymore.

When the papusas arrived I looked up expecting to see Nancy or her mother, but it was Roberto.

"Que pasa, calabaza?"

"What?"

"Ignore my brother. He thinks he is funny. He said, 'What's happening, pumpkin.' It rhymes in Spanish." Nancy shrugged her shoulders, shook her head as she walked by with two dishes in her hands.

"So you know Justin?" he said as he sat down across from me.

Odd opening. Not a "Hello. Do you like the food?" No small talk. Very direct and to the point.

"I do. He mentioned you. But he didn't tell me how he knew you."

"We were roommates, so to speak," said Roberto.

"College?"

"Not quite."

I was silent. Roberto was a hard man to read. He didn't smile. The dark eyes that locked onto mine were sly, yet wary. He sat at an angle in his chair, the front of his body facing the door, head in my direction. I took a sip of water and stared at him through the side of the glass. His eyes were half closed as he stared back.

I noticed he had a tattoo on his neck, a clock face without hands.

"I think Justin has that same tattoo on his neck."

Roberto's expression didn't change.

"You get them at the same place?"

"How do you like the food?" he asked.

"Roberto, why did you come over here and sit down? You don't want to make small talk. I can see that."

Roberto turned his body around in the chair so every part of him was facing me directly. He leaned in and spoke in a low voice.

"I wanted to see what you were about."

"Come again?"

"I'm saying, don't screw with Justin."

"I'm no threat to him."

Roberto looked away, then back at me. "Okay, I'm going to tell you something. It's between you and me. You tell Justin, I'll deny it and you'll regret it."

A thread of fear skimmed down my arms. Roberto scared me. He sat back in his chair and stretched his arms out on the table.

"Family is important, you understand?"

I nodded.

"My sister, my mother—they are there for me all the time. No matter what I've done."

Where was this going? I picked up the papusa oozing with cheese to take a bite.

Roberto pushed my hand to the plate. "No, put that down. Listen." He leaned back in.

"With Justin, there is no real family. He has, had, a brother. He has a sister. His dad was what you might call an absentee father."

"Justin isn't the only one who struggled growing up. And absentee fathers aren't anything new."

Big deal. It was my turn to sit back in my chair and cross my arms.

"Justin's father pretended he didn't exist for a long time. It was easier that way, he always said. His father wasn't married to Justin's mother, but to another lady. It was a small town and according to Lucky, everyone knew anyway, except the kids."

"Wait a minute. Justin told me that Lucky was Richard Waddell's father, not his."

"You still don't get it, do you? Lucky was Richard Waddell's father and Justin's."

"They are brothers?"

"Half-brothers."

"I don't believe it. Does Justin know?"

"Lucky told him years later."

"I thought Lucky was in prison somewhere."

"That's where they met. Justin and I were cellmates in a prison outside of Las Vegas, in Clark County, the High Desert

Correctional Institute. Anyway, Justin was in for some white collar crime. He's a chemist, for Christ's sake. He was working for a lab in Las Vegas and gambling his paycheck away. He started stealing money from the lab's till to pay his debts. Not too smart.

"When we were inside, I introduced Lucky to Justin. Lucky knew immediately who he was. Justin didn't know anything."

"God, what was his reaction?"

"Disbelief, mostly. But later, he said things that he had wondered about as a kid now made sense."

"What about Richard Waddell and Pamela? Did they know?"

"Yeah, they did. Their mother told them when Richard was getting ready to go off to college."

"You're not kidding, are you?"

"No. You wanted to know about Justin, right? These are the facts."

"How does Spencer fit into all this?"

"Spencer was a hustler back in high school, according to Lucky. He liked that. Spencer had a way of making money. It always seemed semi-legit. Guess he was slippery enough not to get caught all these years."

"What a way to meet your dad for the first time, in prison."

"Lucky must have had a conscience. After all, Richard was the golden boy; Justin was the anonymous kid, never quite good enough. Anyway, Lucky kept tabs on Spencer once he married Pamela. He set him up in business, with, uh, an acquaintance. Let's just say, he strongly suggested that Spencer take Justin on as a partner."

"So Spencer gets Justin to come to San Francisco by offering him a job," I said.

"Right, and Justin thinks this will be like a homecoming."

"He connects with Spencer and Pamela. But Pamela's not thrilled."

"Right. Richard shows up about a year ago and Justin offers to help him achieve his athletic goals. Kind of a brotherly offer, you might say. Richard agrees."

"Waddell wanted drugs?"

"Performance supplements."

"Performance supplements…okay…but Justin is really trying to connect with a brother and a sister," I said.

"Waddell and Pamela didn't give him the time of day. They wanted to make him disappear," said Roberto.

Patricia walked over to the table. "Berto, you plan on working tonight or just talking?"

She gave him a backhanded slap to the top of his head.

"Don't bother Justin's new friend."

Roberto got up and strolled back to the kitchen, never looking back.

"Forgive my son, but he must work to pay off his debts to me and his sister."

"Sure. I understand."

Patricia put her hand under my chin, tilted my head up and looked into my eyes. "Justin and Roberto—they are good at heart, but life is more difficult for them than others. Sometimes that happens to people."

She patted my cheek and smiled. Then she walked over to Nancy standing by the cash register.

28

When I pulled into the parking lot at Fort Mason the next morning, I squeezed between the narrow buildings and walked out on a pier overlooking the Bay. The air was still and damp. Heavy grey fog hung on the Golden Gate Bridge towers like a shroud. Last night's conversation with Roberto kept repeating itself in my head. No doubt that Justin was involved with this drug ring. Yet, it all seemed a bit beyond his control. He was chasing a dream and the drug dealing was a way to reach the dream, or so he thought. I needed to talk to him. Maybe Inspector Burrell should know about this. I found her business card in my pocket and left her a message.

I absent-mindedly climbed the steps to the office and there was Bill, quietly sitting at his desk, no arms flailing in all directions, not talking on the phone faster than I can think. He looked at me oddly. He was holding a photograph in his hand.

"Trisha."

"Bill," I said and smiled, sitting down at my desk which was directly opposite his. No reaction.

"Bill? Meeting last night go okay?"

"No. It didn't."

Whatever could make Bill stop moving was serious.

"What's going on?" I asked.

He cleared his throat and then said, "I asked you more than once not to talk about the Waddell death, certainly not to conduct your own investigation into a murder."

Not good, I thought. Not good at all.

"I wasn't conducting an investigation. Just asking a few questions."

"It doesn't matter what you think you were doing. I have heard from Mike Menton, Jackie Gibson and Waddell's brother-in-law. You talked to all of them. I don't know what you said, but they all felt that you thought they were involved with Dick's death. They are extremely unhappy with me and the organization. Menton told me you even questioned his daughter."

"But she called and wanted to talk to me."

"Are you blaming this girl for your inappropriate actions? Daisy Menton is a teenager, a minor. You talked to her without her father's consent. What possibly were you thinking? How many times did I tell you not to talk about the Waddell death or even Jackie's accident? Even the Russian River swim?"

I opened my mouth to answer, but no words came out. Bill kept on talking.

"And there is a message for me from an inspector from the SF Police. You went against what—I—your employer specifically told you not to do. Did you not understand what I was saying or didn't you care?"

"I understood and I cared," I managed to say in a voice that was almost inaudible. There was a bitter metallic taste in my mouth.

"No. Listen…you didn't understand. This organization…this office, my job, your job is paid for by membership and by grants and donations from well-to-do benefactors. Many have been involved with the sport of swimming for their whole lives and they want to support us in anyway they can. Part of what we do is to make sure they are happy. You know we are governed by a board of directors, right?"

I nodded. I had never seen Bill so angry. His eyes were large, pupils dilated; his face was pulsating pink from neck to scalp. He got up from his desk and began pacing throughout the small office, from his desk to the front door to the window, but staying clear of me and my side of the room.

"I am here to tell you that the Board of Directors is not happy—to say the least. This is a small community. It didn't take long for word of your 'investigation' to get around. The Board had questions, many questions like ...well, that doesn't matter. And, if that wasn't enough, perhaps you could explain this."

He held up a photograph of me coming out of Waddell's backyard. It was the same photo that had been sent to me with the same 2 a.m. time stamp. I couldn't breathe. My hands turned ice cube cold. I was afraid I was going to fall off my chair, so I grabbed hold of the desk.

"How did you get that?" I managed to say.

"It doesn't matter. Not at this point. There is no way I could, would offer you a job. Your position has not worked out. I'm letting you go. You no longer work here, as of now. Clear out your desk and then go home. I have to leave immediately for a regional meeting, but I've put a call into the NPS security. They are sending over an officer who will stay with you while you gather your things. Then, he will escort you out. Give your office key to the security guard. I'll send you a check for whatever we owe you."

I watched as Bill walked back over to this desk, locked it, shut down his computer and headed out without a goodbye or a thank you.

A curtain dropped down around me. I couldn't see anything. I could just hear my own breathing and the thud-a-thud of my heartbeat in my ears. What did Bill say I was supposed to do? Clean out my desk and leave. Robotically, I reached for a small cardboard box and put it by my computer.

I had never been fired before. I looked in the small mirror sitting on my desk. The color had drained from my face. I was speechless. I had lost a temporary job.

The shock of seeing my face jolted me back to reality. Staring into the mirror, I realized that it didn't matter what Bill and his precious board thought. I was 99% sure that Waddell was murdered and I was going to find out what happened. They couldn't stop me now.

I only had a few minutes before I had to leave, so I signed on to my computer, logged on to my personal email and started to attach documents about the Waddell death, Jackie's accident, docs that contained phone numbers and names and addresses and general information about the open water swim schedule and its contacts.

I picked up a cardboard box and set it on my chair. Then there was a knock at the door. My NPS escort was no other than Jon.

"This couldn't get any worse," I almost said out loud.

"What happened?" he asked.

"I can't believe it. I've been fired."

"Why?"

"For asking questions about the Waddell death. What do I need an escort for? Did Bill think I would trash the office? Steal all the old trophies in the back room?"

"It's just protocol. Are you ready to leave?"

I looked around the office. I had been there about a month. It wasn't the job of my dreams, but I had a paycheck. What would I do now?

"Yes."

Jon picked up my small cardboard box and we walked into the hallway. I handed him the key. He closed the door and locked it. We walked down the three flights of stairs, our footsteps echoing in the empty stairwell. He followed me to my car and waited while I unlocked the trunk. After placing the small box inside, he slammed it shut, then reached in his pocket and gave me his business card again.

"If you had met with the police earlier, this might not have happened."

"After I talked with Inspector Burrell, did she talk to Bill?"

"I don't know, probably she or someone did some follow up work."

I couldn't look him in the eye. I just got in the car.

Like the night our office had been broken into and he watched as I drove out of the parking lot, Jon stood there watching again. Only this time he wasn't protecting me. He was protecting the building from me.

———

I headed down Marina Boulevard past the wide grassy stretch of the Marina Green. The joggers were still there; some sailboats were leaving their slips for a sail on the Bay. The wind had picked up and the fog had flowed in, draping over Alcatraz and San Francisco Bay like a lumpy damp blanket. I drove not even realizing where I was going until I found myself on the road to Fort Point, the old army barracks almost directly under the Golden Gate Bridge. I pulled off to the side and parked.

Still a little dazed, I picked up my phone. There were three phone messages and a couple of texts.

"Trisha, this is Justin. It's important that I talk to you. Last night's meeting did not go well. I need your help. Can you come by the office maybe late in the afternoon? Give me a call."

I pressed nine to save the message.

I went on to the next one. "Hello, Trisha, this is Inspector Burrell returning your call."

Saved.

And finally, "Trisha, why don't you ever answer your cell phone? Seriously, I can never reach you when I need to. An update on the two ladies involved with Dick Waddell. They are being released within the hour. You want to talk to them, get here by 9:30 a.m.," said Terrel.

It was 10:30 a.m. I texted Terrel immediately.

"Am I too late?"

I could get to the hospital in less than thirty minutes. I started planning my driving route.

My phone pinged. There was a one word answer from Terrel. "Yes."

Could this day get any worse? Maybe. I had to check out the call from Justin. It was an opportunity to confirm what Roberto had told me. I could ask why he was partners with Spencer, a man he said that he didn't like. That might get him talking. Maybe he would fill me in on Holly Waddell, too. With any luck, he'd tell me more than I was actually asking.

But first, I dialed Inspector Burrell's number.

"Detective Burrell," said the low-pitched female voice.

"This is Trisha Carson. I talked with you yesterday about…"

"I know who you are and I know what we talked about. What's up?"

"I was fired today—for asking questions about Dick Waddell's death and everything else."

"Sorry to hear that."

There was a pause.

"Was that the reason you called?"

"No. Last night, I talked to a former cellmate of Justin Rosencastle's."

"Cellmate?"

"Yes. According to him, Waddell's brother-in-law, Spencer, was strongly encouraged to give Justin a job."

"That's what the cellmate told you?"

"Yes."

"Who is the cellmate?"

"I know his first name, but not much else. It's Roberto. He works in his family's restaurant in San Francisco."

"Ex-cons aren't always the most reliable source," Inspector Burrell said. "But okay, let's take the next step. Why?"

"Why would the ex-cellmate tell me or why would Waddell's brother-in-law hire Justin?"

"Let's start with the second part, although I am interested in the first part of the question."

"It seems that Dick Waddell and Justin Rosencastle were half-brothers. Their father, nicknamed Lucky, made Spencer Matthews hire Justin. Spencer is married to Waddell's sister, Pamela."

There was another long pause. I could hear a tap, tap, tap as if Inspector Burrell was tapping the edge of her phone with a pencil.

"I'm curious. Do people just volunteer this information to you?"

"I don't know how to answer that. Look, I'm calling with a specific question. Justin wants to see me this afternoon. Is there anything you want me to ask him?"

"Where are you supposed to meet him?"

"At his office."

"My advice is, 'Don't go.' It could be dangerous."

A cool silence hung in the air.

"You're going anyway, aren't you?"

"Yes, I am."

"It is not a good idea. But, I can't stop you. If you do go, make sure there are people around. Don't spend any time alone with him."

"That's it?"

"What did you expect? That I'd ask you to wear a wire? To go undercover? Find out what he wants and then leave. Got it?"

"Okay."

"Then call me."

"Okay."

"One more thing."

"What?"

"You don't like me very much do you?"

"It's not you. It's the police in general."

———

I had done what everyone had asked me to do. Call the police. The conversation was a waste of time. Inspector Burrell didn't want my help or my information. She treated me like a meddling school girl.

With about five hours to kill, I decided to take a short drive to the Exploratorium, San Francisco's combination science and art museum. There was a new baseball exhibit. I wanted to find out how you hit a ball going ninety miles an hour. Then, later in the day, I would head over to AT&T Park, buy a seat in the bleachers for today's 1:05 p.m. game and try not to think about what would happen next.

29

It was 4:30 p.m., when I pulled open the door to the building that housed JL & Associates. Here it was sunny and warm. No hint of damp fog. As the summer sun dipped behind the tall office buildings, streaks of light boomeranged off the windows until they glowed red and orange.

The building was a San Francisco classic with a worn brick façade and ornate detailed cornices. It had a long narrow entryway with a security guard sitting at a desk near the door. Before I had gone a few steps, Justin was walking down the hall toward me.

"You're here." He took my arm and walked me over to the security desk.

"Hey, Larry. Meet a good friend of mine. This is Trisha Carson. She's going to taste test our new products. Anything going on in the building?"

"Nothing's happening. People are on their way home."

A small television was sitting on the counter tuned to a pre-game show for the Oakland A's. The drone of the commentators echoed through the quiet lobby.

"When are you going to come over to our side?" Justin asked.

"Never. A's fan 'till I die," he said pumping his fist in the air.

The JL & Associates office was a short walk down the hall around the corner from the security guard. A large clear glass window revealed a young man answering phones in a starkly modern reception area.

Inside, the RazzleD logo, etched in frosted glass behind the reception desk, screened off the rest of the office. There were offices off to the right hand side, a lab that could be seen directly behind the frosted glass in the middle and a kitchen, a tasting room and a conference room to the left.

"This is really nice. When you said new company, I was thinking 'startup.' Basic."

"I told you my partners are wheeler-dealers, big money types. They think that first impressions are the only ones you get. They like to bring clients here. The philosophy is if the company looks solid, both on paper and in person, customers will sign on."

I watched as two women working in the lab took off their white coats, hung them up and walked toward the reception area.

"See you tomorrow," they said to Justin as they headed for the front door.

A few staff walked between offices before disappearing into the conference room on the other side of the hall. I could pick up muffled laughter as the door shut.

"You have a tasting room?"

"That we do," he said. "Let me show you."

The tasting room was set up like one in a Napa County winery. There was a highly polished curving bar carved from dark wood, tall green plants, expensive art featuring various athletes and sports, comfortable chairs and a small sofa.

Although we were alone in the room, I could still see the receptionist only 25 yards away. I sat down on a bar stool and glanced at him again. He could hear me if I yelled.

"The message that you left said the meeting didn't go as you expected. What happened?"

"They don't want RazzleD promotional booths at the swims anymore. To tell the truth, I wasn't supposed to be at the Russian River swim."

"There must be a reason. What did they say?"

"They said that the claims for the product's results haven't been scientifically proven. That the testing has been incomplete."

"Are they right?"

"They are being too cautious. We can easily fix whatever their concerns are. But that's where you come in. While we are readjusting some of our formulas—and changing some of the copy on the bottles—we still need exposure. We have a small foothold in the market. If we aren't at the swims, people won't see or try the product. It will impact our sales. Can you talk to Bill, maybe ask him to convince the board to reconsider, let us work the swims?"

"How can you promote a product, let alone sell it, if it isn't what you claim?"

"We're taking care of that. I just told you. It won't be a problem."

Justin paced around the room as he talked. Sounds like Bill and the board were having second thoughts, not only about RazzleD but about those behind it.

"I won't be able to help. I was fired this morning."

"No, shit. Why?"

"It seems that I have been asking too many questions about the Waddell death. People, including the board, have complained."

"I told you to leave it alone."

Justin walked over to the small couch and sat down.

"Who have you talked to?"

"The people on my cards. Remember my cards? Them mostly. And the police."

Justin's body stiffened. He blinked, stood up, walked slowly over to the bar where I was sitting. He ran both hands over the top of his head.

"Why would you talk to the police?"

"Everyone from the NPS security to my sister told me to tell the police my suspicions and then step away."

"How many people did you say you talked to about the Waddell death?"

"And Jackie's accident."

"Okay, and Jackie's accident."

"And the brick through my car window. And the Russian River events."

"Okay, tell me already."

I said the names out loud as I counted on my fingers, "Pamela, Mike Menton, Daisy Menton, his daughter; my sister, you, my sister's boyfriend, the security guard at work, Waddell's coach and my hairdresser. That makes nine. Oh, and Inspector Carolina Burrell. 10."

Justin blinked again.

"You okay?"

"Sure. I didn't realize this had gone beyond writing people's names on cards, that's all."

"I have a question for you. I thought you couldn't stand Waddell's brother-in-law?"

"You're right. I can't."

"Well, then, why is he your partner? In this?"

I spread my arms out and looked around the tasting room, pausing to glance at the receptionist.

Justin didn't miss a beat.

"You're right I don't like Spencer, but he came to visit me a while back with a business proposition."

"RazzleD?"

"Kind of. Think big picture. Anyway, that's what got me to Northern California. I thought this could work, so I signed on."

"And that was it? No other reason?"

Justin went behind the bar.

"My name is Justin. I'll be your guide to JL & Associates products. Today, we'll be sampling one of our most popular products—RazzleD replacement drink."

I laughed. The tension in the room eased for the moment. Justin was very good at changing the topic.

"Come on, tell me. Was that the only reason you came to San Francisco?"

"We keep you going…longer, stronger. How does that work for a slogan?"

"Lacks a little punch, to me."

"Needs work, I agree."

"Do you have family here?"

"Why all the questions?" he asked as he pulled out three small glasses with the RazzleD logo on the side and filled them with different color liquids.

"Try these and let me know what you think. They are all for after a swim/run/bike—hard exercise—maybe a competition or a really tough practice. It is for replenishing the body. The red one is pomegranate. The yellowish-orange one is mango/peach. The light green is what we call green apple. One of them is brand new. Let's see if you can tell which one it is? Take a taste."

I took a sip from each glass. "Mango/peach is my favorite. Green apple I could do without. Which one is the new? Wait, let me guess. Green apple."

Justin laughed. "That obvious is it? We'll have to work on it."

"It's bitter…very strange after taste."

Justin reached into a cooler behind the bar and pulled out a RazzleD bottle with a purple liquid inside.

With Roberto's warning to keep my mouth shut running through my mind, I took a deep breath and said, "Justin, I know Dick is your brother. I know Lucky is your father."

He slowly, very slowly stood up, cocked his head to one side. Then quietly said, "Who told you? Pamela?"

There was sadness in his eyes. I waited.

"Sisters. Can't keep their mouth shut, right? You know, you have one."

I waited.

"This wasn't my doing. I wanted to make a good nutritional product for athletes. Spencer had something else in mind. So did Dick, the wholesome winner, my brother.

"He didn't want to know what was in the products I gave him, as long as they made him go faster. He was a fraud. I thought for a while Lucky cared, but look what he pushed me into. Setting me up with Spencer. What a joke. Got a card from him a while ago. He's back in prison. All it said was, 'You, Dick and Pamela are family. Stay together.' I tried. They didn't want anything to do with me."

Justin walked out from behind the bar.

"Let's go to the lab where I guess I'll be working again."

We walked down the hall and stood outside the large windows looking into the empty lab. Behind me, through the frosted glass, the receptionist answered a phone. The door to the conference room was open and it was now empty. The normal office sounds; people talking, phones ringing, copying machines running—were missing. Stillness inched its way down the hall. I folded my arms across my chest. A shiver went through me.

In the lab, there were long white tables, microscopes, Petri dishes, and big refrigerators with glass doors where different products were kept. It looked like a hematology lab in a hospital.

"Justin, you can still get away from this."

He ignored me.

"I used to do product development. Not so much any more. Now, after last night's meeting, I'll have to do some formula adjustment. My office is down the hall. Come here for a minute. I want to show you something."

"I don't think so," I said, beginning to walk toward the front office.

"You have nothing to worry about. It's a good thing you know about all this. I like you. My brother, my sister—that's another story. This will only take a minute."

I glanced over at the receptionist and knocked on the glass that separated us. The young man turned around. I waved at him. He smiled and waved back.

"See. You're safe," Justin said.

Then, I slowly followed him as he walked to the end of the hall.

He had a corner office with a view of the neighboring building. There was a desk and computer to one side of the room, on the other wall was a floor to ceiling bookcase filled with ribbons, trophies, and plaques. I picked up a glass globe of the world and read,

2nd place, 200 meter breaststroke, 1984, Justin Rosencastle, FINA Worlds, Athens, Greece.

"Nice," I said.

On one of the lower shelves was a heavy rectangular silver plaque given for another world competition around the same time.

"Very nice."

I turned around and my arm hit his chest. Justin was inches behind me. I sidestepped away from him. His emotionless pale light blue eyes followed me.

"I saw a photo of you."

"You did?" he said surprised. He moved back a few feet. "From a past swim?"

I began to creep away from the bookcase, toward the door of his office. Justin mirrored my steps and stood solidly in front of me once again, blocking the door. "It was swimming, but not recent. It was a picture of your high school swim team. You had an Afro back then."

A cautious look crossed his face.

"Where did you see a photo of me from high school?"

"Pamela."

"I told you not to bother her," he said leaning toward me.

"I wasn't bothering her. I was taking back some swim equipment that belonged to her—your—brother."

"I made it very clear that you shouldn't go near her."

"Look, if I want to talk to someone, I'll talk to someone."

Justin tried to brush off the darkness from his face, but it lingered and he couldn't quite hide it with a forced smile.

"What did she say?"

"Not much."

"Spencer was there?"

"Yeah, he was."

"Of course. You know, Spencer always played the odds, even in high school. He was a scumbag. When Lucky was sent to prison, I helped at the ranch. I was driven, compelled to keep the ranch going. I worked twice as hard as Dick who was always off at some swim competition."

Justin turned around and started pacing up and down his office. He seemed a million miles a way. He slapped his hand down on the desk. Whap! I jumped.

"What's the matter?"

"Spencer's an idiot. If Pamela hadn't married him, then I wouldn't be involved with JL. It's her fault. This is not where I wanted to be."

"It's not too late to get out."

"Right, and I go straight back to prison. You know I've been in prison, don't you?"

I nodded and moved over to the two-seater couch in his office.

"Justin, was Waddell married?"

He stopped and looked at me.

"Her name is Holly, right? Holly Worthington?"

"Yet another high school swim team member. They were married right after high school. Classic story. The stud swimmer got her pregnant. Father was a well known rancher. He made it clear that Richard was going to marry his daughter, or else. He did, but then he left town to go to college in Texas. Skipped out. His family knew he was leaving, but they kept it a secret. And then Holly disappeared for a long time. We all thought she followed him. No one ever suspected she'd turn up here."

"And the baby?"

"No baby. She said that to get him to marry her."

"How did you know she was here?"

"Waddell mentioned it. I was dropping off some product at his house. But Spencer had already told me."

"Product?"

"Nutritional supplements."

"That's not what they were."

Justin smiled a strange tight smile.

"What you dropped off was some form of High Test, maybe HT2, a street drug, an illegal drug. Is that what eventually killed him?"

"I hope so," Justin said. "Waddell spent his life using people. Spencer heard him complain about losing his speed and he told me about it. Dick wanted me to develop something for him. He didn't care what it was—legal, illegal. So, that's what I did. He was happy to see the drugs, but never me. He kept asking for more, higher dosages. His philosophy was, if some is good, more is better. Did he ever thank me? Never once. I was treated like a delivery guy, completely disregarded. He wouldn't talk to me at swims, never invited me to his house. I didn't exist. Here I was helping him and he acted like I was invisible.

"When he began to complain about Menton being a threat in his age group, I told him I'd put together something new that was to be taken with what he already had. I told him to try it at the Lake Joseph swim, that he'd fly through the water. I knew he had some minor heart problems. Spencer told me. Early on, I tried to warn him. But he didn't care. All he wanted was to go fast."

"You killed him."

"Nah, not me. His arrogance, his fear, his competitiveness killed him. I only provided the means."

Justin moved over to the couch to sit next to me. I got up and shifted toward the door.

"What about Jackie? Were you involved with that?"

"That was so easy. Waddell was finally out of the way. Jackie and I were going out to dinner after the Cold Water Clash. Then along comes Mike Menton. She cancels, says she has other plans. I could tell from the way they were hanging on each other after the swim that it was with Menton.

"She stopped by the booth complaining of being a little tired. 'I have just the thing,' I told her. 'It's one of our new after race recovery products.' I handed her a capsule and she swallowed it with a swig of RazzleD. About 20 minutes later she drove off a cliff."

"And the Russian River swim?"

Justin chuckled.

"I was pissed. Your board didn't want our products at the swims anymore. I drove up about 45 minutes before the starting gun, set up my table with samples that had an extra special ingredient and gave them away."

"That extra ingredient had something to do with nuts, didn't it? Every single swimmer who was pulled from the water is allergic to nuts, some severely, like my sister."

"Did they die?"

"That's not the point. Why would you go after the swimmers?"

"If I couldn't be at the swim, why should they?"

"What did you put in your RazzleD drinks?"

"You should know."

"Me?"

"Yeah, you. You told me your whole family had nut allergies. Remember? When I needed something to randomly affect some swimmers, but not all, I added peanut oil. It was extremely effective, don't you think?"

I was talking to a lunatic. My eyes quickly darted to the door. How would I get out of there? Justin saw the glance. He moved to the door and shut it. The walls of the office began to close in around us. He slid toward me and I began to back up once again toward the bookcase. I couldn't breathe.

"You're different, I can tell," he said. "You're not like Pamela or Holly or Jackie."

My arms and legs started to tremble and my mind began to race.

"Hey," I called, hoping the receptionist could hear me. "Help me." But my voice was weak; the words came out smothered like yelling in a dream. I bumped into the trophy bookcase. He approached slowly. He reached both arms out to the bookcase, trapping me between him and the shelves. Then, he slid his hands down my arms, took hold of my wrists and quickly pushed them behind my back.

"Stop, that hurts. Let me go."

I felt a warm light kiss on the back of my neck. I turned my head away and gritted my teeth.

"You smell good. Taste good too."

"Stop, I..."

"Quiet...it's okay."

There was no room to move. I was pinned between him and the bookcase. His light blue eyes were glassy, almost transparent. Beads of sweat began to ooze from his forehead. His cheek chafed against mine like sandpaper. He pushed my hands back into a shelf. I could feel one of the trophies. It was the heavy silver plaque. I grabbed it.

He leaned over and kissed my neck again, then my cheek. Then he dropped my wrists, reached under my cotton blouse and before I could stop him, forced up my bra. His hands, cold and calloused, pressed against my breasts.

"Knock it off," I yelled. I pushed him back away from me with one hand and slammed the trophy into his head with the other. He stepped back, dazed. I aimed the trophy at his face and swung again. Blood spurted from his nose. I hit him one more time on the side of his head by his ear.

He staggered backwards until he reached his desk. Leaning against it, he covered his hands with his face. Blood dripped through his fingers, down his arms, soaking through the blue and white stripes on his shirt and fell onto the expensive Turkish carpet. I dropped the trophy and ran. The receptionist was gone; the office was empty. I pushed open the glass door heading into the building's foyer, pulling my bra and blouse back into place.

I could hear his footsteps following me.

As I bolted down the hall, I called out, "Hey, Larry, what's up with the A's?" The footsteps behind me stopped.

"National anthem time."

I slowed to a trot and smiled weakly. I never looked back. I pushed the front door open and sprinted to the corner. I glanced over my shoulder. The street was quiet. I continued jogging to the car, slid in the front seat and locked the door.

With the cellphone shaking in my hand, I called Inspector Burrell's number.

"Be there. Please be there."

It went to voicemail. I hit zero then # and started talking as soon as I heard a human voice.

"I'm been working with Inspector Burrell. Is she still around? It's important. I have to talk to her now."

The line was quiet. Then Carolina Burrell picked up the phone.

"It's me, Trisha. Justin is responsible for Waddell's death. He told me as much. And the other accidents involving the swimmers…that was his doing, as well. I just left him at JL & Associates. Go arrest him."

"Slow down. We can bring him in for questioning. Hopefully, he will tell us what he told you. Are you okay?"

"Rattled. That's all. He tried to attack me. I hit him and ran."

30

It was more than 14 hours since I tore out of JL & Associates and flew across the Golden Gate Bridge to the safety of my bedroom in San Rafael. Now, it was the next morning and my home phone was ringing. Three, four, five rings and it stopped. I put my head under the pillow. It started ringing again, another three, four, five rings and it stopped. Two minutes later my cell phone started chirping.

I didn't want to talk to anyone or see anyone. My head felt like it was stuck in a bucket of cement. But now, I had solid information about what happened to the swimmers and why, from the person who did it. I hope Justin was in jail, nursing a splitting headache and a broken nose.

I checked my cell phone. There were three texts from Lena, saying, "CALL ME" in all caps. I looked at the caller ID on my home phone and saw that one call was from Inspector Burrell and two were from Lena. I didn't play my sister's messages, just hit the talk button and listened as the phone dialed her number.

"Trisha, where have you been?" she asked yelling into the phone. "I came to JL & Associates to work on their website and everyone is in a state of shock here. Justin is dead. He was killed last night."

My hand went up to my mouth. I sat down heavily on a kitchen chair. I couldn't have hit him that hard. I know he was moving. I heard him following me down the hall.

"What? What did you say?"

"Killed. Someone killed him."

"Who told you?"

"Well, when I got to the building, the police were there. They had put that yellow tape across the door to his office. His body must have been taken out earlier this morning."

I looked at the clock. It was 8:45 a.m. I wondered when the body was discovered and by whom. Maybe it was the police and I sent them there. My God, I killed him. I'm going to be arrested.

"I had a chance to walk by the office. There was blood on his desk, on the carpet. Some of the trophies from his bookcase were on the floor. It was awful."

"Do they know who did it?" I really didn't want to ask that question.

"No. Spencer found him last night. They are trying to track down the security guard, but he left early and seems to have taken off for a couple of days. Right now they don't know who did what."

There was a long silence on my end of the phone. I was thinking about the security cameras that Larry had been watching last night, along with the A's game. I'd be on the tapes; walking in, running out. And the receptionist at JL & Associates, the women from the lab, everyone saw me with Justin.

"Trisha? You still there? Did you talk to Justin lately?"

Another long pause.

"Look. I know you're upset. You saw him as a potential boy-friend."

Potential rapist and actual killer, I thought.

My voice came from deep inside an empty well.

"I need to talk to you and Terrel today. Can you set that up? I'll meet you wherever."

"11:30 a.m., at the hospital. I'm meeting T for lunch. Trish, what's wrong?"

"I'll tell you when I see you."

———

Terrel twisted around and looked at me in the backseat of his car, with a 'you did what?' expression on his face. "No. No way. From what you said, you couldn't have killed him. Three half-hearted blows…no way."

He, Lena and I were sitting in his Charger in the hospital parking lot. I didn't want to talk any place where we could be overheard.

"What do you mean halfhearted?"

"Look, your first blow was probably more of a surprise to him than anything. Your arms had been behind you; there was no wind up, speaking in baseball terms. The second hit probably did the most damage, broken nose, maybe broken facial bones and you said the third hit grazed the top of his head. Unless he fell, hit his head on a desk, that shouldn't have killed him."

"Have you talked to Inspector Burrell?" asked Lena.

"Last night. Right after I left Justin."

"Call her again. Talk to her, someone, anyone," said Lena. "Once they find the security guard, he will describe you. I mean, you were even introduced to him. The people at JL & Associates know you were there. The police know you were there. They need to hear your side of the story immediately."

"And then there are your fingerprints…in his office on the trophy," said Terrel.

"I never thought about that," I said. "I didn't go there to kill him. I was cautious, I thought."

"What were you doing home this morning?" Terrel asked. "You better tell your boss you need some time off. Where does he think you are?"

"Free time is not a problem right now. Yesterday, I was fired."

"I don't believe it," Terrel said, sinking down in the front seat and putting his head on the steering wheel. "Who lives a life like you? Nobody I know."

"What were you fired for?" asked Lena. "Never mind, I can guess…talking about the Waddell death, saying it was a murder. Right?"

I nodded.

"I heard some grumblings about your questions from different swim friends. They wondered what you were doing."

I stared out of the side window of Terrel's car. Nothing but cars around us and steel and concrete.

"I want to do one more thing before I talk to the police," I said. "And I'll need your help."

Lena and Terrel glanced at each other and at me.

"Oh, no," said Terrel. "I don't mess with the police. I have seen what happens when you're not straight with them."

"This isn't about the police. It's simple…really. I need your help, Terrel, just for one more thing."

Terrel shook his head. "No. I don't care what it is."

"Please. This is the last thing that I'll do. I promise."

"No."

"Lena, help me here. After this, I'll talk to the police."

"Terrel?" asked Lena.

"Trisha, I thought you were the sensible sister." He banged his head against the steering wheel a few times, then threw up his hands. "This is the last time, then it is over."

"O—VER," both Lena and I said in unison.

"What do you want me to do?" he asked with his eyes closed.

31

The waiting room of the Turk Medical Clinic was cheery. Overflowing with people, but still cheery. That came as a surprise to me. I wasn't sure what the reception area of a community clinic would look like, but this didn't fit my preconceived notion.

I was here thanks to Terrel. I needed to find Holly Worthington and he knew how to get in touch with her. Holly received medical care at this SF clinic. Terrel had called his friend Tariq Kapoor, the physician-in-charge as well as the street drug expert, and asked him to help me find her. Dr. Kapoor was able to track her down through his outreach, folks he called 'scouts.' She was supposed to arrive at the clinic around 2:00 p.m. I was sitting there waiting. It was 2:10 p.m.

Dr. Kapoor came out, smiled at some of the patients in the waiting room. "Anything?"

I shook my head.

"Let me know when she gets here. The two of you can sit and talk in my office. It's very small, but private."

I picked up a magazine, put it down and watched patients sign in, disappear into the back with a medical assistant, reappear and leave. A half hour went by, then an hour. At 3:15 p.m., I caught Dr. Kapoor as he came out to talk to the receptionist.

"I don't think she's coming. Thanks for trying. If she arrives later, can you ask her to call me?" I wrote down my cell phone number.

"I doubt that she has a phone, but she can call from here if she wants," said Dr. Kapoor. "Sorry, but it's not unusual for appointments to be broken. It happens."

We shook hands and I walked out the door, heading for my car parked at a meter two blocks away. Sitting on the pavement at the corner, holding a sign that said 'Hungry, please help,' was a woman dressed in a shabby long black overcoat. The oversized sleeves were shredded at the cuffs. My eyes turned away from the woman as if she wasn't there. I pulled out some change and dropped it into the small cardboard box she was holding out.

"Bless you, miss," she said while looking down the street, past the parked cars.

On a chance, I took out one of the pictures of Dick Waddell—the one that showed him and a young woman holding up swim ribbons—from my backpack. I squatted down beside her. She looked up at me, bit the inside of her cheek and tried to inch back against the wall. Her eyes were red rimmed. Her cheeks were hollow. Grey streaked her stringy brown hair. I held the photo up for her to see.

"This girl in the picture. Is this you?" I asked.

She took the faded color photo in her hand and held it close to her eyes. "Can't see too well without my glasses," she said. She squinted and a smile passed across her face. "Cute young things, aren't they? But, no, not me, missy," she said and handed the photo back to me.

"Are you Holly Worthington?" I asked.

"No, honey. I'm not Holly."

"Oh, sorry to bother you." I stood up. "You okay sitting here?"

"Sure, why not? I like it. This is my corner."

I smiled and turned away, ready to walk back to my car.

"Do you want to find Holly?" She called out to me. I turned in a flash.

"Do you know where she is?"

"Sure. She's over there in the park. Just don't tell her I told you, okay?"

She thanked and blessed a man who dropped two one dollar bills in her cardboard box.

"I won't say anything."

I headed for the corner and waited for the light to change. The park was small with a black metal fence around it. Inside there were climbing structures and young Vietnamese moms watched their kids closely as they played.

Everyone in the park seemed to be connected to one of the kids. No one looked out of place. I scanned the whole park, but didn't see what I would consider a homeless person sitting or standing in the area. Another strike out. Okay, it was O–VER. I had to tell Terrel that I was finished and would call Inspector Burrell again. I walked along the black fence and listened to the shrieks and laughter from the children in the park. Didn't matter that they were in one of the most dangerous parts of the city, they were having a good time. I watched them run through the miniature playground; such unbridled joy and happiness.

I was about to head back across the street when out of the corner of my eye, I saw a flash of something shiny and red in the undergrowth behind the play area, outside of the fence. I walked slowly around the perimeter of the gated park and stood near the shrubs in the back. There, I could see a red and silver shopping cart that was packed to overflowing. White partially filled garbage bags were tied to either side. Two bigger black bags, normally used for yard waste, were tied to the rim at the back of the cart. I took a few steps closer.

"Stay away from me," a woman's voice shouted out. It attracted the attention of some of the mothers in the park. They looked toward the sound of the voice then looked away. From a distance I quietly said, "Holly? Are you Holly Worthington?"

The woman stuck her head out from behind her cart. "What if I am? I'm not bothering you. Go away."

"Holly, I have some pictures of you. Or at least I think they are of you? I thought you'd like to see them. I'll walk over to that flat tree stump and put them there. Then I'll come back here."

She watched me carefully as I moved slowly through the thick grass. I laid the photo of her and Dick and the swim team on the stump. Then I turned around and walked back to the spot where I had been standing.

"Move back more," she said waving me to the corner of the playground. I moved back even farther and watched as she walked over to the tree stump, bent over and picked up the photos. She sat down heavily on the stump.

"Where did you get these?" she asked, never taking her glance away from the pictures.

"Pamela Matthews. You probably knew her as Pamela…"

"Waddell—I know. I know."

"Is it okay if I talk to you? I'm not here to hurt you. I don't even know if I'm here to help you. I just need some information."

She gave a small nod. "Okay."

"Do you want to go someplace and get something to eat?"

"Can't. Someone could steal my cart."

"How about if I go get us something and we sit over there on the bench? That way we can talk and you can keep an eye on your cart."

She agreed and I walked down the street to a small grocery store. I ordered three turkey sandwiches, bought some bananas, two cartons of milk and two chocolate brownies. By the time I came back, she was sitting on the bench. I gave her the two sandwiches. She picked up the carton of milk and stared at it.

"Milk? What do you think I am, eight years old? I want a cup of coffee."

"I didn't get coffee, but I have water." I pulled a water bottle out of my backpack. She grabbed for it. She laid everything in front of her on the bench like she was setting a table. Sandwiches in the middle, water at top right, napkins next to the sandwiches and brownies top left.

She bowed her head for a few seconds; then she started to eat.

She didn't speak, concentrating only on the food in front of her. Even while eating, she sat and moved with a certain grace. There was an elegance and agility of movement that suggested a dancer or an athlete. She was about 5'5" and slender, almost to the point of being skinny. I expected her skin to be pasty, shallow, but she had color, like she'd been in the sun, which, of course, she had been since she'd lived on the streets. Her face was puffy, including the skin around her green eyes. Her shoulder length dark hair was tangled and needed to be washed and combed. Her nails were chipped and dirty.

Did I see the healthy young swimmer of years ago underneath the tattered and faded grey San Francisco sweatshirt and ripped jeans? Barely, but there was something there.

When she finished eating, she shook out the food wrappers and folded them carefully, slipping them into her cart. Then she sat up straight, looked directly at me.

"What do you want?"

I was looking at the picture of her in a swimsuit taken so many years ago. "So, this is you?"

"Yes," she said.

"And the boy standing next to you?"

"Dick Waddell."

"Your teammate, right?"

"Yes, we swam on the same high school team."

"You were good friends, it looked like."

"Too good," she said handing me back the pictures. "What are you here for?" she asked.

"I don't know whether you have heard or not. I'm sorry to be the one to tell you, but Dick Waddell died about a month ago."

Her body stiffened and she stood up.

"No. I didn't know. No one told me."

She looked down at the ground and walked a few feet away from me. Then she retraced her steps back to the bench and sat down. Tears were in her eyes.

"How did he die?"

"That's really why I'm here...to talk about it. His family first thought it was a heart attack. I have information that says he was taking some kind of illegal drugs and that it could be the cause of his death."

Holly didn't say anything.

"Would you know anything about that?"

She shook her head and stared back to the play area and the metal fence. Then, she looked at me with a grim expression on her face.

"I get it now. You think that somehow I'm connected to his death…gave him drugs…killed him. Fool," she said.

"No. That's not what I think. I know who gave him the drugs. It wasn't you."

"You're right it wasn't me. Then tell me, what do you want?"

"I'm not even sure anymore. I know that Dick moved to Northern California about a year ago. The articles I've read quote him as saying it was to be close to family. I thought originally it meant to be close to his sister, Pamela, and her husband, Spencer."

Holly grunted. "Spencer's an asshole."

"But maybe the family he was talking about was you. You were married to him, weren't you?"

There was a long pause. I could see her thinking it over, trying to assess what she could tell me.

"How did you know that?"

I told her about Dr. T from SF Memorial finding the weathered newspaper article announcing their wedding.

She shook her head in disgust. "My private stuff. People think that because I live on the street I don't have a right to my privacy. I do. Makes me sick. No respect…no respect at all."

"He was just trying to find out who you were. That's all. From what he told me, you were incoherent, could hardly speak."

She glared at me. "Yes, we were married after high school. Yes, to your next question. I was pregnant. Yes, to the question after that. He left me. His family let him leave. Leave me in that small town. And yes, to the question after that. I went after him.

"I found him, too. In a dorm room in Texas. He said he was sorry but he didn't want to see me, didn't want to be married and did not want to be a father. He had his swimming career to think about. He had a shot at the Olympics. He gave me what he said was all the money he had, $200. I kept the money and hitchhiked here."

"Hitchhiked? From Texas? But you were pregnant. I know this isn't my business, but what happened to the baby?"

"You're right. This isn't your business. It was so long ago. A different time. I was a different person, I guess."

She stared off into space as if she was looking back through the years, at the teenager who found herself alone during the frantic and dangerous end of the flower-power days in San Francisco.

"It wasn't that strange to be on the streets back then. When I got here I ended up at a clinic in the Haight. Nice people; nice doctors. They took care of me while I was pregnant. They helped me find a place to live, food to eat and kept me healthy. I gave birth to a little boy."

"Really? That's not what I was told Where is he now?"

"Don't know. I held him once. I remember wondering if he would be a swimmer, too. Then I handed him to the nurse and signed a couple of papers saying I was giving him up. A few hours later, I left the clinic. That was that."

"Did Dick know any of this? Did he know you were here?"

"Oh yeah. About four years ago, he hunted me down, just like you did. His first question, just like yours. 'What happened to the baby?' Not 'how are you? What have you been doing for the last 30 years?' Only 'where was the baby?' Did you come to find me to tell me that Dick was dead?"

"That wasn't the original reason. Why I wanted to talk to you has changed—changed one, two, even three times. A few days ago, I overheard Spencer talking to someone else you probably know, Justin Rosencastle."

She shook her head. "Another unfortunate blast from the past."

"It sounded like they were talking about drugs. Last night, I confronted Justin, told him I thought the drugs he sold to Dick killed him. He didn't deny it."

Holly was staring at me. "Girl, you are so stupid. Don't you know what Spencer and Justin do? Look at me. Look at my arms," and she pulled up the sleeves of her sweatshirt to show the needle tracks.

"This is because of them. Back in the 70's, I ran into Spencer at a concert in Golden Gate Park. We kept in touch. He offered me drugs, for free, and a place to crash and food. He wanted to help me so I wouldn't be on the streets or so he said. But it was only so I'd sleep with him. Maybe it was the times; maybe it was me. What the hell did I care? I had nothing going on and I got free dope and a roof over my head. Justin took over when Spencer was tired of me."

I couldn't believe what I was hearing. Not only had Holly been in touch with Spencer and Justin, but they had been dealing drugs of one kind or another since the late 70's. And they treated her like a disposable diaper. Use her and throw her away.

"I think I killed Justin last night. I hit him a couple of times with one of his swim awards."

For the first time in our conversation, Holly started to smile. Then, she threw back her head and laughed and laughed.

"One of the best uses I ever heard of for a swim trophy."

She laughed so hard, I thought she'd fall off the bench. She put her dirty hands up to her face and pushed the tangled hair back behind her ears.

"So let's see—you hunted me down to tell me that Dick was murdered and that you killed Justin? Is that right?"

I didn't know what to say. I pulled out Dick's camera and searched for the pictures of him and Jeremy Reid.

"Have you ever seen this man before?"

She shook her head. "Who is this guy with Richard?"

"I don't know for sure. But it might be your son."

Just then, my cell phone rang. I looked at the number. It was from my sister.

"I have to take this."

I handed her the camera, stood up and walked away from the bench.

"Trish, write this down."

"Why are you whispering?" I asked.

"I'm at JL. No time to talk. I've been researching information in their files for the new website. I found a warehouse address in South San Francisco. Ready?"

"You need to get out of there. They are probably looking for me. They're going to ask you questions. Is Spencer around?"

"I saw him walk out the door."

I hunted around in my backpack, pulled out a pen, shuffled through the bag some more and pulled out a crumpled napkin. It would have to do. "Go."

"3557 South Airport Drive, South San Francisco."

"Got it. Anything else?"

"Can't talk now. Someone is coming." And she clicked off.

This could be the link, the place where they warehoused drugs that were meant for the streets, the suburbs and for swimmers.

I turned around and started back to the bench. Holly was gone. I could see her at the end of the block pushing her cart, ready to cross the street. She never looked back at me. I decided not to run after her. Instead, I walked back to the bench. She had left the camera and the photographs.

On the back of the receipts for our lunch, I wrote, "Holly, if you can tell me anything else about Dick, please call." I jotted down my cell phone and home numbers. Following the perimeter of the fence, I came to the wooded area behind it. I stopped at the indentation in the grass, the area that Holly called home. There were some long pieces of cardboard folded up and stuck between two bushes. I took the photos and my note and placed them between the folds of the cardboard. Then I headed for the car.

———

There on the windshield under the wiper was a parking ticket. I had put enough change in or so I thought. But the afternoon had dragged on and I forgot about the vehicle. Now I had to pay $60 to the City and County of San Francisco. Not happy. Not happy at all since I had no job that would allow me to pay for it.

Well, as long as I had a ticket, I was going to make use of the extra time. I put the citation back under the windshield wiper and climbed into the car. My promise to Terrel was to wrap up my so-called investigation—his words, not mine—by today. Then tell the police my findings. Okay, it was late afternoon, but the day officially ended at midnight.

I laid out my cards one more time. I looked at the one for Holly Worthington and added the address of the park. I transferred the South San Francisco address that Lena had given me from the napkin to another card. I was about to call Terrel just to let him know—let him know what? That I was still asking questions and didn't plan on going to the police for another few hours. Skip that call.

There was one message on my cell phone, from Inspector Burrell asking me to call her as soon as I could. I hit delete.

This whole thing which had started with a simple 'what if a heart attack was not really a heart attack' had escalated. And now, I was probably a murder suspect. Since Justin was dead, there was no way I could prove that he had been providing drugs to Waddell, and had given him additional drugs to kill him. And that out of spite, revenge, jealousy, he had caused Jackie's accident. It would be my word against a dead man's. I don't think that would hold up in court.

I had an idea. I couldn't prove any of what Justin said, but maybe Lena could.

I called her cell again. No pickup—what else is new? This time I left a message. "Any chance of you finding out who the JL clients are? Both the legitimate clients and maybe the clients that are locked behind a set of passwords?"

I'm not sure if this was something Lena could even do. She was a web graphic artist not a hacker. Then I put a call into JL & Associates.

"JL &Associates, how may I direct your call?" said a very friendly female voice. "This is Inspector Carolina Burrell, may I speak with Spencer Matthews please?"

"Can I tell him what this is regarding?" the voice asked with a touch of concern.

"May I speak with Mr. Matthews, please?" I asked again.

"He's not here, but I will take a message."

I left Inspector Burrell's number and then hung up. The call wouldn't seem too much out of the ordinary if the police had been in and out of the office since Justin's death. But it might buy me some time.

"Think I'll take a ride," I said to myself. But first I stepped out of the car, pulled the parking ticket from under the windshield wipers, crumpled it up and threw it on the backseat. Then I headed for South San Francisco.

32

The warehouse was located in a desolate industrial area in South San Francisco that made no attempt at looking like an upscale business park. Wide streets and set back buildings with no signage besides street numbers kept prying eyes from learning too much.

The gloomy overcast in the city morphed into cool drippy fog here. The pavement and streets were wet and a dismal grey. I drove by 5357. I couldn't see a front entrance, even a door. It was a two story building and the blank façade facing the street had no windows. A locked chain-link fence with a high secure gate kept the driveway off limits from anyone driving in. By the side of the driveway, next to the fence was a small call box.

I found a place to park across the street and waited. It didn't take long until a 16-foot rental truck pulled up. The driver stuck his head out of the window of the cab, pushed a button and said a few things into the speaker. Then the gate automatically opened and the truck pulled in and the gate closed. It looked like the vehicle pulled around to the back.

I wouldn't be able to see anything from where I was sitting. The lot next to 5357 was empty, only tall weeds and trash blowing around in the chilly damp breeze. There was a high wooden fence separating the two pieces of property. I shouldn't be seen if I was walking around.

Before I got out of the car, I grabbed my camera. Since it was close to 5:00 p.m., employees were leaving their offices and heading for home. If asked what I was doing, I'd say that I was thinking of buying the property and constructing a small building. I remember my dad always saying, 'Act as if you belong and no one will bother you.' Let's see if it would work.

Not only did it work, no one cared or even noticed. I was just a woman walking around an empty lot taking pictures of weeds, the street side and surrounding buildings. Not one person glanced my way as they got into their cars and drove away.

Toward the back of the lot away from the street, the fence angled off toward 5357, protecting me even more. Some of the warped boards were loose and it was easy to see between them to the back of the neighboring building. But truth be told, there wasn't much to see. A loading dock, cardboard boxes. Guys speaking Spanglish were grabbing boxes off the truck that just pulled in. One man looked familiar, but I couldn't quite place him. His face was hidden by the hood on his sweatshirt.

I could see a shed to the side of the loading dock. Behind it was an outside metal staircase that went up to the top floor. If I could get to the shed without being seen, the corner of the building should protect me while I climbed up the steps.

But I needed to get the guys off the loading dock first. Modern automotive technology was going to come in handy. I pulled out my automatic car door opener and hit the alarm button. My car exploded with sound. It beeped loudly. The front and rear lights flashed. The beeping became more frantic and an annoying whoop-whoop siren started up. I heard the men at the loading dock talking about the noise, gesturing toward the car. I hit the panic button again and the volume increased. It blasted up and down the street.

Four men walked down the driveway. They pressed a button, and opened the gate heading toward my car. I glanced at the loading dock. It was empty. Now was my chance. I squeezed through the fence. Moving quickly to the back of the shed, I darted over to the staircase. I could see the men curbside surrounding my car, peering inside.

I sprinted up the steps and tried the metal door at the top. It was locked. I continued climbing and stepped onto the roof. As I moved away from the roof's edge, I hit the car's open door button and the noise stopped. Then I pressed the lock button and the car relocked itself.

"This car is haunted," I heard one of the men say.

The others laughed as they walked back to the loading dock. "It's a ghost car, coming to get you."

One man shoved the other and they climbed inside the back of the truck, and continued pulling out boxes. The worker in the hooded sweatshirt stood by the loading dock stacking the boxes. I knew who he was. The guy who tried to steal my backpack.

"What was that all about?" said a voice standing almost directly below me at the door I had just climbed past.

"Car alarm," said one guy. "Nothing else."

"You sure? I don't like empty cars outside my building."

"It was across the street, boss. Nothing in the car. Doors are locked. Car computer went loco, maybe."

"Okay," said the voice as it moved back inside the building.

I looked around. On the roof were a large heating and air conditioning unit and various small vents. It was a tar and gravel roof and I had the distinct impression that each step I took could be heard below. I bent over to untie my shoes and take them off.

There was a door that opened unto the roof, probably the way workmen reached the heating units for repair. I walked over, put my hand on the door knob and turned it as quietly as I could. It moved in my hand. The door wasn't locked. I pulled it open very slowly, wondering if it would creak. It really wouldn't have mattered if it did.

There was plenty of noise coming from two stories down. Still holding my shoes, I moved inside the building. I'm not sure what I was expecting to see but this wasn't it. I thought I would find a loud busy plant bottling the sports drink, RazzleD and packaging nutritional supplements. I also expected there to be a separate section—a protected room—for getting the street drugs ready for distribution. But that's not what I was looking at.

Off to the side was a pile of smallish white garbage bags, folded over and taped shut. From my vantage point, I could see men working at two conveyor belts; solid white bricks were on one, off-white bricks were on the other. Men stopped and started the belts as they inspected each block.

I was probably looking at kilos of cocaine and heroin. I couldn't tell. Whatever it was didn't have much, if anything, to do with nutritional supplements. Each of those slabs moving down that conveyor belt was worth tens of thousands of dollars. I had heard Terrel once say that years back, a brick of approximately 700 grams of Asian heroin, cost about $70,000. Once it was cut and resold, it was worth about $280,000.

Sitting in a small alcove in the corner of the room were two big burly men with rifles propped up against their chairs. Another man was leaning up against the wall and chatting with the other two. Tucked into his waistband was a pistol with a mother-of-pearl handle. While they talked, they kept an eye on the men working and on the non-descript plastic trash bags filled with drugs worth millions of dollars.

Drugs and weapons. How naïve could I be? This was beyond dangerous. I had to get out of here, now. I was dead if they found me. Inspector Burrell was right. This was a job for the police. I backed up as quietly as possible to the door, when the conveyor belts stopped. I held my breath.

"Shit…what the fuck?" I heard a man below me. "This is a piece of crap."

"Something happened to the belt. Jimmy gonna take a look. So let's go get something to eat," said one of the men.

The voice came out of an office on the floor below me. "Forget about it. Keep working. We have to make a delivery tonight."

"We've been at this for nine hours. Quick break. We need food," said the workman.

"All right. Pick something up and bring it back."

I could hear the phone ring in the office below me.

"Inspector who called? Why didn't you call me immediately? I don't like this. I'm coming back to the office. Get this inspector on the phone and see if you can find out what she wants."

The man on the phone below me was Spencer, Dick Waddell's brother-in-law. Still on the landing, I could hear him making another call.

"Hey, Tip. Need to tell you something—I got a lady inspector nosing around at my office—probably related to Rosencastle's death. Don't know. She left a message with the receptionist. Idiot didn't call and tell me about it until right now. Nothing to worry about, just wanted to let you know. Right. I'll call you later."

With that, he moved quickly down a flight of stairs and walked over to a man working on the machinery at the end of the conveyor belts. "Jimmy, get this working by the time the guys get back, you understand."

Jimmy mumbled something that I couldn't hear. Then Spencer opened the door by the loading dock and walked out into the damp air. That was my cue. I inched quietly out the door and was back on the roof. I stood behind the heater unit and watched him. He walked by the truck, looked in, and nodded. 'Almost empty,' I heard him say. Then he moved toward the back of the yard where his car was parked. He glanced to his left and stopped.

"What the…"

Tilting his head, he walked over to the fence, to the section I had climbed through. A slat was clearly missing. He shook his head. "Jimmy, get out here."

The short heavyset Jimmy in a dirty white tee shirt came to the edge of the loading dock.

"What's up?"

"How long has this fence been broken?"

"What are you talkin' about?" Jimmy asked, jumping down from the dock and walking over to Spencer. He bent over, reached through the hole in the fence and picked up the piece of wood on the other side.

"This looks like it has been pulled off," he said turning the long slat of wood over in his hands. "Probably kids."

"Where was security? Get Renaldo and Ken. Show them this and then fix it. Have one of the guys stay out here until we're finished."

Jimmy headed inside the warehouse. Spencer squatted down by the fence. He stuck his hand through the opening. He picked up a small white card. It was one of my cards from the Nor Cal Swimming Association. It had fallen out of my pocket.

Spencer looked around the yard, by the truck, down the driveway, at the loading dock. His eyes moved to the top of the building. I stepped farther back and bumped into the door. The impact surprised me and I dropped one of my shoes. I gritted my teeth and winced. Did he hear that? I bent down slowly and picked it up.

I heard his car start up and saw it head for the gate. I let out a sigh and tried to calm my rapid breathing. The gate opened. Spencer drove out and the gate closed.

I started down the steps on the side of the building. I could hear Jimmy deep inside the building, talking to the guards in the alcove. A quick look and I saw that his back was facing the truck. I only had a few seconds before the three of them walked out to the loading dock. I sprinted behind the truck, then to the back of the shed and shimmied through the gap in the fence.

Breathe in, breathe out, deep in; deep out. Surveillance yoga, I thought. It took a few minutes, but my breathing slowed down. Quickly, I put on my shoes and headed for the car, now the only car parked on the street across from the warehouse.

33

Spencer was on his way back to the office. If Lena was still there and looking into the underpinnings of their website and he walked in on her…I swallowed. Not good. She needed to get the information to the police and I needed to tell Inspector Burrell where I spent the last few hours and 'Oh, by the way, I probably killed Justin by whacking him with his trophy.'

I called Lena. No answer. I called Terrel. This time he picked up.

"You been to the police yet?" He doesn't mess around. No 'Hi, how are you?'—pure business.

"Not really."

"In other words, no."

"That's correct, no. But I'm calling Inspector Burrell as soon as I hang up. Lena could still be at the JL office which is not good. Spencer is on his way there. Their plant in South San Francisco is only a cover for what they really manufacture."

"And that would be?"

"White and dirty white bricks. Drugs, right?"

"Sounds like it."

"They had guards with weapons."

"Please tell me you're not still at this place?"

"No, I've left."

"And what is Lena's part in this?"

"Well, she found the South San Francisco address and gave it to me. Then I asked her to check for a list of their clients, both those that looked legitimate and not so legitimate."

"I've heard enough. Call Inspector Burrell's office immediately and tell her everything that you've told me. I'll get a hold of your sister."

"Okay."

Terrel was right. He had been right all along, but I never listened. I screwed up, because of a few bad experiences in my past. I called Inspector Burrell's office and left a message with the sergeant who answered the phone. Now the police had the warehouse address in South San Francisco and a description of who was there and what. I didn't say anything about Justin Rosencastle. I wanted to talk to Inspector Burrell about that in person.

If I couldn't get Lena on the phone, I was going to drive to JL & Associates and find her. I headed for Highway 101. Before I had gone more than five miles, my cell phone rang. Lena's photo came up on the screen.

"Did Terrel just call you?"

"Terrel? No."

"You okay?"

"Certainly I am." Her voice sounded odd, a little strained.

"Still at JL?"

"No. Listen to me. I was driving home and my car died. I'm at Fort Mason. Just inside the parking lot."

"You sure everything is okay? You sound strange."

"I'm upset about my car. If Terrel or his father can't fix it, this is going to cost me more money than I have. Can you come get me?"

"It will take about 45 minutes, but I'll be there. Stay by the car, okay?" Lena hung up. Pain in the ass is what she is, but she's out of the JL office and she won't be going back.

With Lena conveniently stuck in a broken down car, I felt much better. I switched on the radio and found the current Giants game. They were in the middle innings and leading the San Diego Padres, 4-2. From Highway 101, I traveled north on Van Ness Avenue, a major thoroughfare that takes cars from one end of San Francisco to the other. Not that much traffic. Relief was washing over me like a cool waterfall on a hot day.

It was that half hour after dusk, when it wasn't day anymore, but not quite night. San Francisco Bay was covered in a moody thin fog. A strong cold wind blew off the ocean dropping the temperature to the fifties. Welcome to summer in San Francisco. I could see sections of the two orange towers of the Golden Gate Bridge stretching into the darkness. There were still a few joggers making their way around the Marina Green and a few sailboats heading out of the marina for what would be a bumpy nighttime sail.

I pulled into Fort Mason but didn't see my sister's Camry. I drove slowly through the large parking lot. It was partially full. Customers at Greens, the vegetarian restaurant, were going in for dinner. Parking spaces in front of the Magic Theater was filling up. Where were Lena and her car? I drove by my old office building slowly and rolled down the window. At the other end of the parking lot, I could see the NPS security car. I wondered if Jon was driving.

Was it only yesterday that I had been fired and Jon had escorted me out of the office? It seemed like weeks ago.

Then I headed outside the parking lot toward Gas House Cove, the marina gas dock that backed up against Greens. I could see Lena's car parked near the gate closest to the dock. I pulled over slowly and parked next to it. She wasn't inside.

I rolled down the window and called out, "Lena." No response. The only sounds were the halyards clinking against the masts of the sailboats in the marina and the low rumble of traffic going by on Marina Boulevard.

I got out of my car, leaving the door open, walked over and looked in the window of the passenger side of my sister's car. She wasn't inside. The car door was unlocked. I shook my head in disbelief. If she was going out for a walk, she should lock her car. I walked around the car looking at the tires. No flats.

The parking lot was almost empty. I scanned the marina docks. "Lena?"

Still no response. Maybe she went across the street to the Safeway to get something to eat. The long low grocery store was lit up as bright as a cruise ship coming into port at night. I took a few steps back to my car and pulled out my cell phone. "I'm here. Where R U?" I texted her. Grabbing my backpack, I hunted around in the bottom until I found her spare set of car keys.

I went around to the driver's side, climbed in, put the key in the ignition and turned it. The car started. What could be wrong? I backed it up slowly—no problem—then drove around the empty parking lot. No engine lights turned bright red on the dashboard. The car didn't make any stranger sounds than usual. Even the wipers and the radio still worked. What was the problem? I pulled next to my car, turned everything off, got out and locked it.

Where could she be? I sat on the hood of her car and waited. I'd been there almost 30 minutes in the dark and I was cold. That's when I heard her calling me.

"Hey, Trisha, I'm over here. Come on down," she said.

There she was, standing at the end of the first dock.

"What are you doing down there?" I yelled.

"Ran into some friends. Come over for a drink."

"No, I'm going home. Your car is fine. Whatever was wrong has fixed itself."

"You gotta come."

Her voice sounded a little slurred. Strange. My sister rarely drank.

"Let's go home, Lena. Come on, I'll drive you. We can pick up your car later."

She turned back and said a few words to someone in the sailboat tied to the dock next to her. I heard a faint 'okay' as she began to walk down the dock toward the gate. Her balance was off. A few times, she had to stop or she would have taken a step off the dock and into the water.

I was annoyed. "What is wrong with you?"

The tide was out and the gangway leading up to the parking lot was steep. I walked over to the gate as she climbed up the walkway. I tried to open the gate, but my side was locked.

"Lena, you are so irritating. You call for help with your car and then you go and have a few—maybe more than a few—drinks on someone's sailboat. Open up the gate and let's go."

"Come on down," she said loudly. Then she whispered, "Run away."

"What?"

"Run away. Men with guns."

"What are you talking about?"

"Just get out of here."

Pins and needles spread through my fingers and climbed the back of my hands. My throat tightened up.

Behind her, I could see two sailors walking down the dock. One was pulling a white cooler. The other was carrying two large sail bags. The stiff cloth crinkled in his arms. Their laughter grew louder as they approached the steep gangplank.

"Going out?" one said to my sister.

"Yes, she is," I said.

From down the dock, a heavyset man climbed off the sailboat that Lena had been standing by. He walked quickly toward the gate. He was bald and had a rust-colored goatee. He was the man from the hospital parking lot; the man who had been following me. There was someone else on the boat. I couldn't quite see who it was; but the shape was thinner, smaller. The face was lost in shadows.

Lena pulled open the heavy gate. I grabbed my sister's arm and yanked her toward me, making sure that the gate shut right in the faces of the two stunned sailors.

"Run!" I said.

The man moved faster down the wooden dock. The sharp movement of his steps caused it to sway from side-to-side and the water to splash over the edge. He started up the gangplank as the two sailors juggled the cooler and sail bags so they could pull open the gate again.

"Get out of the fucking way."

"Buddy, calm down."

The gangplank was narrow and the three bodies bumped against each other. One sailor, a small man still wearing yellow foul-weather gear dropped the sail bags. They narrowly missed falling into the water.

"You idiot. Watch what you're doing."

The man elbowed his way past the first sailor, opened the gate and was about to run out, when the other sailor grabbed his arm and pulled him back. The gate slammed shut.

"What's the hurry, pal?" he said with a firm grip on his arm. The sailor backed him up against the gate.

"Move," said the man, as he tried to push back.

The sailor was almost a foot taller, but he stepped back slowly when he felt a gun press into his stomach.

"Whoa, wait a minute. Don't do anything stupid," said the sailor as he walked backwards slowly down the gangplank. The man glanced over at Lena and me as we climbed into my car.

"Shit," he said and he pulled open the gate.

My hands were shaking when I started the engine. I could see the man bolting across the parking lot toward our car. I floored it and heard a shot fired. Pop! The back window shattered.

"My God," I said.

I kept on driving, not sure where I should go. Pop! Another shot. It must have hit a tire, since I started to swerve. I couldn't control the car. We spun sideways and I slammed into a car that was pulling into the lot.

"Lady, what are you doing?" someone yelled.

"Trishy, we havetaget outta here," said Lena, slurring her words. She turned around to look out what was once the back window. "He's right there."

"Who is he?"

"Dunno. Doesn't like me. Doesn't like you."

I slammed the car into reverse and yelled out "Sorry, really sorry" to the passengers in the car that I hit.

"Where are you going? Get out of the car," I heard one of them call after me. A short, dark haired woman threw open the passenger side door and lurched out of the car with a piece of paper and a pen. She squinted as she tried to write down the license plate of our retreating car.

"Maybe she'll call the police," said Lena is a voice that seemed to be getting smaller and weaker. She rested her head on the seat at an angle, but she kept her eyes on the man with the gun. He had stopped running after us. His eyes darted from the passengers in the car we just hit to the sailors opening the gate. Everyone had pulled out their cell phones and were punching in numbers.

He sprinted back to his car. It sprang into motion, but he didn't follow us. Instead, he drove across Marina Boulevard. His car moved past the stores on Buchanan Street and he disappeared into the darkness.

While watching him fade into the side street, I slowed down but kept driving our limping car. Tha-thump, tha-thump, tha-thump. I glanced back at the end of the pier where the sailboat had been docked. From the shadows, a tall thin figure climbed out and ran down the dock.

I stopped the car and watched, transfixed.

"It's your fault," he yelled at us, almost in tears. "It's your fault that he's dead."

The two sailors now standing in the parking lot and the passengers from the car I hit looked at the teenager on the dock and then at our car.

"I don't believe it. It's Nick, Daisy Menton's boyfriend."

"I know," said Lena, her eyes almost closed. "Told me he was working for Justin. Sold drugs at his high school. Made big bucks."

He was almost at the gangway when he threw his arms up in the air and let out an anguished yell.

"He was my friend."

The words echoed through the marina. Then he slowly walked back to the end of the dock and climbed into the shadows of the sailboat.

I began to drive away.

"Where are you going?" asked Lena.

"Back into Fort Mason. I saw a NPS security car earlier."

The car jerked and thudded as I aimed it into the neighboring parking lot. Daisy told me how easy it was to get drugs at her high school, but I blew it off. Just like I blew off her insistence that Nick was involved.

I pulled into a space not far from Greens, turned off the ignition and looked at my sister whose head was dropping to her chest.

"Lena, what's wrong?"

"Shot."

"You were shot?"

"Notwithagun," she said running her words together. Her right hand went to her upper left arm. She pantomimed sticking a needle into it. "Wouldn't kill me," he said. "He wanted me"—she pointed to her chest—"to get you. Get you on the boat." She stuck her finger in my chest.

"I have to call an ambulance. You're sick." I glanced out the window at the parking lot. There were a number of cars moving around, but I couldn't see the security car. Lena let out a groan and her body fell toward me. My cell phone dropped to the floor of the car, as I tried to hold her up.

"Oh, Lena. Don't go to sleep."

Her eyes opened slowly. They tried to focus on me and couldn't.

"Sing," I pleaded with her. "Sing, row, row, row your boat."

As if on cue, I could hear her mumble the song she always sang as a child when she was trying not to cry, or trying to keep her mind off what was hurting her, both mentally and physically.

"Rowwwww, roooo–boat," she mumbled.

"Like this," I said. "Row, row, row your boat."

She joined in, "Gently down the stream."

"Keep going."

"Merrily.......merrily......merrily. Life is but a dream."

"Again," I said. "Lena, I'm going to get out of the car and make a call. You keep singing. I need to reach the police."

I could hear her start the round again, missing a few words here and there, but picking up steam as she went.

I opened the car door, got out and then bent back over to hunt around on the floor for my cell phone.

"Got it."

I was keeping my eyes on my sister as I punched in 911. There was a click and I knew I was about to hear a voice when the cell phone was knocked from my hands. It disappeared into the darkness of the floor of the car again.

"Think you and your sister would like to take a ride?" said Spencer who stuck a gun in my back and grabbed my neck with the other hand.

I could still hear Lena singing as he walked me around to the passenger side of the car, still with the gun at my back. He opened the door and dragged Lena out. His car was parked off to one side.

"Get her out," he said, "and shut her up."

I put my arms around my sister and helped her walk to his car. A cold damp wind blew off San Francisco Bay.

"Gentlydownthe stream."

A couple walking by smiled at us as they passed.

"Too much to drink, huh?" the man in khakis and a windbreaker asked.

"She gets like this every once in a while," Spencer said. "Come on, hon, let's get your sister home."

I stared at the couple, trying to send them a mental message. "Help us...please, help us."

But they kept walking.

I opened the back door.

"No, up front next to me." I eased her into the passenger seat. Reached over to fasten her seat belt.

"Get in," he ordered, motioning toward the backseat with the gun.

"Your boat...your boat...gently down," Lena mumbled off-key, her head sagging toward her chest.

I climbed in and sat down. Spencer slammed the door behind me, then crawled into the driver's seat.

"You do anything strange and your sister is dead," he said looking at me through the rear view mirror. His eyes burned black and vicious.

I nodded and looked out the window. Where was security?

Spencer drove slowly, almost too slowly, toward the parking lot entrance. He stopped. Then flipped on his left blinker. The car moved down Marina Boulevard and turned up Beach Street next to the Safeway.

"What do you want with us?" I asked.

"What were you doing at the warehouse today? Sightseeing?"

He cast a quick glance into the rear view mirror.

"You couldn't keep away, could you? You've been nosing around since that ridiculous brother-in-law of mine died. Couldn't leave it alone, could you?"

Lena started singing the childhood song for the nth time. "Rowing...row...rowed my boat."

"You killed Dick Waddell. That's what Justin said."

That's not what Justin had said, but I wondered how he would respond.

"Justin's an idiot. Was an idiot. He killed Dick. It was his idea. I just got him the stuff to do it with. He concocted the formula, then readjusted it to make sure that Waddell wouldn't finish his next swim. Justin was stupid. I did him a favor. Took him in. Bankrolled a business aimed at athletes. What does he do? Start knocking off people he doesn't like. You know, we have cameras and listening devices in all our offices. I heard what he told you last night."

"Did you talk to him after I left? He was alive when you saw him, wasn't he?"

"Did you think your pathetic blows killed him?"

Spencer sounded incredulous. He kept his eyes on the road as we traveled up Bay Street and stopped for a red light.

"I didn't know."

"Don't flatter yourself. One of the guards called me when he reviewed the tape after you came running out of the office. I showed up about an hour later. There he was at his desk with ice packed around his nose. He told me what happened. But I already knew. Jackass. You know that idiot liked you, thought you could be trusted."

"Liked me?" I shuddered. What would he have tried to do if he didn't like me?

"I had him taken care of. Guy was always running off at the mouth about something to someone." He glanced back at me.

"You mean, you killed him."

"Don't know anything about that."

Lena had stopped singing. She picked her head up, looked around, blurry eyed.

"Lena" I said.

She turned toward the backseat. Quick as can be, Spencer shot his hand off the steering wheel and slapped her across the cheek. She let out a moan; her head jerked back and came to a rest against the window.

"Leave her alone," I said, moving forward, speaking right into the back of his head. He reached down by his legs and pulled up the gun and aimed it at Lena's chest.

"Shut up or both of you will die right here."

I sat back in the seat. If I opened the door and threw myself out, he might kill Lena. I thought about the scene in the *Godfather* when Pauli is strangled by the guy in the backseat. But that car had been parked. If I tried to choke him, he might drive into oncoming traffic, killing us all.

How to get me and my sister out of here alive was the main objective.

"Where are you taking us?"

"A little sightseeing."

He turned left on Bay Street.

"If I'm going to die, I want to know the reason."

"Very simple. You and your sister are a nuisance. You know where I work. You've been there. You've seen our products. Not a good thing. Your sister hacked into our computers. She was printing out a list of our distributors and some very big clients when I got back to the office today. And that was after I found the Swim Association card on the ground by the fence and then noticing your car across the street. I'd seen your car at Waddell's house. What do you think I am, stupid?"

"Look, this isn't Lena's fault. I asked her to find out who your clients were. She doesn't know why," I lied. "Let her go. Stop the car and push her out. She's not involved with this. I am."

Spencer gave a short ugly laugh.

"You're like that dumbass boyfriend. Drugged girl ends up in middle of Bay Street and doesn't know how she got there. Ridiculous."

I looked out the window. My options were narrowing as each minute passed. The safest thing for me to do was keep him talking.

"Why is the teenager, Nick, involved?"

Spencer shook his head.

"Another one of Justin's pet projects. The kid and his girlfriend were always hanging around the RazzleD booths. Justin saw him as a drug pipeline to high school athletes. Actually, not a bad idea. He's smart, a quick learner. But that's over now. Kid will disappear, just like you and your sister."

The car turned left on Van Ness and was heading down toward the parking area that bordered Aquatic Park. Through the trees, I could see the long white boat-shaped Maritime Museum off to the right, its curved edges erased by heavy fog. Although the evening was damp and cool, the nightly improvised drum concert on the concrete steps that bordered the beach, was in full force. Spencer slowed the car to a crawl as he made his way down the hill to the entrance of the Municipal Pier. He pulled into a parking spot.

"Get out. We're going for a walk."

I climbed out of the backseat and moved toward the passenger side to help Lena.

"You okay?" I whispered. Lena began to sing 'row, row row your boat' softly again. There had to be a way out. I slowed down every movement I made to give me time to think. Spencer came over and took my right arm as I tried to guide Lena with my left. My steps were sluggish and labored. I stopped again and again. Spencer jerked at my arm.

"Keep moving," he said.

We headed toward the gate of the long curving Municipal Pier that separates Aquatic Park from San Francisco Bay. It was still open. In front of us, the wharf melted into a breathing dangerous darkness. I didn't want to move forward. The wind whipped at our light clothing. Food wrappers and newspapers blew around the pier in circles.

Spencer pushed me and Lena through the gate to the pier.

"Quickly, move."

He kept nudging us forward. She stumbled and I bent over to pick her up.

Off to one side, the lights of Ghirardelli Square twinkled through the fog; on the other side, straight out in San Francisco Bay, the navigational lights blinked on and off from the dark mound that was Alcatraz Island. In the distance was the Golden Gate Bridge. The russet towers looked paper thin. Only the bottom third was visible. A row of amber lights danced along the deck of the bridge, connecting San Francisco with Marin County. A few red lights marked the cables of the famous suspension bridge and appeared now and then through the thick fog at the top of the towers. It was almost too grand to look at. Especially now.

The two-toned bellow of the bridge's foghorns tumbled through the mist.

"Please don't do this," I said.

Off in the distance I heard the shriek of a police siren. Then another. They were getting louder. If the police were coming in this direction, Spencer wouldn't have time to go much further. He pushed me and Lena toward the Bay side of the pier.

"Climb over."

"I can't."

"Climb over," he said again, thrusting the gun closer to Lena's face. I sat my semi-conscious sister down on the concrete bench and went to the rail. My hands were shaking as I lifted one leg over, then the next. I was standing on a small ledge, holding on.

My hair whipped in front of my face. I could barely see the dark shadow of a container ship moving underneath the bridge. Spencer pushed the gun against my back. He glanced over to my sister who had collapsed on the bench and slowly rolled off onto the concrete floor of the wharf.

Two more police cars were heading down Van Ness toward the pier. Red, yellow and blue lights from the flash bars on the roofs pulsed through the trees. The ear-blasting whine of their sirens was close, very close.

I heard the gun cock behind me. I wasn't going to wait until I was shot. I was going to jump. Right then, the pressure of the gun against my back eased slightly. I turned my head. Spencer was glancing at my sister on the concrete floor of the pier. Then his eyes tracked to the direction of the pulsating lights and sirens. He paused a second. That's all it took. Lena rolled up into a tight crouch and lunged at his legs. She tackled him like a 49er line-backer. His knees buckled and his head jerked back. His left arm grabbed at the air, while his right hand, still holding the gun, sunk into my back.

I let go of the rail and plummeted toward the black water twenty-five feet below. The gun exploded behind me. Who was he shooting at? Me? Lena? Didn't matter. No one would hear that shot down here. No one would know what was happening.

I tumbled into the water with a loud splash. Cold, so cold. I felt my lungs collapse. I couldn't breath. I tried to grab bites of air, but nothing was coming in. No air. I sank below into the darkness. Too cold. My skin felt like it was being stuck with millions of pins. The pilings of the pier were close and the black waters of the Bay were moving me closer. I had to swim or I'd hit them. I took a few strokes away from the pier and glanced up. My skin was burning.

I couldn't see Spencer or my sister. I didn't think I'd been shot. Nothing hurt, except for the impact of me hitting the water. Was my sister still alive?

It was a flood tide and the water was coming into San Francisco Bay, moving me eastward toward Berkeley. Good sign. At least my body won't end up out at the Farallones, the remote islands about twenty-eight miles west of San Francisco in the Pacific.

My jeans had absorbed all the water they could and were beginning to drag me down, pulling me under the water. My shoes felt like anchors. I held my breath, stuck my head underwater, trying to reach my feet. It was pitch black. I couldn't see my hands in front of my face. I curled up into a ball, leaned my back into the water and lifted one foot at a time, until I could push off my shoes. I was getting colder. I had to move, but my arms stiffened up. I took a few strokes and stopped. My arms were useless, weighed down by my clothes. The backwash off the pier slapped me in the face and I swallowed the salty water coming in from the ocean. Coughing and sputtering, I kept my face out of the water as I swam following the curve of the pier. I knew there was an entrance into Aquatic Park. Could I see it in the dark? Would the tide push me past it?

Above me, flashlights pierced the darkness. I tried to yell, but I swallowed water instead. I had to keep moving. My body was numb.

Then, I heard a voice.

"Trisha, Trisha. Where are you?" It was Lena. My semi-comatose, singing, tackling sister was yelling at the top of her lungs.

"Here. I'm here. Down here." Did they hear me? Could they see me?

The tide kept pushing me along. Moving me closer to the pilings of the wharf. They were black and slimy. They smelled of rotting seaweed and tar. Barnacles ripped my hands when I reached out to push myself away. I gasped. Snapped my arms back and started kicking as hard as I could away from them. I only went a few feet before I began to wonder what was in the water with me, under me. Sea lions hung out here. I didn't want to touch anything, living or dead.

Now, two powerful flashlights shone down on me. I looked up but all I could see were lights. No faces, just searing white light.

"Follow the lights," said a male voice. One light stayed on me; the other turned into a moving narrow path on the dark Bay. Still keeping my head out of the water, I stroked and kicked, following the light.

"Now," said the voice, "swim to your right, through the entrance." I turned sharply and hit one of the piers. Pushed off and bounced against it again. I took a few strokes and I was finally in the calmer waters of Aquatic Park. In front of me, I could see the twinkling red and blue "G" of Ghirardelli Square. Off to my left was the shadow of the tall three-masted sailing ship, the Balclutha at Hyde Street Pier. I knew where I was. I almost cried. The beach was so close.

But I was cold. I couldn't feel my feet or my hands. My arms were thick and heavy, like two lead pipes. It was too much of an effort to lift them out of the water. The lights from the buildings near the shore grew fuzzy. They danced in front of me, teasing me. 'We're just out of reach,' they seemed to say.

I took one stroke; then stopped. Then another; then stopped again. In the distance, I could hear the low grumble of an outboard engine. It grew louder. Through the darkness, a jet ski with a rescue sled off the back was approaching.

"Grab my hand," yelled the driver.

The man reached down, seized my wrist and pulled me onto the sled. I managed to grasp the thick handles spaced along the sled's edges.

"You ready?" he asked with a look back in my direction. Then we roared toward shore.

———

Two police cars, their lights swirling, and an ambulance were waiting when the rescue watercraft pulled up on the beach. I turned over and looked at all the concerned faces staring down at me.

"Lena? Is my sister okay?" My tongue felt too big for my mouth and the words came out slurred. I don't think anyone understood me.

The area in front of the Maritime Museum was lit up like a stage set. Glaring lights and deep dark shadows were everywhere. Tourists were cordoned off to one side but watched the goings on with curiosity. Another car drove up onto the sidewalk and stopped close to the ambulance. It was a NPS security car. Driving it was my friend, Jon. Sitting next to him in the front seat was Lena, no longer singing about anything to do with a boat. She jumped out of the car and trotted over to the circle of emergency technicians surrounding me. Jon followed her.

I sat up.

"How you doing?" said one of the paramedics as he squatted down beside me.

"Cold...colder now, than in the water," I managed to say.

My arms were shaking badly.

"Night swimming is frowned upon, you know," said Jon, "especially in your clothes."

"Not funny," I said through chattering teeth. My lips and jaw were numb. Even my tongue was thick, like I just had a shot of Novocain at the dentist's. My hands looked like witches' claws. I couldn't make a fist. And if I wasn't looking directly at them, I'd swear my feet were in the Bay with my shoes.

One of the EMTs gave Lena a dry pair of sweatpants and a sweatshirt and she helped me change in the back of the ambulance. I began to warm up quickly once the wet clothes were off. Then, she climbed out of the ambulance and the medical professionals climbed in. They checked my vital signs, blood pressure and heart rate. And they looked into my eyes.

"You're going to be fine," said one of the EMTs.

I sat on the back bumper of the ambulance and someone stuck a cup of hot tea in my hand. Lena threw her arms around me and almost knocked me over.

"You're okay?"

"I guess."

"I thought I lost you."

She looked closely at my face. Then she smiled.

"Cold, wasn't it?"

"Yes."

"I know. I swim in Aquatic Park sometimes. It must be about 59 – 60° now. Not too bad. Your body gets used to it over time."

"Thanks. I'll pass."

"I didn't know you could swim."

I looked at my sister in disbelief.

"Of course I can swim. Who do you think taught you?"

"You?"

"Yes, me. I came before the swim coaches."

She looked a little surprised. I glanced over at Jon.

"When did you show up?"

"I saw your car pull into Fort Mason with a flat tire. Before I had a chance to see if you needed help, I saw this guy stop. Then the two of you got into his car. I couldn't tell exactly what was happening. I thought I'd better keep my eyes on all of you, so I followed the car. When he started leading you toward the Municipal Pier, I called for the SF Police."

"I called 911, too," said Lena.

"And how did you do that?" I asked. "You could barely talk. Where did you get a phone?"

"The phone was yours. When you dropped it in the car and you and Spencer were walking to the passenger side, I reached over and put it in my pocket."

"So you weren't really drugged?"

"Yes, but it was wearing off. I have to thank Spencer for bringing me completely back. When he slapped me, it was like a wake up call. But I could tell from the conversation that it might be better for me to appear semi-conscious."

I looked at her in amazement. "Smart move," I said.

"Normally that gate on the pier is locked; when you didn't turn around…well. It was hard to hear the gunshot because of the drumming going on at the steps of the Maritime Museum. But I could make it out. I radioed the police again and reported gunshots. It wasn't looking good. You're both lucky to be alive," Jon said.

"You weren't shot were you?" asked Lena.

"No. When you tackled Spencer, he pushed me, still holding the gun. I was afraid he'd pull the trigger, so I jumped."

"You jumped at the same time his gun went off. It went flying. I was running down the pier and was able to kick it out of his reach. The police were right behind me," said Jon.

"They arrested him, cuffed him and read him his rights. He's on his way to jail, as we speak," said Lena. "The guy is a complete psycho."

Jonathan and I nodded.

"He's a murderer. He had Justin killed. You heard him say that, right? And he's a drug dealer."

I stood up. A dark fuzzy curtain dropped over my eyes. Flashing lights erupted inside my head. The paramedics were watching me closely. When I began to sway, they moved in.

"We're going to take you to the hospital, just to make sure everything's okay."

34

It was a quiet night at the Emergency Room at San Francisco Memorial.

"Incoming," called out the nurse to anyone who was listening.

"What's up?" said Dr. T.

"Someone went swimming in Aquatic Park at night, sounds like hypothermia," answered the nurse.

With that the double doors swung open and I was rolled in on a gurney.

Terrel looked at me.

"You have got to be kidding."

I smiled weakly. The paramedics handed off the paperwork to Terrel while I was pushed into a room. I could hear him.

"Say again, she did what?"

I was perched on the edge of the bed when he walked in.

"Here's the problem," he said sitting down on a stool by my bedside. "I have to treat you because I'm a doctor and you're a patient. But I don't want to. You understand? I am angry, very angry. You were supposed to call the police, remember?"

He stuck a thermometer into my mouth before I could answer. Then he put a blood pressure cup on my arm and inflated it. He was watching the numbers on the screen by my bedside when Lena walked in.

"Why am I not surprised?" he said looking at Lena.

"Everything okay here?" she asked.

Terrel did not look happy.

"Let me clarify this for you. This is important, so pay attention."

Lena and I looked at each other and then at Dr. T.

"Drug dealers…bad. They hurt people. They kill people. You listening?"

We both nodded and waited.

"That's it?" I asked.

"That's enough," he said.

He took the cuff off my arm and pulled the thermometer out of my mouth.

"What's this?" he said, looking at my arm.

There was four inch gash.

"I don't know," I said.

"When was the last time you had a tetanus shot?" he asked me.

I tried to remember. "Years ago. I stepped on a nail when I was about 13. I think it was then."

"Well, you've got a deep cut on your arm. Maybe you scraped your arm on a nail from the wharf's piling. We're going to clean it up and give you a tetanus shot. Then you're ready to go home."

"T, it's over now," I said. "Spencer is in police custody. I did call Inspector Burrell right after I talked to you. I gave the police the address of his warehouse and they are probably there now. It really is finished."

Terrel didn't say a word to me, but walked out of the room. When he came back he had a syringe in his hand.

"I hope this hurts," he said.

35

Lena and I spent most of the morning the next day talking to Inspector Carolina Burrell. Although officers had gone out immediately to the South San Francisco warehouse, it was vacant when they got there. The gate was unlocked. The only things on the loading dock were some empty water bottles. Inside, the conveyor belts were still in place, but there was nobody around to use them.

Spencer's office on the second floor had been stripped bare. His computer was gone; and his two small file cabinets were empty.

I had asked about the person named 'Tip', but Inspector Burrell avoided the topic. Since the evidence had disappeared, she wasn't sure that drug charges would hold. The list of clients and what looked like dealers, and the two sets of books, one legit, one not which Lena had downloaded from the JL & Associates' computer could be important. Time would tell about that.

But the death of his associate and friend, Justin Rosencastle, was another matter. She wouldn't say much to us but, so far, Spencer was being held without bail.

That afternoon, Lena and I were back in San Rafael. It was a lovely warm afternoon. We decided to walk down to the Sun Valley Market for a soda. It gave me a chance to tell Lena everything I had learned about Justin.

As we strolled down the tree-shaded street, Lena looked over at me.

"If Dick had accepted Justin as a brother, maybe they'd both be alive now," said Lena.

"Hard to say. They were on their own self-destructive paths."

"You saw the paper this morning, didn't you?" Lena asked.

"Yeah. The headline was something like, 'East Bay Sports Nutrition Entrepreneur Accused of Killing Partner.'"

"It didn't mention us by name, just something about unsuspecting bystanders involved. It didn't mention anything to do with drugs. We helped bring this guy down. Don't you think we should get some recognition? At least our name in the paper?"

"Probably not such a good idea. Since it looks like Spencer is part of a drug ring in the Bay area, he may have friends. I wouldn't want those friends to know any more about us than they already do."

"Good point." We walked into the neighborhood market, picked up some drinks and headed for the small tables outside on the brick patio.

"Do you think Spencer could be charged with the death of Dick Waddell and for Jackie's accident?" Lena asked, taking a sip of her iced tea.

"I don't know. It was Justin who provided the actual drugs. Terrel said that the autopsy results finally came back. Waddell's heart muscle wall was slightly thickened and enlarged, which isn't unusual for someone his age. But if you add street drugs to that... well.

"We know he swallowed a capsule full of cocaine, although he probably didn't know what he was taking—or didn't want to know. It was just something called HT2 that made him alert and fast. Terrel said that the cocaine increased his heart rate and blood pressure and constricted the arteries that supply blood to the heart. He had a fatal heart attack in the water. If that wasn't enough, the final toxicological results showed he was taking synthetic testosterone."

"Why couldn't he compete on his own merits? We all slow down as we age," said Lena.

"His unreachable standards got in the way. Really sad. This whole drug ring…maybe the task force will learn something when they look at the 'real' set of books that you hacked into. How did you do that anyway?"

"My newest talent. I'm on an internet group that is extremely helpful. Really, it wasn't that hard. You know, the drinks, the RazzleD line of fluid replacement drinks aren't bad. I tasted a few when I went for my interview. I don't know if they were any better for an athlete than a glass of water, but they tasted okay. Do you think there are other athletes out there who were Justin's clients, so to speak?"

"I wouldn't be surprised. But I'm not looking for them. I have to find another job."

"So it's over?" asked Lena, as we gathered up our half full bottles and started the short walk home.

"Well, almost. I do have one more thing to do. It involves another ride to the East Bay."

36

When I pulled into the Matthew's circular driveway at Opal Valley, a gardener was working in the front yard. He nodded, smiled, and gestured to the garage. I parked there and walked over to the front door. Out here in the Livermore Valley, it was steaming hot, over 90°. The white glare of the sun seared my skin as I stood at the front door. Glancing around, I couldn't see or hear another person on the street. Occasionally a car passed by, but that was it. Looks like money buys you solitude, whether you want it or not.

I rang the bell and a middle-aged Latina, short, full-figured with an apron tied around her waist, answered the door. She looked at me suspiciously.

"Yes?" she said.

"I'd like to see Pamela."

"She is busy. Who are you?"

"I'm Trisha Carson. I was working on a memorial presentation, a tribute for her brother. I have some things I wanted to give back to her. You're Renata, right?"

"Si." Her expression changed and she looked at me quizzically. "Then you know Senora Matthews?"

"I do. I understand how difficult things have been for her."

"Okay, come in. She is outside in the back of the house. She is not doing well right now."

I thanked her and walked past the huge living room with the floor to ceiling windows that overlooked the golf course. I glanced up the staircase, half expecting Spencer to step out of his home office with a phone to his ear. I continued by the palatial kitchen, the family room and the paneled study where I had looked through old photos of Dick Waddell.

"The door is this way," Renata said and she pointed to the double doors in the family room.

Outside, a tall deep green hedge between the golf course and the house gave privacy to the backyard. The difference between the two landscapes was striking. On one side were wide open fairways, sand traps and greens baking in the sun. But on the house side, there was a cool, peaceful English garden.

Pamela sat on a simple white Adirondack wooden chair on the patio. On the wide armrest was a glass of ice water. She looked up. Her eyes were red-rimmed. Her face pale and puffy.

"Haven't you done enough?" She spoke in a weary whispery voice. I almost couldn't hear her.

"Pamela, this is not my fault." I walked over and sat down beside her.

"My brother is dead. My husband is in jail. Even Justin is dead."

She stared at me out of sunken eyes in a face overcome with sadness.

"I don't know what to do. I really don't know what to do."

"I'm sorry, but I'm not much more than a bystander in all this," I said.

"Oh, come on. You know that's not true. The police think Spencer killed Justin. But that was really your doing, wasn't it? That's what Spencer told me."

"I didn't kill him. Your husband did that. You know, you must know that he was a ...he is..."

I didn't know how to tell her that her husband was a drug dealer.

"He develops nutritional supplements. He wants to help people. That's all he ever has wanted to do—help them achieve their top performance."

"Pamela, you're kidding yourself. He's been involved with drugs, illegal drugs, street drugs, call it what you will, since before he came to the Bay Area. His drugs killed your brother."

"I don't believe it."

"It's true."

"You're lying. Spencer would never hurt Dick. Never."

I sat back and looked out at the garden. She would have to figure this out in her own time. And it really wasn't the reason I was here anyway.

"Do you remember Holly Worthington?"

"How do you know about Holly?"

"I met her the other day. She's homeless and living on the streets in San Francisco."

I told her what I knew about her sister-in-law. She listened quietly, not sure whether to believe me or not.

"I think that through your husband, Dick found out that Holly was in the area and that she had a child. That's why he came here to live. Yes, he wanted to be close to you, but he wanted to see Holly and maybe try and find his son."

"So you're saying that Spencer has known about Holly and this child?"

"Yes, for at least 15 years, if not more."

"And I have a nephew?"

"He was given up for adoption years ago. But yes, you have a nephew. I think his name is Jeremy Reid."

I gave Pamela Richard's address book and camera.

"It's all in here. If you want to contact her, call this number and ask for Dr. Tariq Kapoor. He can help you."

I gave her Dr. Kapoor's card. I laid the photos I had planned on using for Dick's tribute on the table next to the camera.

"I came here to give these back to you." On top were the two smiling teenagers, Dick and Holly, holding their blue ribbons.

"Good bye, Pamela," I said.

She didn't look at me. Instead, she picked up the photo and stared at it.

37

The text, like all text messages was brief, but telling.

"Get here now. L is driving me crazy."

Terrel had driven Lena to her next open water swim. Unlike so many of them that had her up at 5:00 a.m. in the morning for a two hour drive, this swim was only 30 minutes away. Keller Cove was located through the tunnel at Point Richmond, one of the first exits off the Richmond-San Rafael Bridge. I was up when they left. While she fluttered around the house throwing swim suits, goggles and towels into a bag, I made myself a cup of coffee, picked up the morning paper and went back to bed. A quiet serene morning was what I hoped for.

But Terrel's text had something else in mind for me. So I threw on my sweats, dumped the coffee in a to-go cup and headed out in the early morning once again to an open water swim. Who would be doing the swim evaluation? Would it be Bill? How awkward?

Oh well, I'm a big girl. As I drove across the Richmond-San Rafael Bridge, I could see a slash of brilliant morning sun below the lumbering grey fog in the distance. While the sky was still overcast, there was a good chance that the sun would be out before the swim started.

Once through the Point Richmond tunnel, I started to look for a place to park along the road. I was late and parking was not going to be easy. I drove past Terrel's black Charger and pulled into a spot about a ten minute walk from the beach.

The sidewalk skirted a cliff, high above the beach area. As I looked down, I could see the swimmers bundled up. Out in the water, the East Bay Regional Park lifeguards looked like two-inch high action figures, setting out huge yellow and orange inflatable buoys. The shiny buoys popped out dramatically against the deep grey sky and the surprisingly flat grayish green water of San Francisco Bay.

Down on the beach, Terrel and Lena were sitting off to one side, watching the timers check their equipment. Terrel walked over as he saw me approaching.

"She is out of control. I keep telling her to maintain the situation, be calm. But she's not hearing a thing."

"She's nervous. It all goes away once the swim is over. What time is the start?"

"About 10 minutes from now. They just went through the starting instructions."

Terrel looked at me. I knew what he was about to say.

"Don't you dare leave."

He turned away and looked up at the sky.

"Here's the problem…"

I cut him off.

"Please stay, even if she is a pain in the ass, right now."

As if on cue, Lena came over to us, threw off her swim parka and said, "I can't find my goggles. Oh my God, I left my earplugs in the car."

With that she was gone, running back to her swim bag, digging into it until she found the goggles. We watched as she jogged back to the water and walked in up to her knees. The announcer said that her wave would start in three minutes.

"Don't like these. Can't see anything," she said, as she jogged back past us again to her swim bag. She threw her dark goggles on the sand and dug around in her bag until she found the clear ones.

"Better. Much better," she said, as she passed us for the fourth time. She made it back to the edge of the beach as the timer gave the one minute signal. There was a countdown from 10 seconds to zero and the swimmers ran into the water, splashing and cheering until it was deep enough to swim.

"She likes this?" asked Terrel, looking after the swimmers disappearing around a point of land.

"Yeah, she does. She'll be back to her normal obnoxious self once she runs across the finish line."

The sun had come out and the beach was warming up quickly. I looked around. Off to one side was Jackie. Her arm was still in a cast and so was one leg. She was quietly sitting by herself. Menton's daughter Daisy stood by the food table cutting up bagels. The gangly Nick was missing. So was the booth for RazzleD.

I walked over to the finish arch with Terrel. We stood about ten feet from the water's edge watching the long line of swimmers now spread out in the distance.

"Hey, Trish, hear you're unemployed," said the owner of the timing company glancing up from his laptop at the finish line.

"Guess so."

"Don't know if you're interested, but we're expanding. We have more events to time than we have staff. I want to set up and train another crew."

"What are you saying?"

"I'd like to talk to you about working for us."

"Really?"

"Yeah." He reached into his pocket, hunting around for a business card.

"Call me, maybe midweek, after I get these results finalized." He handed me his card.

"Thanks. I will."

Terrel looked over and shook his head.

"Seriously, you want to sit out on a beach with a computer and then deal with swimmers like Lena who complain about the results? Why don't you find something that you really like? Go work for the San Francisco Giants."

"Just how would I get a job like that?"

"You'll figure that part out," he said.

I patted him on the arm and started up for the walkway to the street. I made a slight detour aiming for a large green trashcan that was close to the food table.

"Hey, Daisy," I said.

She glared at me and then stabbed one of the bagels in front of her.

"What happened to Nick?" I asked.

"He's not in school anymore, because of you. You're a snitch," she said, turning her back to me.

"He was doing things he shouldn't have been doing."

With that, I reached into my backpack, grabbed all of my cards relating to the Waddell death, tossed them into trash and walked away. No need for these anymore.

Standing at the top of the hill, I saw the swimmers rounding the first buoy and heading down the longest leg toward the

Chevron pier. Even from a distance, I could make out Lena's lopsided, but effective stroke. By the finish arch where Terrel was still standing, I noticed a tall man with a clipboard. Was he the event director or maybe he was the evaluator? It really wasn't my concern anymore. I climbed into my car, switched on the radio and headed for home.

———

Made in the USA
Lexington, KY
24 April 2013